The GLITTER of Gold

by

J.M. PHILLIPPE

Blue Zephyr Press
2661 N. Pearl, #360
Tacoma WA 98407

This book is a work of fiction. Names, characters, and incidents are products of the author's imagination or are used fictiously. Any resemblance to actual events or persons living or dead is entirely coincidental.

Cover art by **LILT**.

ISBN-10: 1-7320863-7-0
ISBN-13: 978-1-7320863-7-1

Acknowledgments

I would like to take this opportunity to thank folks who have helped me bring both The Glitter of Gold and my prior Galactic Dreams novel, Aurora One, to life. Thank you to my tech advisor, Ryan Mahle, and my readers Aisha Butler and Peter Swanson for stepping up at the last minute to help me out when I needed it. Thank you to Crystal Durnan of Anima Editing for her patience, support, and grammar expertise. Thank you to Juel Lugo for her constant encouragement and ability to step in and help with ideas and resolve world-building disputes. Thank you to all my friends and family who are my most constant and dedicated fans, especially Lance Yomtob who always remembers to tell me he's proud of me. But mostly, thanks goes to my incredible and generous fellow world-builders, Karen Harris Tully and Bethany Maines. Working with the two of you to create a universe we all get to play in has been an amazing and joyful experience, and I can't wait for Galactic Dreams Volume 3!

Table of Contents

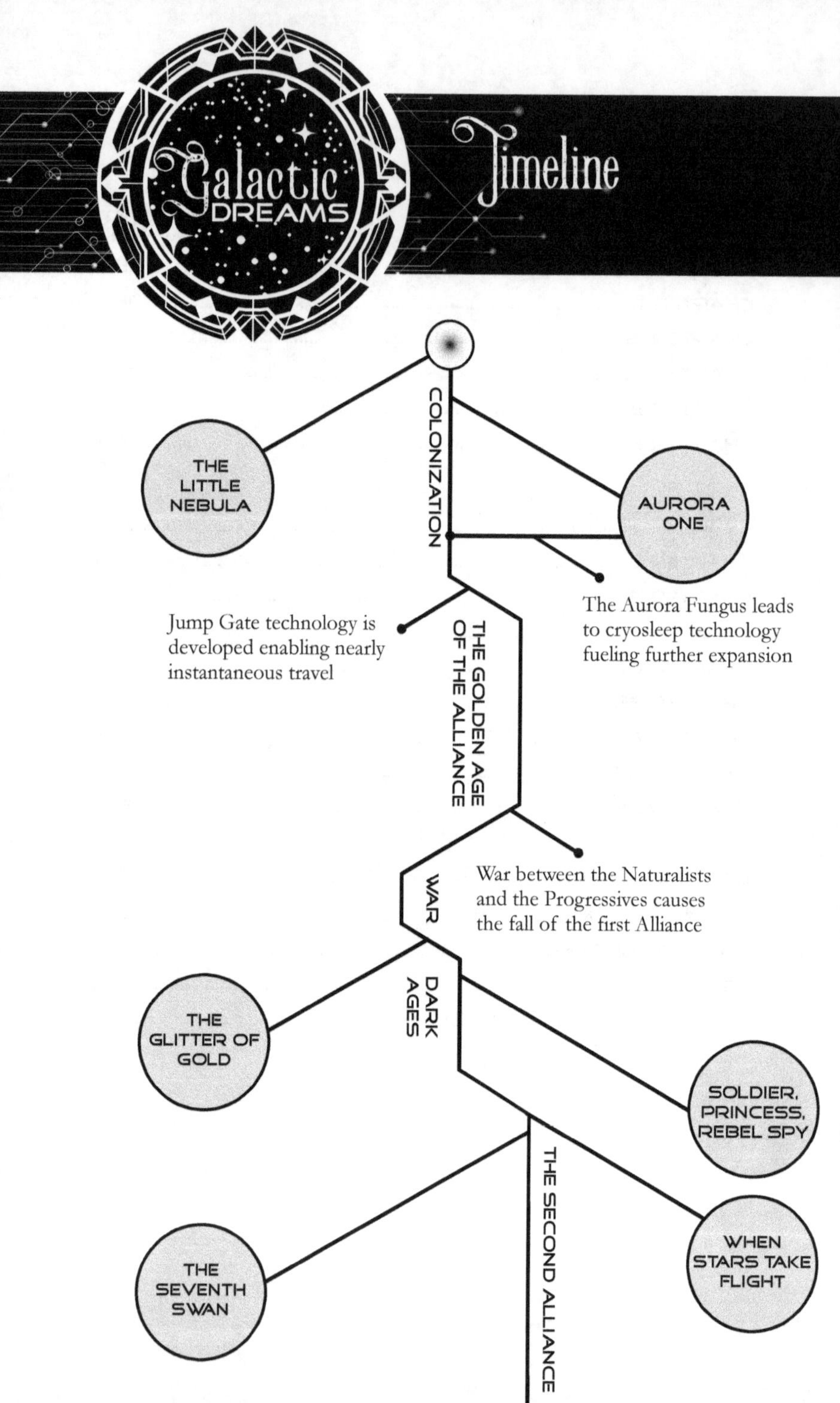
Galactic DREAMS
Timeline
COLONIZATION
THE LITTLE NEBULA
AURORA ONE
The Aurora Fungus leads to cryosleep technology fueling further expansion
Jump Gate technology is developed enabling nearly instantaneous travel
THE GOLDEN AGE OF THE ALLIANCE
War between the Naturalists and the Progressives causes the fall of the first Alliance
WAR
DARK AGES
THE GLITTER OF GOLD
SOLDIER, PRINCESS, REBEL SPY
THE SECOND ALLIANCE
THE SEVENTH SWAN
WHEN STARS TAKE FLIGHT

Introduction

WHAT IF...

...in the future the stars must fight to save humanity?
...an algae farmer's daughter and a spy make a deadly bargain to save everything they both love?
...a silent engineer on an empty moon can save a prince from an ancient evil?

Welcome to the universe of Galactic Dreams, where fairy tales are reimagined for a new age—the future. In each Galactic Dreams Volume 2 novella you'll find an old tale reborn with a mixture of romance, technology, aliens and adventure. But this time, each Prince and Princess, each band of intrepid heroes, is fighting the same enemy — an entity so vast that he can span centuries and not everyone is guaranteed to survive.

Galactic Dreams is a unique series of science-fiction novellas from Blue Zephyr Press featuring retellings of classic tales from different authors, all sharing the same universe, technology, and history.

We hope you enjoy this adventure.

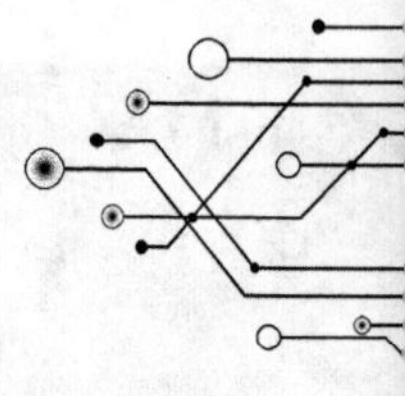

PROLOGUE
The Chosen One

"Once upon a time," Corhalae said as the children in front of her squirmed and then settled. "There was a beautiful nebula named Luminous, and she swam through the galaxy, surfing the atmospheres of planets and creating aurora borealis."

"She was a star?" one of the little ones asked, a round thing with hair sticking up and a runny nose.

"Not quite," Corhalae said. "She was an energy being."

"Stars aren't energy?"

Corhalae was getting annoyed by this little one, who she saw wipe at their nose with the back of their hand. Boy or girl, she didn't care. At this age, they all looked the same, and she wasn't interested in things like that. She was looking for some sign of intelligence—for one of her descendants to be *clever*.

"Quiet and listen," she told the child. "One day, Luminous saw in the stars that a great and horrible war would come to her solar system. She decided that she needed to become human in order to prevent it."

"Stars can't become human," the same child said, and Corhalae felt an old frustration—and an old power—stir within her. Another small child shushed the first, taking their hand either out of a sense of comfort or control, Corhalae couldn't tell.

"So the young nebula went to the great and powerful Ix and made a deal."

Corhalae's eyes floated over the gathered children, looking for any change in their behavior at the sound of Ix's name. Whatever hold the dark energy being had on her kin, it either had not kicked in just yet or was too subtle for her old eyes to see. She tried to sense it instead, reading their auras.

There. Tiny dark threads among the light colors of youth: pinks and blues and yellows infected with the tiniest slivers of shadows. Corhalae sighed.

"Luminous was made human. She met a prince and fell in love. Together, they worked to overthrow Ix's power, and stop him from a path of wanton destruction. They got the help of the Matriarch…."

"Who?"

But the child sitting next to the noisome one was already quieting the other and Corhalae ignored the outburst.

"The Matriarch," she repeated, "who trapped Ix, and buried him inside an asteroid, throwing him far across the universe."

"Did he die?"

Corhalae met the eyes of the inquisitor, the comforting child. All children's eyes seemed big in their small heads, but this one's eyes also seemed knowing, and perhaps, troubled. They sat with a stillness that belied their age, and their small face was thin, and serious.

"No, he did not. Ix is still out there," she said. "And he wants to be free."

"Who will free him?"

There was something about this child, something in the aura. Could this be the one that Corhalae had been looking for?

"We will," she said.

"Why? Isn't he evil?"

"Yes, he is."

The child's face scrunched up in thought.

"Then we can't free him."

"We won't have a choice," she said. "You see, Luminous wasn't the only one to make a deal with Ix, and not the only nebula to turn human."

Corhalae sighed, remembering what it was like to be caught in Ix's energy field, her radiance stripped away, her raw and naked human body thrust mewling and crying to planet Earth. It would be decades before she could remember who she really was, and by then she was too ashamed to find her sister, Luminous, and ask for her help.

By then, the nightmares had already started.

"What was the deal?" the child asked, eyes wide.

"To become human."

"What did the nebula trade?"

"Service." She watched to see what the child would do with this information. The little face looked solemn, and sad.

"For how long?"

Yes, this one was clever. Corhalae felt hope rise in her old heart, hope she hadn't felt in generations.

"For always," she said. "And not just the nebula-turned human, but all of her children, and her children's children, and all the other children to come."

The child looked scared.

It took a long time for Corhalae to understand, for her to

see. It was in her blood. So it was in theirs too, her children's children's children, all called, all shaped by this need to seek, to find. To serve.

They would be the instruments of her master's release. They would be the instruments of the universe's doom.

"This is a boring story," the other child said, huffing and wiping at a still-runny nose. "Can we go play now?"

"Yes," Corhalae said, "everyone who does not want to finish the story can leave."

Small bodies climbed or sprung to their feet, as their personalities dictated, and dashed off toward the other room and all the toys in it.

All the small bodies but one.

"Why did you tell us this story?" the remaining child asked.

"It's my story," Corhalae said. "And it is yours." She motioned for the child to come closer, and it obliged—she thought maybe it was a boy—and he sat cross-legged directly in front of Corhalae.

"How do we stop Ix?" the child asked.

Corhalae still had some magic left in her old bones, and she gathered it up with her strength. The young one would need every gift she could bestow in order to break free of the deal she'd made. She was too old for the task herself, too bent and frail. As it was, transferring her magic would cost her the rest of her life, not all at once, but she could feel her final days approaching.

She hoped it would be enough to save the family, and the universe.

She hoped that she wouldn't die in vain.

"I won't," she told the child. "But you will."

PART 1: A Poor Man's Daughter

Once there was a miller who was poor, but who had a beautiful daughter. Now it happened that he had to go and speak to the king, and in order to make himself appear important he said to him, "I have a daughter who can spin straw into gold."

The king said to the miller, "That is an art which pleases me well, if your daughter is as clever as you say, bring her to-morrow to my palace, and I will put her to the test."

And when the girl was brought to him he took her into a room which was quite full of straw, gave her a spinning-wheel and a reel, and said, "Now set to work, and if by to-morrow morning early you have not spun this straw into gold during the night, you must die."

Jacob and Wilhelm Grimm, Rumpelstiltskin

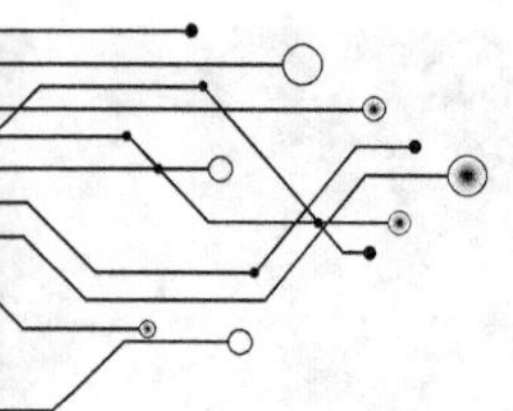

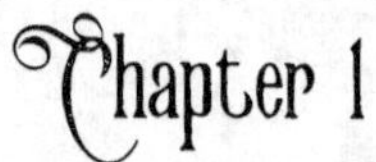

Chapter 1

THE PROMISE OF GOLD

Gwynn Flaxenhart pressed in the final code and held her breath. For one glorious moment, she watched as the pale green crystal in the chamber withstood the pressure and energy flowed into the converter, causing a series of lights to glow brightly. She tried to keep one eye on the clock and the other on the lights. Five seconds. Ten seconds. Fifteen.

Maybe, maybe. She was afraid to hope after so many disappointments. But…twenty seconds. Twenty-five.

The light began to flicker, and her eyes flew back to the crystal. Was that a crack?

"No no no no," she muttered, leaning over the console to look at the readings her computer was taking. "It's not a crack, it's not…."

But the readouts were confirming what her eyes were seeing—the energy level generated by the crystal was dropping. Thirty-two seconds. Thirty-four, and the lights were very dim.

At thirty-six seconds, the crack in the crystal expanded suddenly, and the pale green surface shattered, pieces crumbling smaller and smaller as the pressure continued.

"Stupid *tamade* crystal!" Gwynn said as she shut the chamber down.

She looked up at the clock, and realized she was running late—again. She cursed and saved her data, shutting everything down. Then she jogged to her quarters, which had been conveniently built near her lab.

She had a lot of complaints about the new *Flaxen One* space station that her father spent a small fortune on, but the design was not one of them.

Once in her quarters, Gwynn slipped out of the basic pants and shirt she wore around the lab and grabbed at the dress hanging on the back of her closet door, slipping it on over her head and sealing the back of it by pressing a button in the bodice. She turned on the mirror function of the closet door and swept her longer blonde hair over the patch of shorter purple hair on the right side of her head, a thick stripe that stretched from her temple to just behind her right ear. The blonde covered most of it, and she sprayed it down with a light setting spray, hoping it would hold. Finally, she pulled the white slippers that matched her dress onto her feet and stood up straight to survey the finished product.

Enzo, her father's right-hand man, had told her to dress in the family colors: white and yellow. But the yellow of the Flaxen Moons was a dull, buttery shade that made Gwynn look washed out and sickly. As such, most of the dress was white, with yellow accents contained to a thin sash at her waist and some light beading at the v-neckline. The fit wasn't great—too tight around her hips and butt and too lose in the bodice—but it looked good enough, Gwynn supposed.

She didn't know why she was bothering to even attend the latest of her father's attempts to lure an investor in to help keep Flaxen Moons going. Bertram Flaxenhart was not the business man his father was, and a series of bad decisions, including building an all-new station to house state-of-the-art living quarters and a top-notch lab, all running on a very large and very expensive tuotarium crystal, had left the family on the verge of losing everything. He spent wildly and invested poorly and had absolute faith that somehow Gwynn was going to get the family out of the mess he'd created.

By creating tuotarium crystals. Out of algae.

Gwynn sighed.

It wasn't the science that she minded, which was at least interesting. It was the very idea of the task of creating crystals at all. There were hundreds of thousands of strains of algae just on their farm, and another hundred thousand or so that had been discovered on various worlds throughout the galaxy that she didn't have samples of. Sure, it was possible that one of them, under the right pressure conditions, and in the perfect solvent, could create a tuotarium-class crystal as powerful as the one that ran the station. But Gwynn had been working on this project for two years and had barely gone through a fraction of the strains. It could take decades to find the right combination, particularly since they couldn't afford to hire anyone to help Gwynn with the research.

She finished her look with a little makeup, and then headed toward one of the side rooms off the giant clear-domed room in the center of the station. The ballroom was Bertram's pride and joy, hosting balls one of the few parts of his job that he liked. Not that Gwynn blamed him—she didn't enjoy being stuck at Flaxen Moons either, and she hadn't trained to be an artist, like her father had. But after his father was killed in the Genome War and his older brother, Brandon, was killed in the same accident that Gwynn's mother died in, Bertram was left all alone to take on the task of keeping the family legacy going.

At least until Gwynn came of age. But she was still months out from her twenty-fifth birthday and her full rights and responsibilities as heir to Flaxen Moons. Not that this got her out of any of the family functions, but at least once she was of age, she'd have voting rights. Maybe then she could help Enzo and his husband, Myles, try to curtail her father's spending.

Gwynn arrived at the room that the welcoming celebration for the latest would-be investors was in and felt her heart sink. She was much later than she had planned, and the room was already filled with people, most of them wearing some version of green and gold. She guessed those were the corporate colors. She was intrigued when she saw a young person turn and spotted what appeared to be green glittering sparkles across both cheeks, just under the eyes. Gwynn loved to track the fashion trends in other solar systems. But she couldn't let herself get distracted. She spotted Enzo's tall and thin form at the far side of the room and could guess that the bright yellow thing next to him was probably her father. All she had to do was get to them.

Gwynn tried to make her way through the crowd of people as unobtrusively as she could, but there was a rather wide-shouldered man blocking her way, his rich clothes and long tunic in gold and green making it appear as if he was wearing a uniform. Gwyn couldn't tell if he was security or someone higher up. The way his shoulders were filling out the tunic suggested security; he certainly looked foreboding from behind. She looked back to see if she could get around him and go the other way—her father had to be wondering where she was—but a sparkle-cheeked man filled in the gap Gwynn had just left. After standing on her toes and trying to see if there was another way around, Gwynn realized she only had one option left: she was going to have to ask the man to move.

"Excuse me," she said quietly, hoping she wasn't going to have to raise her voice to be heard over the din of the crowd.

The man looked over his shoulder, puzzled.

"How did you get back there?" he asked.

Gwynn gestured over the crowd that filled up the space around them.

"There was an opening, earlier," she explained. "It then filled up. I'm trying to get to the front."

"You've gotten pretty close," the man said, turning fully to face her. She saw then that he wore thick gold chains and had a corporate emblem emblazoned on the front of his tunic that she vaguely recognized. Not security then. He was probably a good ten years older than her, with a thick black beard that was as neatly shaped as his black hair. Light blue eyes looked out from under thick black lashes, proof of a regressive gene, Gwynn thought, if not a genetic modification. They didn't seem to go with his skin color, which was a few shades lighter than his hair and had a warm yellow undertone.

"If I don't make it all the way, my father isn't going to be too pleased with me," Gwynn said, still trying and failing to look past the man.

"You must be Gwynn then," the man said, smiling and reaching out his hand. "Gair Ingram."

Gwynn stared for a moment, taking in the reality of meeting the owner of the TenDek Corporation, one of the richest men in the galaxy. He was younger and better looking than she had imagined him when reading about him on the AltFeed. She shook off her paralysis and offered her own hand, which he took in a firm grip, stepping slightly closer to her as he shook it.

"Your father speaks so often of your brilliance, he seems to have forgotten to mention your beauty," Gair said. Despite being positive that he was just playing the corporate game with his compliment, Gwynn found herself blushing.

"Mr. Ingram, my apologies," she began, willing her face to cool down. "I hadn't realized who we were meeting today."

"Gair," he said. "And I appreciate your honesty. I suppose we are only the most recent in a long-line of suitors. Who wouldn't want to invest in the future of such a place like Flaxen Moons? The history of these algae farms stretches all the way back to the first colony ships. It would be very exciting to get to be part of that legacy."

"It is very exciting indeed," Gwynn said, not sure what else to say. Gair Ingram had a very different reaction to being asked to invest in Flaxen Moons than anyone else Gwynn had spoken with.

"And I have to say, I am very much looking forward to working with you." He smiled warmly at her.

Gwynn tilted her head to the side, as if trying to hear his words differently.

"Your father has mentioned...?" Gair began.

Gwynn's face grew hot again, but this time with anger and not embarrassment. She forced a bright smile anyway.

"Of course," she said, hoping Gair couldn't tell she was lying. "I just hadn't realized that he'd proposed working with you directly."

"Well, not directly," Gair said. "I don't actually do much with the ReDev team. But a project as big as this will definitely be under my oversight."

"Of course," Gwynn said, her mind racing. ReDev was probably what his company called research and development. But a large project? The only large project that Gwynn had been working on was....

"The crystals," she blurted out.

"Your father said that you are already getting results?" Gair asked.

Gwynn took a step back, her eyes searching out some exit from this conversation, from this feeling of being cornered. What had her father done? What had he said?

"I would love to speak more about this," she said, finally spotting an opening to Enzo and her father. "But I really must let my father know I'm here so that we can officially begin things."

"I am very much looking forward to officially beginning things," Gair said with a twinkle in his blue eyes. For a second, Gwynn was distracted by her panic enough to wonder—was he flirting with her?

Corporate game, she reminded herself.

"As am I," she said back, not really paying attention to her own words. "Until then." She gave a small bow of respect, which he returned, and then he moved aside so that she could get past him. She took a direct route to Enzo, in his own white and yellow outfit, her father a slab of butter next to him in head-to-toe yellow. Gwynn tried not to think about if Gair was watching her, and willed herself not to look back, but as she twisted sideways to get past yet another be-sparkled shareholder, she caught Gair's profile in her peripheral. He *had* been watching her.

She ducked her head down a little to hide her face and any emotion that may be crossing it, and then kept her back to him the rest of the way to her father.

"Dad," she said, urgently, so that only Bertram could hear. "What is going on?"

"Oh good, you've made it!" Bertram said, clapping his hands together. "Enzo, go ahead and signal for the others to start moving people into the ballroom." He made a shooing gesture at the older man, which annoyed Gwynn, but Enzo's face remained placid as he did what he was told. "Gwynnie dear-heart, you look lovely," Bertram said, finally looking at his daughter. "So much white though! And are you covering the purple in your hair?"

"Dad!" Gwynn said with more force, grabbing his arm and physically moving him behind one of the many planted palm trees found all around the compound for more privacy. "What have you told them about the crystals?"

"It's just a proposal, dear-heart, don't be so concerned."

But something was nagging at the back of Gwynn's mind, and it clicked as her father tried to turn away.

"He said *will*," she said. "Gair said will—that this project will be under his oversight. Is this really just a proposal?"

Bertram looked uncomfortable under her gaze.

"I didn't have a choice," he said. "The debts we have—we won't make it another lunar cycle without their support. And there was only one thing they wanted."

"It's what everyone wants," she said, panic mingling with anger. "The ability to make tuotarium crystals changes everything."

"Right, and you said you were getting results," Bertram said. "No one is expecting any miracles."

"Making tuotarium crystals from algae would be a miracle," Gwynn retorted. "I've made power crystals, but none of them last longer than a few seconds. I don't know how to do it! I don't even know if it can be done."

Bertram pulled his daughter close then, his voice low and urgent.

"We have nothing. Nothing! I can't sell this place for what I've borrowed against it. If I don't find a way to pay our debts, it's worse than just losing the farms. I'll go to jail. The debtors will go after you as the heir and make you an indentured servant until you pay off your share. And Enzo and Myles—where will they go? They are too old to start over anywhere new.

"We just ran out of time," Bertram said. "With this deal, we buy some more."

"How much more?"

"Until the day after the Hart Ball," Bertram said. "You don't have to make a lot of crystals—just one, just a proof of concept.

Then you hand over your research, and then we get Flaxen Moons back."

He seemed so confident that it was hard for Gwynn to remember just how horrible of a deal this was.

"And if we don't deliver? What does TenDek get then?"

"Everything," Bertram said.

"Dad, this is a horrible deal!"

"Shush now, dear-heart," he said, looking around the room to see who had heard her. "And anyway, it's too late. The deal has been made."

"How did you let it get this bad?" Gwynn asked. "I don't understand. We'd made a deal. You were going to wait until my birthday, let me have a vote."

"We wouldn't have lasted that long," Bertram said sadly. "Flaxen Moons wasn't in great shape when your grandfather died. He kept things going, sure, but he always had a lot of creditors too. This farm thrived during the Genome War, but without soldiers to feed, we lost a lot of business. And with the Alliance a shell of what it was, the trade routes are more dangerous than ever. Only the large corporations like TenDek with the Blue Band and the security they provide can afford to do any large-scale trade. Maybe your uncle Brandon—he might have been able to turn things around without the help of a corporation. He had the head for this stuff. But...."

Gwynn shook her head. She didn't want to think about that.

"You can do it, Gwynnie, I know you can," Bertram said, patting her on the shoulder. "You're the smartest person I ever met, even smarter than...."

Gwynn shrugged her father's hand off.

"Don't say it," she said.

"We have to get the celebration started," he said. "Dear-heart, try to have a little faith. Things will work out, in the end."

Gwynn couldn't think of anything else to say as she watched her father walk to Enzo and help him herd guests into the ballroom where tables had been set up at the center so that the diners could look up and see the stars. Sure, she thought, everything is going to be fine. So long as I can figure out how to make miracles happen.

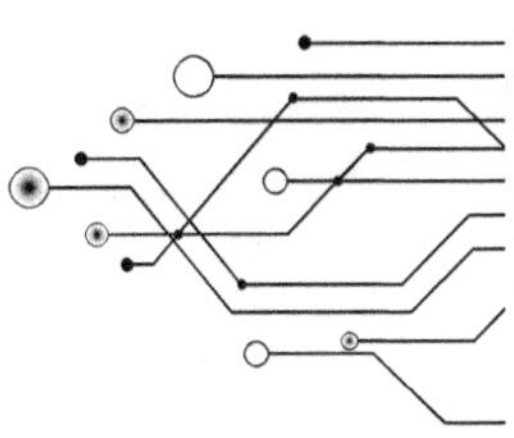

Chapter 2

THE FLAXENHART LEGACY

Gwynn found her footsteps leading her away from the lab. She knew what would greet her once she got there, and she wasn't sure she could face it just then. TenDek Corporation had sent over a small contingent of scientists, presumably to help Gwynn with her project. In fact, the entire station was now staffed in a way it had never been since it was built. There were cleaners and cooks and maintenance workers. The dormant algae farms were systemically being brought back online, with new farmers being hired, and the old ones all promoted to oversee the newbies.

But it was the scientists that were getting to Gwynn. There were at least twice as many as the lab comfortably held, all of them going over Gwynn's old research, redoing her experiments to see if they got the same results, verifying her conclusions. She was being consulted as an expert on both algae and crystals, and the questions were getting more and more complex. It was getting harder and harder to hide the fact that she didn't have any idea how to do what they assumed she was close to doing—turning algae into tuotarium crystals.

Gwynn pushed open the door to the Flaxenhart Museum and took a deep breath, letting it out slowly as the door closed behind her, leaving her in relative darkness and quiet. This was the only part of the station that hadn't been filled with staff and people, Enzo and her convincing her father that having the museum up and running would be a distraction to the more important work.

"After the crystals are made," Bertram had said, nodding. "That's a much better idea."

Gwynn had given up trying to convince him that it wouldn't happen. At first, with all the scientists and improved resources, she actually felt as confident as he did that she could do it, make the crystals. But as the others went over her data byte by byte, she found her confidence in her abilities waning.

So she wandered through the main entrance of the museum and over to the exhibit on the history of algae farming. She stared at the models of the first generation photobioreactors that were on the colony ships and noted how little had actually changed in the intervening years. Growing algae took the same basic things, no matter how fancy of a way it was made: light, water, carbon dioxide, and nutrients. Just like crystals took the same basic things: a base material, a solvent, pressure, and time. So simple, and yet....

"I wasn't sure about this place at first, but I find myself visiting again and again."

Gwynn whirled toward the voice behind her. Gair Ingram was wearing a simple shirt and pants, both made of rare materials and which Gwynn knew cost more than anything in her entire wardrobe. Still, the green in the shirt brought out his eyes, and she found herself smiling at him. Smiling at the head of TenDek had gotten easier the more she practiced it, and she had been getting plenty of practice the past while. It had also been harder for her to remember that, technically, he was the enemy, the man who would take everything she held near and dear away from her and her family.

"I didn't realize the history of algae farming fascinated you so," she said, leaning casually back against the rail that separated her from the models.

"I didn't either," he said, walking forward to lean his elbows against the same rail, putting his head slightly lower than hers. And very close. He looked up at her, blue eyes sparkling under dark lashes. "But it has become a very dear subject to me," he said.

Gwynn had to look away from his gaze. He had a tendency of saying things in a tone of voice that brought heat to her cheeks.

"And what makes it so dear?" she asked.

"How much it has shaped your life," he said, standing up. Now she struggled to avoid looking at him, his body so close to hers. "And how it might lead to something that will change everything."

"Gair...." She stood up too and struggled with her desire to both run away and stand closer. "You put too much faith in me."

"Only because I know just how brilliant you are," he said, reaching out a hand to lift her chin with a single finger. He looked her squarely in the eye. "I know you can do this, even if you sometimes doubt."

In that moment, she didn't have any doubts. She felt confident, and brilliant, and more than a little sexy. He was so close—all she had to do was lean her head in, and....

"Gair!" a loud voice said from the other room. "Are you in here?"

Gair dropped his hand and didn't quite sigh as he stood up straight and faced the doorway to the exhibit room.

"In here," he said.

Elidor Ingram and his constant shadow, Warren Frey, entered the room. Gwynn stood up straighter, suddenly self-conscious under the latter's gaze. Warren had a way of looking at her that seemed to take in details even she was unaware of, and she always wondered how he saw her. It didn't help that he was good-looking, with a long nose and square chin, dark, sun-browned skin, adorable freckles, and quite a lot of green in his blue eyes. Gwynn wanted to impress him, but always felt young and gangly in front of him.

"We need to go over security for the ball," Elidor said. "Hello, Ms. Flaxenhart." He bowed politely. Elidor Ingram was clean-shaven and wore his hair in spikey curls that stuck out from his head in what appeared to be a haphazard way, but Gwynn suspected was very intentionally shaped. Gair's baby-brother looked younger but acted older, his brown eyes always so serious.

Gwynn bowed back at Elidor and wondered why he seemed to always choose to greet her with her mother's family custom, and not her father's. She fought the urge to flop more of her blonde hair over the purple, as though that physical reminder of her heritage was to blame.

"Mr. Ingram," Gwynn said stiffly back. It felt strange to her to call one brother by his first name and the other by his last. Apparently Gair agreed.

"I don't think we need to be so formal," he said. "Elidor, we have been guests of Gwynn and her family for a week. Surely we're on a first-name basis by now."

"I am," Warren said. "Hi Gwynn." He gave her a little wave, and she waved back for lack of a better response. "This place is really neat." He looked around appreciatively, stepping closer to get a better look at the models behind Gwynn and Gair. "The farms used to look like that?"

"On the colony ships," Gwynn said, automatically falling into tour guide mode. She'd given the tour of the museum to countless investors before her father found the Ingrams. "They were able to make algae from light and water and a simple nutrient solution. Then the algae in turn worked as an air filter, taking in carbon dioxide and putting out oxygen. Most ships integrated the algae farms as part of the air filtration system: food, and air, all from the same source. And since there are so many types of algae, including ones that were already in popular rotation as food—mostly the seaweed varieties—there are a lot of types of food products you can make from it."

"Oh, I know," Warren said. "I'm pretty sure I've had just about every variety. There's not a soldier alive who doesn't know the Flaxenhart logo. Every food cube we ever ate came stamped with those three moons."

"We try our best to give them good flavor," Gwynn said, feeling apologetic.

"Don't worry," Warren said. "People from places like I come from? Getting three square meals of any food is amazing. A variety? That felt like heaven when I first enlisted."

Gwynn looked him over with new interest. He seemed too young to have fought in the Genome War, but then he was that in-between age where he could be fifty and have lived well or thirty and lived hard. She was born at the official end of the war, but troops stayed active in some of the further out systems for another five years before the Second Treaty promised poverty relief in those colonies, and people finally put down their arms against the remaining Progressive troops. If Warren had routinely eaten Flaxenhart Food Stuffs, then he fought for the Progressives. Her father had refused to supply the Naturalists because of his love for her mother—Naturalists tended to attack people with visible evidence of modifications even after the war ended. That was the thing—almost all modified colonists were Progressives by default. They were too easily targeted not to be.

One more reason for Gwynn to resent her heritage.

"Well, I'm glad you liked them," she said to Warren. "My family takes a lot of pride in creating quality goods."

"I gotta say, it's a real treat being here," he said warmly. "The Flaxen Moons. Who doesn't want to know how the algae is made?"

Gwynn looked over at Gair to see how he was taking this display of enthusiasm and was surprised to see him grinning.

"Exactly! As soon as we have the first crystal prototypes, I think we should re-open the museum. I know many people would want to see such an important part of history firsthand. This farm has been around since the dawn of the Alliance." He turned to Gwynn. "You're part of an amazing legacy."

Gwynn was taken back by his enthusiasm but found herself smiling at him. He made everything about her life seem so much more exciting than she saw it. She wasn't stuck on a boring algae farm—she was part of a grand legacy. She liked the way she looked in his eyes.

"Speaking of," Elidor said, his tone much less excited than his brother's. "We need to talk about security at the Hart Ball."

"Yeah," Warren chimed in. "Lots of people in and out. Lots of corners to cover."

"I'm sure Enzo can help you with anything you need," Gwynn said. "He's my father's right-hand man. He sort of runs things."

Sort of was an understatement, but she wasn't comfortable being that open about her family business in front of Elidor and Warren. She probably shouldn't be that open with Gair either, considering he was a business partner and not a friend, but she struggled to think along those lines with him.

"Enzo?" Warren asked.

"Enzo Drystan? Have you had a chance to meet him?"

Elidor looked hard at Warren, who simply shrugged back.

"Not the Enzo I knew," he said.

Gwynn tried to figure out why there was tension in the room, and why Elidor kept looking at Warren, but couldn't decipher their expressions.

"Well then, let's go find Enzo and get this all worked out," Gair said.

"I actually have another task I need Warren for," Elidor said.

"Then I guess I shall have to start the discussions by myself," Gair said. He had a tone that Gwynn hadn't heard him use before, and she wondered just how close the brothers were.

"We will join you as soon as we can," Elidor said. He turned and bowed to Gwynn. "Gwynn," he said with the same formality he'd been using to call her Ms. Flaxenhart.

Gair followed suit, adding a wink to his bow, and Warren gave her a small salute and a large smile.

Then she was alone in the museum again, wondering about what to do next. She was running out of time—preparation for the ball had already begun. But she was also running out of will-power. Maybe it would be better for someone like Gair to take over the farms. Her family held them for generations and only managed to run them to ruin.

But even thinking those thoughts felt like a betrayal. She knew she couldn't just give up, let the Ingrams have her family home, her legacy. She owed it to the people who came before her—all the people featured in this museum—to fight with everything she had left.

If she lost, as least she would know she tried everything she could.

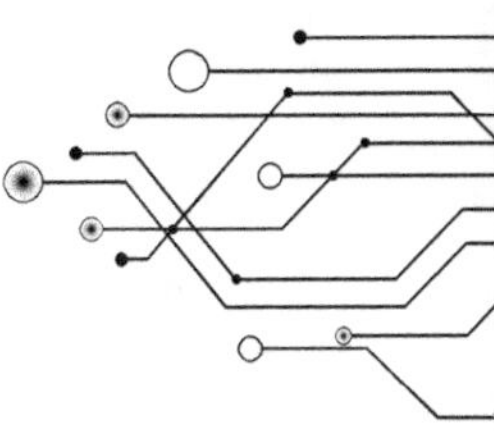

Chapter 8

THE CORPORATE SPY

She was going to get caught. It wasn't a matter of if, but when. She'd played out every scenario she could as she hunched down below the smooth white counter, and not a single one was going to get her out of this mess without a guard, a tech, or the over-eager dock attendant she'd made too much of an impression on coming in spotting her with something she wasn't supposed to have. Aderyn Ryder's original plan was to get in, get a copy of the data, and get out. But none of her research had indicated that the lead tech had a severe case of paranoia and a bio-locked workstation that was impossible to hack into with the genetic material Aderyn had on hand, which did in fact include that of the lead tech, Jareth Ankler. Just not Jareth's pet lizard, who Aderyn had found out he'd grown from a Grow Your Own Reptile! kit and genetically modified to keep small enough to live in a special pouch under his shirt at all times. Said lizard, it turned out, was also the key to every lock Jareth created. Specifically, the lizard's saliva was the key. The lizard's saliva was also lethal to anyone who was not Jareth.

And also, it was a lizard, and Aderyn never really liked lizards. So instead of trying to go through the nearly impossible task of getting Jareth alone, getting the lizard safely back to the workstation, and getting the lizard's spit on the lock without also accidentally poisoning herself, Aderyn did the next best thing: she broke the protective casing of the workstation, yanked the data core out, and ran.

The problem was that said core was tagged with a tracking chip and any attempt to take it out of any exit would immediately set off every alarm in TenDek Corporation. She estimated she had maybe ten minutes until her smash and grab of the data core was discovered, and if she didn't find a way out of the main building and back to the ship dock—with the core—not only would she be facing serious jail time, her client would very unhappy.

Aderyn had the kind of clients that it wasn't safe to make unhappy.

Aderyn pulled up her 3D map of the TenDek Research and Development Space Station on her com bracelet, using her other hand to twist the floor map around, tracking different paths with her index finger. The secret to any good escape was to control the information—video feed, sensor information, ID chip logs—any information that told people who what and where other people were. The truth was, most people didn't look up from their coms anymore, counting on their resident AIs to tell them if the people around them belonged or not. Aderyn had convinced the TenDek AI that she was a visiting shareholder. That would get her to an exit, but not through, not with the core's chip triggering the alarm. She gestured at her projection until it zoomed in on something interesting: there was a recycling room one floor down that Aderyn was pretty sure she could get to. Maybe she didn't have to leave with the core, so long as they both made it out. It was an inkling of a plan, and that was enough to push her into action, tapping into the local video feed to make sure her path was clear before sliding out from behind the counter and smoothing her jacket down where it had bunched up. The core was safe in the satchel draped across her body, but she could practically hear her escape clock ticking down.

She walked calmly and with purpose, keeping her pace steady and unhurried, despite her desire to run. She would be passing three open offices on this floor before getting to the stairwell, and she needed the people inside those offices not to have any reason to notice her going by. Her outfit had been carefully selected to match her persona—a boring, overpriced suit that did little to flatter her curves and that marked her as a mid-level shareholder who was wealthy enough to let do what she wanted, but not wealthy enough to bother sucking up to. Her hair was twisted up in such a way that the bright purple streak was hidden, only showing the dark brown, and her makeup was conservative, with only some sparkle brushed across her cheeks in the way that was all the rage in the Dekken Solar System. She wore brown contacts over her amethyst eyes, as her eye-color would have made her stand out too much. She was shorter than most Dekken women, which was impressive considering she was considered tall for an Osterian, man or woman. Still, she hoped she blended in enough that these little differences didn't mean as much.

Maybe, if any of the workers she passed were bright or curious enough, they may have wondered why anyone who wasn't staff wasn't being escorted. Aderyn trusted her research that suggested that most of the people at TenDek Research and Development were neither of those things—too stressed out and preoccupied with their own drama to pay attention to anyone else's.

Still, she breathed a sigh of relief when she got to the stairwell without incident, using her swiped ID chip to gain entry, and only then allowing herself to jog lightly down the stairs. She gained entry to the next floor with another quick scan, trusting her memory of the 3D map to lead her to a doorway about halfway down the hall on the right-hand side. This door didn't have a lock, and Aderyn slipped inside easily.

The recycling room for this part of the TenDek compound was mostly filled with old coms tech, vid-screens, and empty food packages, but Aderyn could tell at least one workstation had been torn out and sent down here to be stripped into parts. The core would blend in well with those bits, and she hurried over, noticing as she did a small reflective square on each item in the room. Even the food packaging had these squares, and as Aderyn picked one up to look closer, she felt her heart sink.

Of course the TenDek workers tagged their recycling. They wanted to prevent the very thing that Aderyn was trying to do—slipping important tech into the recycling chute to smuggle it out of the compound. After using her com bracelet to get images of a few more of the tags, Aderyn's computer told her that not only was each item tagged, each tag directed the item to the appropriate recycling center. The good news was that Aderyn could use a tag to send the data core where she wanted it to go. The bad news was that she had no idea how to make the recycling tags. She wandered over to the main workstation in the room and stared at the login screen.

The question now was whose ID should she try to use to log in? She had a handful of worker IDs and passwords with her, which is how she had gotten as far as she did. And while she was pretty sure anyone could come and log in their own recycling, she doubted anyone of any status in the organization did. She turned on her com bracelet's 3D projector again and flipped through the various IDs she had stolen, trying to find someone of the appropriately low status. She narrowed it down to two potentials and cross-referenced their IDs with their schedules. Most AIs noticed when the same person logged in to two different parts of their compounds at the same time. She needed one of the two to not be logged in.

But unfortunately, that was not the case. They both appeared to be at their respective workstations. Aderyn scrolled through her IDs again, this time looking for anyone marked currently offline. Again, she had two possibilities. One was the head of the bioengineering department, and the other the very same lizard-holding lab tech who had made this job so very complicated. Of course, Jareth probably never logged in his own recycling. She imagined it would be very hard for him to explain why he suddenly had, particularly the day the data core went missing. It gave her no small amount of satisfaction to picture his discomfort as she typed in his ID and password, swiping his replicated DNA sample across the sensor to verify his identity. It was a public workstation—no poisonous lizard spit allowed.

She hoped.

Aderyn exhaled when the computer granted her access and brought up a simple menu. She picked the name of a recycling center in orbit around the same planet as the research and development station and labeled the data core as a broken motherboard.

When the computer asked her if she'd like to disable the tracking chip, she grinned. Yes, she selected. Most definitely yes. The computer secured the recycling sticker on the data core at the same time it disabled the tracking chip, replacing one way of keeping tabs on it with another. Sadly, the sticker was no easier to remove than the chip itself had been, but Aderyn programed her own computer to track the sticker, noting its unique ID code. She hoped it would be enough once she got to the recycling center.

The only thing left to do was drop the core into the appropriate bin so that a drone could start it on its journey.

Aderyn's hand hovered over the bin. Once she let go, so much could go wrong. She hadn't anticipated this path, hadn't figured out all the variables, all the possible outcomes. If she lost this core....

"Stupid lizard," she muttered. Then she let the data core go. A scanner at the entrance of the bin beeped once to register that it was tracking the core as it slid down and out of sight. Aderyn just had to trust the AI would get it to its destination safely.

Now, to make sure she did, too.

Aderyn quickly logged out of the workstation, then brought the vid-feed up on her com bracelet to check that the corridor was clear. Moments later, she was outside the nearest lift, trying not to pay too much attention to the time.

Footsteps were approaching, and Aderyn could see the general shape of a man in her peripheral. She kept her head straight, her gaze bored.

"Nice sparkles," the man said as he settled in next to her. Aderyn let her eyes drift over to him, picking up on a strong profile with a long nose and square chin, before rolling her eyes in a clear gesture of dismissal. But her eyes took in other details: his suit was nicer than hers. His hair was shorn short, only slightly longer on top than on the sides. His blue-green eyes were bright and alert, and his skin was sun-browned with a smattering of dark freckles across his face, proof that he'd spent time planetside in the near past.

And he was staring at her. Blatantly. Obviously. She shifted uncomfortably under his gaze, trying to figure out how her character would handle a situation like this.

"Do you mind?" she asked sharply, turning to look pointedly at him.

"Not at all," he said, smiling warmly back. "I like the purple in your sparkles," he added. "But I think they were probably a mistake."

"A mistake?" Aderyn asked. Her mind raced as she took in other details, like the way his suit jacket puffed out just so, as though it was concealing something hard and probably metal underneath it. She found her eyes searching for his hands: short nails, rough calluses on the knuckles, a few scars nicked along the edges that looked an awful lot like the remnants of old defensive wounds. Her eyes glanced down to notice the width of his stance and how he was carrying his weight. Then her eyes were back up, finally seeing his face and the warm smile. It was a handsome face. The nose didn't look broken or crooked, but she figured that just meant he had good health care. He was a fighter, and he had good health care, and that meant he was probably very, very good at his job.

"Purple isn't a Dekken color," the man said, gesturing to the brush of sparkles at her cheeks.

"Who said I was Dekken?" Aderyn asked, shifting her weight slightly, the hand furthest away from the man slipping into her bag, her fingers searching out her taze-stick. She grasped the stubby handle firmly and slowly started to pull her hand out.

"All the shareholders are," the man said. "It's in the bylaws." He opened his jacket then in one swift move, revealing the gun holstered underneath it. "Stay still, and I won't have to draw this."

Aderyn froze. Option one, pull the taze-stick out as quickly as she could and hope she could swing it around at the man before he got his gun pointed at her. Option two, play this out and find a different opportunity to try to escape.

But the core was already on its way. She needed to hurry if she wanted to catch up to it.

She smiled.

"I am not sure who you think I am," she said as sarcastically sweet as she figured her persona could be, "but if you dare pull that thing on me, I will have your job. Maybe even your head."

"You really don't want to do this," the man said, his hand hovering just over the gun.

"Want so rarely comes into it," Aderyn said, dropping her persona. "But I do it anyway." She jerked to her left, slamming her shoulder into the man's while whipping her taze-stick out of her bag at the same time, pressing the release to make the stubby stick a long thin baton crackling with electricity. The man was more solidly planted than she'd hoped, and he recovered quickly, swinging his gun up toward her just as she slammed her taze-stick down on his arm.

His hand went rigid, and then his arm, and suddenly he was still as a turned off work-bot in front of her.

The lift arrived and Aderyn backed away from the man, his eyes wide with fear and pain as she retracted her taze-stick back into its dormant and smaller state.

"It won't last long," she reassured him. "But the recovery can be a bitch." She stepped into the lift, turning to keep the man in view, and watched as his eyes swiveled to follow her. "Oh, and thanks. I like the purple too," she said. The lift doors closed.

Aderyn checked the time on her com bracelet. She was going to be cutting it very close, and she willed the lift to go faster. Her skin felt as electric as her taze-stick, and she had to take several deep breaths to calm her heart beat. It had been a very near thing.

But while the man was willing to pull his gun on her, she could tell he was reluctant to pull the trigger. His hand froze with his index finger just outside where it should have been if he'd wanted to kill her. For some reason, that made her smile. She shook it and her nervous energy off, smoothing out her suit jacket again, and plastering the appropriate haughty look on her face.

The same dock attendant from earlier greeted her. Batilda, her name-tag read. Poor thing.

"Done already, Ms. Carmenère?" Batilda asked, jumping up and hurrying toward Aderyn.

"My meeting was cut short," Aderyn said, pushing past her to get to the transport shuttle. "Some issue with one of the workers." She waved her hand vaguely. "They are making me reschedule."

She gave the attendant her most offended look. "Someone is definitely going to hear about this." She kept walking and hoped Batilda would get the hint.

"Oh, I'm so sorry to hear that," the woman said. She stopped walking suddenly and looked down at the com pad on her wrist. "Oh," she said again. "It says here there's been a security breach. All ships are to be grounded." She looked up, clearly uncertain.

"That certainly doesn't apply to me," Aderyn said. "But if this place isn't actually safe anymore, I really need to leave as soon as possible."

"But it says...." Batilda looked up, clearly distressed. "All ships." She held her wrist out toward Aderyn as if to show her. Aderyn's hand reached for her taze-stick again, already knowing it was a bad idea. Only the attendant could unlock the docking gear and open the hangar doors. There was no way to both be on the shuttle and launch it at the same time. Her pet AI, Gilda, wasn't advanced enough for that yet. If Aderyn took out poor Batilda, she would be stuck on the TenDek station.

As Aderyn's eyes stared at the screen Batilda was holding out to her, they widened in surprise.

"Actually," she said, "it doesn't."

Batilda pulled her hand back quickly, staring at the new instructions scrolling across the screen.

"All ships except Ms. Carmenère's," she read out loud. "Oh, well, that worked out then!" She grinned up at Aderyn. "I'll get you underway in no time!"

Aderyn smiled back, genuine relief flooding her face. She hurried to her shuttle, practically throwing herself into the pilot's seat and pulling the hatch closed behind her. It was a cramped space, but then again, the shuttle was only meant for short-term travel for one or two people max. Skip-hops, the Dekkens called them, because they were only good for short trips between ships or orbiting stations, like the TenDek one. Aderyn ran her skip-hop through the pre-launch sequence and waited for the dock attendant to give her the all-clear. She watched as the hanger doors ahead of her opened.

Soon, all the lights above her were green, and her craft's com sent Batilda's voice echoing around the cockpit.

"You are free to launch, Ms. Carmenère!" she said cheerily. "Safe travels!"

Aderyn waited while Batilda engaged the em-sails—electromagnetic spacecraft launching system—shooting her forward like a rock from a sling-shot into the open vacuum of space. She engaged the thrusters of the skip-hop, slowing her momentum and gaining control of her direction.

Aderyn looked down as a message pinged on her com bracelet, and she tapped the screen to read it:

YOU OWE ME ONE.

It was signed IMP.

The only problem was, Aderyn had no idea who that was.

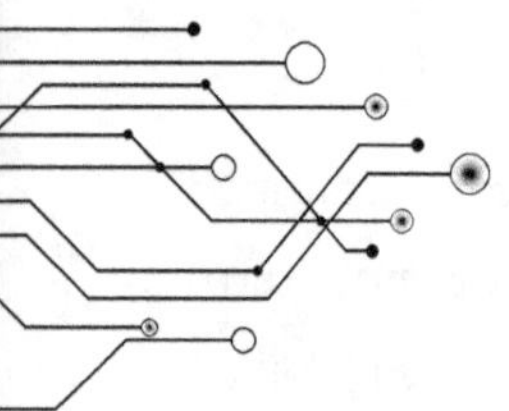

Chapter 4

THE RECYCLED HEART

Aderyn set the skip-hop to autopilot so that she could free her hands up. It took her longer than she wanted to find the signals going in and out of the recycling center, and longer still to trace those signals back to their source and set loose her pet AI, which worked its way into the recycling center system, giving her full access. She scanned the inventory and confirmed that the data core had arrived at the facility, and where it was likely located. Fortunately, the batch of items it was in hadn't been moved to the conveyor system to be taken apart by mechanical arms, all the useful bits stripped off, and the remainder melted down and reshaped. However, it was placed with a collection of things that were scheduled to be stripped within the hour, which didn't give her a lot of time.

Aderyn then switched to the docking manifesto of the station, adding one of her aliases and the registration number of the skip-hop, which would allow her to land with minimal questions. It wasn't unusual for folks to look for specific parts at the recycling stations. Anything not marked as proprietary could be purchased from the station, at a profit to the company that ran the recycling center—in this case, TenDek. TenDek seemed to run everything in this solar system. Aderyn had been very careful to mark the data core as something available for purchase.

She then resumed control of the skip-hop to maneuver it into the landing dock. Her skip-hop struggled to engage with the em-sails magnetic field, making for a rough landing. Aderyn quickly changed her clothes, struggling in the cramped space, so that she could better match the ID she had chosen, shoving her hair under a helmet with a removable visor and scrubbing at the sparkles on her cheeks with a cleaning solvent. The hangar doors closed while she was still trying to get glitter off her face, and she cursed whoever came up with this particular cosmetic trend. She gave up when her sensors indicated that someone was walking toward her skip-hop and hoped that she either did a good enough job or that it was a popular enough trend that even folks like she was going to pretend to be wore the stuff. She opened the hatch to the cockpit, and pulled herself up, looking toward the deck attendant.

Blue-green eyes over a smattering of freckles greeted her, making her freeze. This time his gun was out and pointed at her, but his smile was wide and bright. She couldn't be sure from this distance, but she was guessing his finger was definitely on the firing mechanism this time.

"I'm sure you're planning something," he said. "But I'd prefer that you just stay still and keep your hands where I can see them. Up above your head would be best of all."

Aderyn did as she was told since her taze-stick was in the bag slung across her shoulders, and every other plan she had involved her getting back in the skip-hop. But again, without anyone there to launch her into space, she really had no way of using the damned thing to escape.

"How'd you beat me here?" she asked, slowly straightening up until she was standing in the cockpit.

"I did tell you not to move," the man said.

"It was an awkward position," she countered. "I was getting a cramp." She tested his patience again by sliding one leg up and over the edge of the open hatch, resting it firmly on the small ledge below. He narrowed his eyes and kept his hand steady. She followed suit with her other leg, holding her hands out awkwardly for balance, and ended by sitting on the edge of the cockpit, her hands still in the air. "This is much more comfortable," she informed him.

"You do like pushing things, don't you?" he asked. He seemed amused.

Aderyn could hear footsteps sounding behind the man, and her eyes searched for their source. She noted that the man didn't seem surprised by the sound. He didn't turn or react as another man walked up beside him.

"This is her?" the second man asked. Aderyn sighed deeply.

"Elidor Ingram," she said. He was wearing a nondescript jumpsuit, looking more like he belonged at the recycling center than she did, and had a satchel draped across his right shoulder. His face was smoothly shaved, and his hair styled so that some of his dark curls seemed to spring out from his head like small stalagmites. She was sure it was supposed to give the impression that he didn't really care for his appearance, letting his hair do what it wanted. She was also sure that someone had intentionally spiked his hair like that, and not a single curl was out of place.

"You know me?"

Aderyn was surprised by his surprise. He was the younger

brother of the richest man in the Dekken Solar System, and he didn't think he'd be recognized?

"I did my research," she said simply.

"You got pretty far," he said, pulling an object out of the satchel—the stolen data core. Aderyn could see light reflecting off the recycling sticker. "I am actually fairly certain you would have recovered it and delivered it on time, which is impressive."

"On time," she repeated, her mind whirling. "Interesting."

The man with the gun grinned.

"I told you," he said to Elidor.

"You did indeed," Elidor said. "Mr. Frey speaks very highly of you," he told Aderyn. "Despite your most recent interaction."

"I have questions," Aderyn announced, testing the waters by slowly bringing her hands down into her lap.

"You're pushing things again," Mr. Frey said.

"You're not going to shoot," she said dismissively. "And you're not going to arrest me because if you were a security force, you would have announced that by now. You have to, by law." She rolled her shoulders back as if working a kink out, and stretched her head from side to side, loosening her neck.

"You have questions," Elidor said, his eyes narrowing.

"Who hired me?" she asked.

"I did," Mr. Frey said.

"Why?" Aderyn responded.

"I asked him to," Elidor said. He looked back down at the data core, and tossed it up in the air, catching it easily again. "This was supposed to be a copy."

"Of something I am positive you already have access to," she said. "Unless your brother has been keeping things to himself."

Elidor's eyes turned sharply back to her.

"Are you positive he won't shoot you?" he asked.

Aderyn stared at the other man, assessing. His arm seemed relaxed, as if he could hold his gun up all day, and he continued to have a bemused look on his face. There was something in his eyes though that she hadn't fully registered before.

"Not unless you order him to," she said after a moment.

Elidor glanced over at Mr. Frey, whose gaze was steady on Aderyn.

"Perceptive," he said. "Mr. Frey, you can lower your gun now."

Mr. Frey did, holstering it under his jacket.

"Does Mr. Frey have a first name?" Aderyn asked.

"Warren," he said, blue-green eyes sparkling. "And it's a pleasure to finally meet you, Ms. Ryder." He gave a small bow of respect, and Aderyn found herself bending forward in return, an almost automatic response.

Her family bowed. Others in the Osterian Solar System bowed. But not in the Dekken system, she had noticed. They preferred handshakes, grasping each other by the wrist. Warren knew both her name and where she was from. Aderyn tensed, her hands open and ready in her lap.

"What happens now?" she asked, skipping all the less important questions. Warren's gun was away, but that didn't mean anything. She knew how fast he could draw it.

"You get paid," Elidor said, putting the data core back into his satchel. He nodded at Warren, who pulled a small data disc out of his pocket. He stepped a few feet forward and tossed it at Aderyn.

"The information you wanted," he said.

She caught the disc one-handed, feeling its smooth surface in the palm of her hand.

"And that's it?"

"You still have questions," Elidor said.

Aderyn nodded.

"Don't ask them. Not to anyone."

"It wouldn't be a good idea," Warren added, smiling again. "You have a reputation for being smarter than that."

"Oh, and Ms. Ryder," Elidor said. "I may require your services again. Mr. Frey will let you know when I do." He turned then and walked away, leaving Warren and Aderyn staring at each other, Aderyn wearily and Warren comfortably.

"I think he likes you," Warren informed her as Elidor got out of hearing range.

"Why not steal it yourself?" Aderyn asked. Warren put up a finger and made a tsk tsk noise.

"What was the deal again?"

"No questions. To anyone."

"Good." He bounced a little on his toes, as if stretching his legs, still seeming completely at ease with the current events.

"My taze-stick..." she said cautiously, not sure how to ask a question without asking a question.

"Nanites," he said back. "They make for a quick recovery. But you were right—it was a rough one. Interesting piece of hardware. Not sure I've seen anything like it."

"I made it," she said with a shrug. "It's usually more... debilitating."

"It did the job," he said, grinning again. She couldn't fathom how he could be so amiable after what she'd done, or why it seemed like she was going to get away without any retribution.

"So now I just—" She motioned back to her skip-hop.

"Oh yeah, I'll launch you," he said. "Open the doors, all that. You're free to go."

"Great," Aderyn said, standing up cautiously. She backed into the cockpit one leg at a time, the same way she got out, keeping her eyes on Warren and his too-casual stance. He gave her a small salute—she wondered if that was the greeting in whatever region of space he was from—and walked toward the dock attendant's station. Aderyn slid into her skip-hop and closed the hatch firmly behind her, relieved that it would offer protection in case Warren decided to shoot at her after all. Of course, now all he had to do was intentionally bungle the launch, and she'd be just as dead.

She started the pre-flight check anyway, waiting for all her panels to turn green.

"This is Warren." His voice was staticky over her com, but clearly still genial. "I am opening the hangar doors now. You will be clear for launch in ten, nine, eight, seven...."

The countdown wasn't necessary, or even standard, but it added tension to the moment and Aderyn wondered if maybe Warren was just playing with her, making her last moments more unbearable for his own amusement.

"Three, two, one," he finished. "Safe travels, Ms. Ryder."

And then the skip-hop was flung forward through the

atmosphere shield and into space. Aderyn ignited her thrusters and checked her engine, and everything was in working order. She maneuvered the skip-hop around so that she could look back at the landing dock of the recycling station. If there was another ship there, it hadn't arrived the same way she had.

She checked her com, but there were no new messages from the mysterious IMP, and in fact no new messages from anyone. She turned the skip-hop around and powered it up for a long burn, heading for her ship, the *Herald*. Her mind raced with possibilities, trying to put all the pieces of the last several hours together, trying to remember everything she could about how she got this job, and what information she was given then. She knew that she wouldn't be able to talk about this with anyone.

She'd keep her word and not ask anyone any questions.

But she sure as hell was going to find the answers.

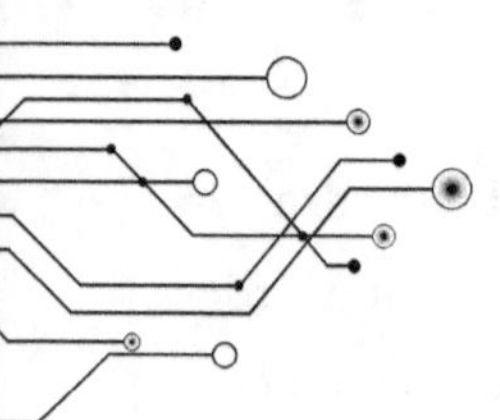

Chapter 5

THE PERFECT DELIVERY

Aderyn stumbled as she walked off her STP—ship-to-planet transport shuttle—and grabbed the side of the shuttle to help her balance, cursing planetside gravity. Spres Prime was part of a small cluster of planets orbiting a young star, which shined bright yellow in the sky, warming Aderyn's skin and dampening her face with sweat. The humidity was much higher than she was used to, and she felt strange breathing in the fresh, moist air. She had the impulse to ask someone to adjust the environmental controls, since obviously they were less than ideal.

Aderyn tried not to make a face and wiped at her forehead with the back of her hand, peering out into the sunlight and trying to spot Tuari.

He was standing not too far away, obviously amused by her display of re-adjustment to being planetside, based on his wide grin.

"Don't say anything," she said as she straightened up and made her cautious way over to him. She always felt clumsy on Spres, the gravity being just far enough off from Earth Standard that she never felt like she picked up her feet the right amount.

"If you came planetside more often, you wouldn't have such a hard time adjusting," he said, pulling her into a tight hug. "Good to see you, *shi'áád*."

"And you, *shiką*," she replied, returning the hug. She pulled back to look him over, noting that he looked leaner than the last time she saw him. He was wearing his hair up in a top-knot, loose strands dangling out from it, giving him a messy look that suited him. "Are you well?"

Tuari's people had dedicated themselves to cleaning up the ravages of the war from the planets and systems it had impacted the most. Naturally nomadic, they travelled in large tribe-ships, and worked with the survivors of any given planet to help them rebuild using sustainable and environmentally-sound means. But their anti-genetic modification stance meant they weren't as well suited to the clean-up efforts as the Ryders, who had natural protections against the increased radiation leftover from warheads and explosions, and Aderyn always worried about Tuari's health.

"Well enough," he said, laughing. "Your eyes don't miss anything."

"I'm going to worry until you tell me," she said, trying to see if he maybe looked paler than her last visit. It was hard to tell when he was sun-browned, but something did seem to be different.

"I've just been working too hard," he said. "Come, tell me your worries so that I can forget about mine." He put his arm around her shoulders easily, being only a little taller than her, and led her away from the shuttle pad and toward a hover vehicle nearby.

"This looks like a new design," she said and as they approached a side door slid open to let them inside. It was a small, sleek thing with a large glass front and generous windows on each side that looked like it would only seat two comfortably—one in front of the other—and seat three if they were very close friends.

Aderyn climbed in, moving to the back so that Tuari could take the front in case he needed to take over for the autopilot. "This reminds me of the skip-hops in Dekken."

"It's called a hover-cradle," he said, getting in and settling in front of her. "It will move over almost any obstacle in its way and can wind easily through the trees. I helped design it." He moved his hands over the control console, and the hover-cradle hummed and smoothly moved forward. "And just what were you doing in Dekken? A bit out of range for you, isn't it? That's two jump gates from here."

"My work has a tendency to take me all over," she said, glad that with his back turned he couldn't see her face.

"Even to Spres Prime," Tuari said over his shoulder.

"So, I didn't fool you then?"

"Your whole 'just coming by for a visit' thing? That was fairly easy to see through."

She watched over his shoulder as the hover-cradle entered a forested area and they glided under shade. Aderyn could tell this was an old forest based on how little light came down through the tops of the trees, and all the plant-life was shade-loving fern-like things. For a moment she was enchanted by the way the light and shadows danced around them, and her eyes caught on the fluttering wings of birds and flying insects they passed. Planetside could be very lovely.

Then the deep greens gave way to blackened trunks and scorched earth much faster than Aderyn would have anticipated. The hover-cradle shook slightly as it made the transition from one type of terrain to the other, almost like an animal shivering.

"How has the work been going?" she asked quietly.

"Rough. It always goes rough." There was a tightness in Tuari's voice that made Aderyn ache to reach out and touch him.

She gripped her right hand with her left instead and took a slow breath. That wasn't her place anymore. It would do neither of them any good to fall into old habits.

"I didn't think Spres was hit so hard," she said. "There's only, what? Three habitable planets here?"

"It's a trade hub," Tuari said. "Or was. And will be again, if we can help it."

"I saw three large stations in orbit."

"We started there," he said. "The citizens of Spres Prime fled there, those that could. There was a lot of overcrowding, but the stations themselves were in good repair. We got people planetside as soon as it was safe, hired a lot of the locals to help with the work."

"Radiation?" Aderyn asked. She hadn't felt much of anything after she landed and walked to the hover-cradle, but if the radiation had been localized, she wasn't sure she would. She had never got the hang of sensing radiation further away as some of her relatives had.

Of course, they all felt the radiation on Oster. It felt like warmth, from the inside out. It was eventual death for anyone who was not Osterian. But it was just a background sensation for everyone who was.

"Pockets," Tuari said. "We're taking all necessary precautions. It was mostly blast weapons here. Not as much atomic activity.

Not like Spres Second. People will be living in stations over Spres Second for generations."

"Why don't they leave?"

"Believe it or not, most people don't want to leave their homes." Tuari turned enough to grin at Aderyn.

"You left yours," she countered.

"With my entire family on a collective mission to help others recover from the ravages of the war." He pinned her with one of his classic pointed looks. "If home is where your family is, I am always home."

"I travel with my family, too," she said. "The Ryder clan is close."

"Not all of your family."

She looked away from him and watched as the hover-cradle made its way past a crater with edges dark and shiny like glass.

"How is Gwynn doing?" she asked.

"You could ask her."

"I try. She doesn't take my calls."

She watched in her peripheral as Tuari faced forward again, clearly uncomfortable.

"She seems distracted," he said. "I know she's under a lot of pressure, but the last several weeks she hasn't really made a lot of time to talk."

"Do you know what she has been busy with?"

"She always just says 'algae experiments'," he said, his voice weary. "Then she always promises to share more later, and never does."

"Is worrying the reason why you've lost weight?"

Tuari ignored her question, as he always did when she fussed about his health. Aderyn couldn't help but wonder if he had been impacted by the radiation sickness his family was prone to.

"We're here," he said instead.

Tuari's hands flew over the control console of the hover-cradle, and it shuddered slightly and turned sharply, settling down on a grassy patch of ground outside what looked like a large-scale campsite. The land here was less damaged than that which they'd passed, and Aderyn could see people, many of them with the same sharp features and long hair Tuari had, walking to and fro with purpose among large temporary shelters. The dome-like tents were made of thick materials and shimmered with the energy of the force-fields that were woven into their fibers. The tents had the ability to filter out harmful particles, creating cleaner, safer air inside, free from radiation.

As Tuari slid open the door of the hover-cradle, getting out first so that Aderyn had room to climb out after, Aderyn could feel a familiar tingle across her scalp. She shook her hair out as she stood up, exposing more of the purple strands that acted as a radiation filter, transmuting the low-levels of radiation around her into a gentle warmth, creating a small bubble around her that was noticeably freer of radiation than that around Tuari. She resisted the urge to pull him into her bubble, both to keep him safe and to feel his body pressed into hers. She could tell, now that she was out in the open, that the radiation here wasn't too bad—so long as the workers were taking appropriate precautions and the right meds, they could withstand long-term exposure relatively safely. Probably she was worrying for nothing, as it was clear that

Tuari's people were doing everything they could to prevent radiation sickness.

"I don't suppose you want to tell me what your business is?" he asked.

"If you can keep secrets, so can I," she responded. He gave her a wry grin and led her through the camp to a smaller tent on the outskirts.

"Chianna is in there," he said. Aderyn stared at him, searching his face for answers to the questions she was afraid to ask. "My cousin is not as good at keeping secrets as you are," he said. "She made it clear she wanted to know as soon as you arrived. I am a very smart man—I can even do simple arithmetic."

Aderyn made a face at him, and he laughed.

"Come find me after," he said. "My father wants to see you before you leave."

She reached a hand out to him, and he took it, squeezing it before letting it go. Then he turned and walked away.

Aderyn smoothed her shirt down and ran her hand over the lump at her hip that was her holstered taze-stick. Chianna may have been Tuari's cousin, but Aderyn never fully trusted clients.

She pushed the indicator to let Chianna know someone was outside. After a moment, the door opened, and Aderyn stepped inside.

"I thought you'd be more discreet," Chianna said as Aderyn's eyes adjusted to the lower inside light.

"Lovely to see you too," Aderyn said. Chianna was older than Tuari, and thicker—her side of the family tending toward stocky. She wore her hair in a single braid down her back and plain brown and beige clothing that looked practical and well-worn. Her arms were crossed against her chest, and her face seemed locked in a permanent scowl.

"You do have it, don't you?" Chianna asked.

"I wouldn't have come without it."

"And you didn't look to see what it was?"

"That's not how I work," Aderyn said, annoyed. "And you know that, which is why you went through me."

"No questions asked," Chianna said. "That's your way."

"Which is serving you well right now."

"And?"

"And I need something from you."

Chianna huffed and shook her head.

"That was not our deal. You were paid in advance."

"I just need to know how you knew this information would be in those hands." She was very careful to make it a statement, and not a question.

"That is more than I am comfortable telling you," the other woman replied.

"Things went off-plan," Aderyn said, again carefully. "But it didn't seem to matter. I was paid in full."

Chianna seemed caught off guard by this information.

"Did you see the hands?" she asked, also carefully.

"A surprising sight," Aderyn said, stepping further into the main area of the tent and looking around, her eyes taking in everything and nothing. "It almost seemed like I shouldn't have had to do what I had been hired to do."

She glanced over her shoulder to see Chianna's reaction. The older woman frowned and uncrossed her arms.

"I am not sure what you mean."

Aderyn believed her.

"I have questions that I'm not allowed to ask, that it's not safe to ask. But I also need answers."

"That's not my concern," Chianna said.

"Any name would be a good place to start."

"You are very blunt," Chianna said. "I thought you were better at this."

"Oh, I'm good enough," Aderyn said. "And I still hold what you want."

Chianna scowled. "Do you want me to wrestle you for it?"

"Could be fun," Aderyn said, smiling. "A name would be more fun though, at least for me."

"You've already been paid," Chianna said, her face flush with anger.

"I'll owe you one then," Aderyn said. "That's a promise."

Chianna considered this.

"One word," she said. "IMP."

Aderyn's pulse quickened, and she opened and closed her hands to try to get some energy out.

"I really wish I could talk you into giving me more," she said.

"Are you going to give it to me or not?" Chianna asked, her hands in fists at her side. Aderyn took the small disc out from the pouch at her side and tossed it at Chianna, getting no small amount of satisfaction in watching the other woman scramble to catch it in surprise.

"Don't worry, it's tougher than it looks," Aderyn said as Chianna glared at her. "As am I."

Chianna looked down at the disc, and Aderyn watched with interest as conflicting emotions seemed to pass over her face. Relief, anger, and was that shame? To her credit, she took a deep breath, steadying herself before meeting Aderyn's gaze.

"Then we're done here," she said. "You can go back to your ship."

"I'm going to go find Tuari, and say hi to Akechata," Aderyn said. She grinned at the glare that Chianna gave her in response.

"Tuari's father is too generous with you and your...kind," Chianna said, making a show of staring at the purple in Aderyn's hair.

"He's the head of your tribe—maybe you should follow his lead." Aderyn felt her patience wearing thin. "My family's willingness to adapt is what has saved us from the same sickness that plagues yours."

"And at what cost?" Chianna asked. "The Spres system was all but destroyed thanks to the war, thanks to people like you refusing to accept how things ought to be."

"The Naturalists started the war," Aderyn said, feeling heat rise in her body. "Because they don't know how to be tolerant."

"And how much change should we tolerate? How much until we're not even human anymore?"

"Human enough to get you what you needed," Aderyn said.

Chianna scoffed, shoving the disc into a pocket.

"You should have been more discreet," she said.

"So should you," Aderyn said. "Tuari walked me directly here."

Chianna stared at her in surprise.

"I'll go find your cousin then," Aderyn said, turning back toward the entrance. "Be well, Chianna."

PART 2: A Bargain Made

When the girl was alone the manikin came again for the third time, and said, "What will you give me if I spin the straw for you this time also?"

"I have nothing left that I could give," answered the girl.

"Then promise me, if you should become queen, to give me your first child."

Who knows whether that will ever happen, thought the miller's daughter, and, not knowing how else to help herself in this strait, she promised the manikin what he wanted, and for that he once more spun the straw into gold.

Jacob and Wilhelm Grimm, Rumpelstiltskin

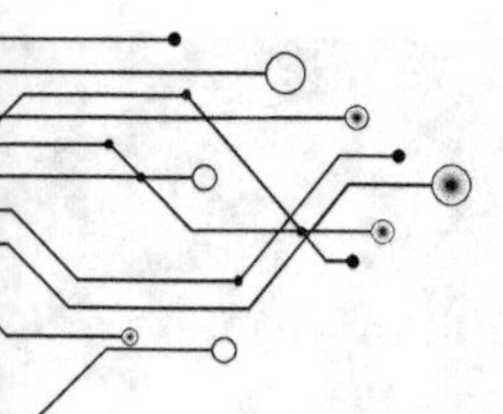

Chapter 6

THE GENEROUS OFFER

Gwynn had taken to working from her quarters, her frazzled nerves making her patience too thin to bother with other people. She had been sequestered in her room for the last several days now that all her old research had been thoroughly examined, telling everyone that she was doing more of her own work. She'd even had a pressure chamber installed near her workstation. She'd tried making a few crystals, continuing the methodical approach she had been taking before her father's ridiculous deal, but none of her results were promising, and the number of variables she was looking at were still too high to make any sort of educated guess about what combos were more likely to bring her closer to her goal.

In desperation, she had signed on to the AltFeed, scouring discussion boards and data hubs for any posted research on tuotarium crystals. She had been looking for share-tech, but most of what she found was people claiming to have original pre-war formulas for making crystals out of almost any organic material, and they were all willing to share it—for a price. Gwynn might have been tempted to try buying one of those formulas if she had any hope of affording them.

The history of the tuotarium crystals—a subclass of crystals that all formed the same high-energy structural bonds—was wrapped up in the history of the colonies themselves. They had been discovered right around the time jump gates were first discovered, though there was some debate about which discovery came first. The combination of a new, efficient, and accessible energy source and the means to travel vast distances ushered in the golden age of The Alliance. Scientists during that time even figured out how to make tuotarium crystals through very expensive and very complicated means that only the wealthiest in the Alliance could afford.

And then the Genome War happened, and those formulas were destroyed by terrorists trying to stop the continued expansion of human colonies across the galaxy. They also destroyed any crystals they could get their hands on, trying to turn back the clock on technology. The remaining tuotarium crystals in the system became even more valuable, particularly the large ones big enough to power whole cities. Anyone who could make crystals would quickly become very wealthy.

Gwynn hadn't even been that interested in the money when she first started. She knew her family needed more, and that was definitely an interest of hers, but mostly she was after the recognition she imagined she would get as a scientist. She hadn't exactly left Savenel Science Academy in good standing when her father called her home. She still felt like she had a chance to prove to everyone just how capable she was.

But not if she couldn't actually deliver.

As she scrolled through, her feelings of helplessness increasing, a private com message popped up in the corner of her screen. It was from a user named IMP.

I CAN HELP YOU MAKE TUOTARIUM CRYSTALS.

SURE, she wrote back. EVERYONE CAN.

This is a legitimate offer, Gwynn. I will help you save Flaxen Moons.

Gwynn shivered then and turned to look behind her to see if there was someone there. Maybe this was Tuari playing a trick on her? She never used her real name on the AltFeed, and she took all the security precautions Tuari had taught her, with active firewalls and no ability for anyone to trace her account back to her. She should have been completely anonymous.

But tricks weren't Tuari's style. For a second, she imagined that Aderyn was contacting her, but this wasn't her cousin's style either. Besides, she hadn't spoken with Aderyn since the incident at Savenel—the reason why her performance began to slip, why things all started to go wrong.

Gwynn pressed reply, and typed out: Who are you? How do you know who I am?

I just want to help. I have been watching your family for a long time.

You realize how that sounds? she typed back.

It was a moment before another message came in.

I understand that it will be hard to trust me, but I can prove my intent.

Gwynn shook her head.

There is no way. There is nothing you can do.

But then a new message popped up with an article embedded in it. It was something Gwynn hadn't seen before, and it was all about algae solutions—and crystal formation. From the publication date, it appeared to be written pre-war, which seemed impossible. There had been a concerted effort by the Naturalists to track down and destroy any mention of tuotarium crystals that could help people learn to make them. They wrote virus AIs specifically for that task.

Where did you get this?

I have access to everything you would need.

Gwynn skimmed through the article. It was the real deal. This alone could help her research jump to the next level, help her better understand what she was trying to do.

If she hadn't gotten access to it two years ago....

It wasn't much good to her now.

You are running out of time, IMP wrote. The Hart Ball is in a few days. Please. Let me help.

It was chilling that IMP knew her timeline, but everything about the conversation scared Gwynn—but also gave her hope.

What would it cost?

Gwynn was almost surprised to see her own text appear below IMP's. Was she really contemplating this? She should run and get someone, tell them that security had been compromised.

Access to your research.

That's all? she typed back.

For now, came the reply.

Gwynn stared at those words, feeling the weight of them. She should call Tuari and talk it over with him. He'd offer words of support at least, warn her against such a rash choice. She could reach out to Enzo and his husband, ask them what they thought of this deal. He'd always been good at giving advice.

She could call her Aderyn. Aderyn had ways of finding things, of figuring things out. She could probably figure out who IMP was, tell Gwynn if this was a good idea or not.

But Gwynn didn't need anyone else to tell her this was a bad choice. Trusting IMP was stupid. This was a horrible idea.

But then, horrible ideas ran in the family.

AGREED.

She hit send and leaned back in her chair. The follow up message gave her instructions about how to package her research and where to send it.

Her hands hesitated again. But it wasn't like she had gotten anywhere with this same information. She couldn't imagine why IMP would even want it since whoever IMP was, they had access to better research than she could send.

Gwynn sent everything IMP asked for. The message took a long time to transmit—it was rather a lot of data. It surprised her to see it all bundled together like that, to see the fruit of two years' worth of labor all in one place. She really had done a lot, even if it hadn't gotten her anywhere.

Then she got a confirmation that the data was received, and a final message:

GIVE ME TWO DAYS.

She wanted to ask what, exactly, she was going to get in two days. She wanted to know what guarantee she had that she would get anything back at all. She had a million questions.

CAN YOU REALLY DO THIS?

I PROMISE, IMP wrote back. I WILL NOT LET YOU DOWN.

Gwynn was surprised by how relieved she felt even seeing

those words. It had been a long time since anyone had promised to take care of her and her needs.

THANK YOU.

She smiled at the response: IT IS MY PLEASURE.

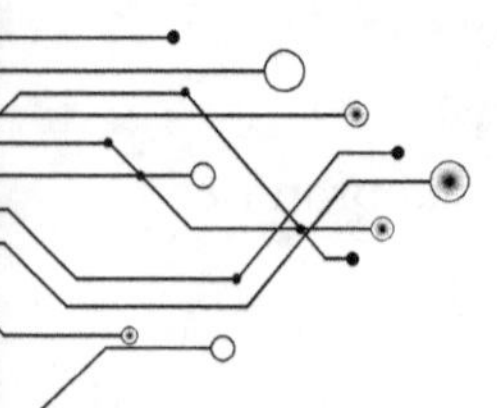

Chapter 7

THE ONGOING SEARCH

Aderyn sat in one of the four chairs of her STP and patched her com bracelet into the *Herald* in orbit around Spres Prime, using the STP's com system as a relay.

"Gilda, find anything?"

"I have searched all records and networks I have access to, and could not find any information on any person, username, or artificial intelligence named IMP," her ship's AI told her. "I could search the AltFeed," she offered.

"No," Aderyn said. "I don't want you to take the risk."

"I have searched the AltFeed before," Gilda reminded her.

"Not for something like this," Aderyn said.

"You believe this search is dangerous," Gilda surmised, her computerized voice flat and unemotional.

"Someone or something powerful is putting various pieces into play toward an unknown outcome," Aderyn. "That is definitely my idea of dangerous. And whatever or whoever IMP is, they have been able to completely hide their trail. That suggests high intelligence and skill."

"You are worried that IMP is smarter than me," Gilda said.

"I am worried that IMP is more nefarious than you," Aderyn replied. "You're young yet. There's some things I want to put off you knowing for as long as possible."

"I want to help," Gilda said. Of course you do, Aderyn thought. I programmed you to want to help.

"Can you connect me with the *Cardinal de Richelieu*?"

"Of course I can," Gilda said. "Connecting now."

Aderyn watched the STP's vid-screen anxiously, hoping that Treasa would answer.

"Addy, what the hells?" Treasa said as greeting. "Do you have any idea what time it is?"

"The time for you to be on watch," Aderyn said.

"If you were waiting for me, that means this can't be good."

Aderyn watched as her older cousin twirled stands of her purple hair around her fingers. Treasa had more purple than most in the clan, on account of strong blood lines on her father's side. Her actual hair, a deep auburn in color, looked like a decorative stripe among all the purple.

"Something came up," Aderyn said.

"Obviously," Treasa said. "Do I need to get Mom involved in this?"

"Gods, I hope not," Aderyn said. "But I was on a run, and something weird happened, and I need help tracking someone down."

"How much do you want to tell me?"

It was a legitimate question. The Ryder clan appreciated what Aderyn did for a living, trading information for goods the same way her father had, but they also understood the boundaries of her work.

"For now, just the name. I may need to share more if this gets any more complicated."

"Got it. What's the name?"

"IMP," Aderyn said. "All capitals, like an acronym or an

abbreviation maybe. Could be a user name too. May be connected to Dekken, TenDek, or even Spres."

"That is not a lot to go on," Treasa said. "You're a better tech than me—you haven't found anything?"

"I haven't had access," Aderyn said. "Gilda came up empty on all the usual channels. I was hoping you could get Glenda involved. I haven't done a search of the AltFeed."

"You worried about needing Glenda's level of protection?" Treasa looked skeptical. "Gilda is a pretty advanced AI. She's got a lot of bells and whistles."

"I am worried," Aderyn said. "Someone is pulling a lot of strings to get folks to dance, and I want to know why. But I can't find the why until I find the who."

"I'll put Glenda on it," Treasa said. "Tell her to take extra precautions. She's got a fair amount of paranoia in her programming."

"Courtesy of dear old Dad," Aderyn said, nodding. "If this gets much weirder, I may bring him out of retirement."

"Aunt Deedra would never forgive you," Treasa said.

"I'm not sure I'd forgive me. Mom just got him convinced to give up the life. It's barely been a year since they settled on L'Mondeau."

"So we'll do this without him then," Treasa said. "Let Uncle Coburn raise his sheep or whatever in peace."

"Alpacas," Aderyn corrected. "He likes their wool better."

"Where are you these days, anyway?" Treasa asked. "Or are you allowed to say?"

"I'm on Spres, believe it or not," Aderyn said. "Came by to see Tuari and his family."

"How's his father doing?"

"Not well," Aderyn said. "I wish they would let us help."

"They're Naturalists—they don't want our kind of help."

"They never fought in the war," Aderyn said.

"No, but they hold the views. If they didn't, then you and Tuari...." She let her voice trail off. "Anyway, I'm sorry to hear about the old man. Akechata is good people. Stubborn people. But good. And Tuari himself?"

"Looking tired," Aderyn admitted. "Maybe a little thinner."

"Which means you're worried," Treasa said. "Think you'll ever find someone else to worry about?"

"Who has the time?" Aderyn countered. "I'm years away from settling down."

"Mom doesn't think so," Treasa said.

"She didn't have one of her visions, did she?"

"I don't know. She just said something the other day about 'Addy's young man.' But it wasn't Tuari."

Aderyn didn't want to think about that. Her Aunt Leona, head of the Ryder clan, had The Gift, and her telepathic ability sometimes veered into an uncanny ability to be right about things happening in the future or far away.

"Well, I don't have a young man," Aderyn said. "Or a young woman. I am young people free."

"Uh-huh," Treasa said. "I kinda wish I was."

"Oooh, can I see?"

Treasa gave Aderyn a wry look, but then leaned back anyway, bringing a large round belly into view of the vid-screen.

"You're huge!" Aderyn said, grinning. "Can't be much longer now."

"We should be in orbit around Oster in a few days," Treasa said. "Mom says we'll make it, and the birth will be planetside, like I'd hoped. Which reminds me—she says you have to go to the ball."

Aderyn groaned.

"Can't someone else go?"

"Mom and Kionna are staying with me, Uncle Jonas is still on Lyric with his wife's family, and I don't think Great Aunt Arleen's folks even know Gwynn," Treasa said, rubbing her stomach. "That leaves you as our representative."

"Does anyone have to go?"

"Mom says yes," she said. "She wants to make sure we don't let Gwynn think the Ryders have forgotten her."

"What if Gwynn wants to forget about the Ryders?"

"She's young, only turning of age this year, right? She'll come around. And we need to make sure we're here when she does."

Aderyn nodded her head reluctantly.

"Ug, this little one is kicking my bladder," Treasa said.

"Go, and give hugs and kisses to everyone for me," Aderyn said.

"I'll put Glenda on IMP, and let you know as soon as she has anything."

"I should be there," Aderyn said, staring at Treasa's belly.

"You were here for the last one. And at the rate I'm going, there will probably be another one not too far from now. It's a birth. They happen. You do your thing."

"So you don't miss me at all, is what you're saying," Aderyn said, mock pouting at her cousin.

"I am hanging up now," Treasa said, and Aderyn laughed. "Love you and miss you!"

"You too," Aderyn said. "Be well."

The vid-screen went blank and Aderyn felt a rush of homesickness. Most of the time she loved her life, loved the travel and the adventure and never knowing what was going to happen next. But times like these, knowing that the clan was heading back to Oster for Treasa's birthing, she wished she'd chosen differently.

But Treasa was right, there would be other birthings.

"Do you think Glenda is a better AI than me?" Gilda asked.

"I think she's an older AI than you," Aderyn responded. She was probably to blame for Gilda's tendency to question her usefulness—something in her seeped into Gilda's programming. "She has more redundancies than you do, more layers of protection. You have a better music collection."

"Would you like to hear any music now?" Gilda asked.

"Not right now, thanks. I'm going to sign off. Let me know if you get any communications from the *Cardinal de Richelieu.*"

"I will," Gilda said.

Aderyn disconnected her bracelet from the STP's com system, and walked to the door of the craft, pushing open the hatch to climb out under a starlit sky, two bright moons hanging heavy over the tree line in the distance and reminding her of Treasa's belly.

"Reach Glenda?" Tuari asked. Aderyn nodded and wandered

over to where he was leaning against the side of the hover-cradle, taking the spot next to him.

"Treasa says hi," she said.

"She on Oster yet?"

"Almost. Aunt Leona says they'll make it."

Aderyn watched Tuari's face as he absorbed this information. He didn't like to talk about the special gifts many of her family members had. For a moment, some of the old wounds split open, every argument they ever had about the differences in their families coming to mind.

"Aunt Leona says I should go to the Hart Ball, too," she said, still watching his face. "As the family representative."

"We could go together," he said.

"We could. Take my ship."

"Father doesn't really have any to spare, so otherwise...."

"You need the ride, is what you're saying."

"Yep."

She watched him look out at nothing, or something, anything that wasn't her.

"I'll go," she said, turning her own gaze upward, to the moons and stars. "For Gwynn."

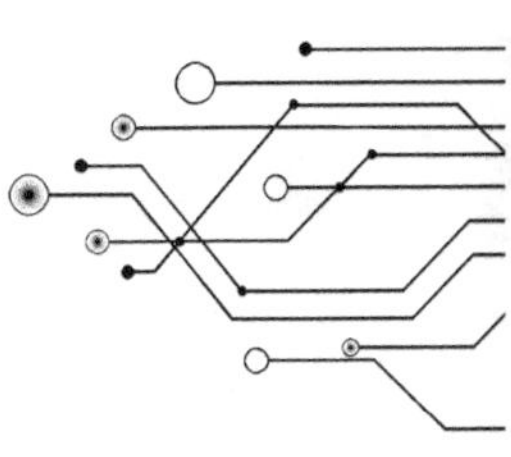

Chapter 8

THE BIG LIE

Gwynn stared at the dress, almost too afraid to put it on. The package it came in was carefully preserved at the side of her room, the delicate tissue neatly folded back inside the box. The dress itself was hanging in a clear protective material on the back of Gwynn's closet door. It was a pale green, two shades lighter than the TenDek corporate color, with white and golden-yellow decorative beadwork at the bodice and along the hem. Flaxen colors, woven into the design of the thing, making it a perfect blending of the two organizations, a visual representation of the merger.

And it was hers. The most expensive and fancy dress she ever owned. Gwynn removed the plastic and ran her hands over the smooth and silky material. She'd tried it on the night before, and it fit like a second skin, the cut of it giving her the appearance of a smaller waist and fuller bust than she actually possessed, the color bringing out hues in her eyes she wasn't sure she'd ever seen before. Gair had stopped by after, to be sure she received the dress, and suggested that for once she not style her hair to hide the purple.

"Be who you are," he had said. "All of who you are. You come from two noble families. Let both be seen in you tomorrow."

She had listened and instructed the hairdresser her father hired to find a style that showed her purple streak—though not too much of it. She was pleased with the result, her hair piled up on top of her head with more volume than she thought it could have, making her look and feel like a princess. The mask that she would wear for most of the night continued the theme of the dress and was a light gold color decorated with green and yellow jewels. Also a gift, also very expensive. Gair suggested that it might end up in the museum someday, helping mark the occasion that TenDek announced their partnership with Flaxen Moons.

And that is when the familiar anxiety chased away all the pleasure that Gwynn had been feeling at his gifts and his visit. She cited the lateness of the hour and made her excuses, and he gallantly left her to rest.

It was time for Gwynn to put on her gown and walk with her father to the dais at the center of the ballroom, which would rise above the crowd so that Bertram could give his annual speech.

But Gwynn hesitated. She didn't think she deserved the dress. She fiddled with the gold-banded com bracelet at her wrist, a gift from her father during better times.

She wandered over to her console, sat in her chair, and typed in the commands to take her to the AltFeed.

No new messages.

There had been no new breakthroughs in the lab, either, with even the other scientists starting to look discouraged now that they finished reviewing all her prior work. It's not that they didn't think making crystals was possible, they just also realized, the way Gwynn had, that it could take decades to go through all the possible combinations to find the perfect one. And Gwynn didn't have decades. She had hours until she had to deliver a proof of concept, a crystal, however large, that could hold energy and convert it using the same standard converter all the other tuotarium crystals used.

Gwynn ran through some of her favorite discussion boards, tried to see if there was anything new on any of them. Then she pulled up her conversation with IMP, trying to see if she could get any more clues as to who IMP was, or why they wanted to help her.

She couldn't take the not knowing anymore and sent a message through the same direct com field IMP had first contacted her in.

ARE YOU THERE?

She waited several minutes, and when she didn't get a reply, was just about to log off.

I AM HERE.

Gwynn was surprised by how relieved she felt.

IT'S BEEN TWO DAYS, she wrote back.

TONIGHT, IMP replied. I CAN GIVE YOU EVERYTHING YOU NEED.

HOW?

HAVE FAITH.

Gwynn snorted with frustration. That wasn't really an answer.

AND THE COST? she typed instead.

A FAVOR, TO BE COLLECTED IN THE FUTURE.

WHAT KIND OF FAVOR?

YOU HAVE HOURS LEFT—DOES IT REALLY MATTER?

Gwynn frowned at that. But it's not like IMP was asking her to sign anything. IMP also had yet to deliver. At this point it felt a lot like she was trading nothing for nothing.

EVERYTHING I NEED? she asked.

AS PROMISED. I NEVER GO BACK ON A DEAL.

Gwynn couldn't tell if that was comforting or supposed to remind her that this was more binding than she realized.

WHERE? she responded.

THE WORKSTATION IN YOUR QUARTERS. YOU WILL GET A MESSAGE WHEN IT IS TIME.

What she needed was an actual crystal, made from algae, and she didn't see how IMP was going to be able to deliver on that.

But she was also out of options.

DEAL.

THEN IT IS AS GOOD AS DONE, IMP wrote back.

THANK YOU, she responded, not having anything else to write.

She got the same message back as last time: IT IS MY PLEASURE.

Gwynn looked at her clock then and realized she had pushed the time about as far as she could, and she really did have to get into her dress. She signed off from the AltFeed and walked over to the gown.

It was simple to get on, constructed with self-sealing tech in the back she could activate from a sensor hidden in her bodice. She turned the reflective function of her closet door on so that she could see the final result: gown, hair, and make up. She felt ten years older, a proper adult and not a gangly adolescent.

A door chime distracted her from her self-admiration, and she called out "enter" without thinking.

Enzo smiled at her from the doorway.

"You look amazing," he said. She turned toward him with a smile, smoothing her hands over her dress.

"I don't think I've ever worn anything so nice," she said.

"You deserve it, sweet-one," he said. He was looking sharp himself in a black tuxedo with white vest, and Gwynn couldn't help but notice that it seemed better made than the one he'd worn the year before—which was the same one he'd worn five years in a row before that.

"This is new," she said.

"The Ingrams have been very generous," Enzo confirmed. "Elidor saw to the fittings for all Flaxen Moons staff himself."

"They are both such gentlemen," she said, mostly thinking of Gair.

Enzo patted her hair and stood back, smiling at his effort. "There—perfect." For a moment he looked wistful, and Gwynn thought she saw tears in the corners of his eyes.

"Don't start," she said. "Then I'll start, and then I'll be all red-eyed for the ball."

"I won't," he said, turning away to hide his face and wiping discreetly at the corner of his eyes.

"Enzo," she said quietly. "What my father has promised...."

"You're worried," he said. "I think you have reason to be. This deal he has entered into—all the benefit is for TenDek."

"He was desperate," Gwynn said, frowning. "But maybe it's not as bad as that. They are the ones pouring a fortune into Flaxen Moons, restarting the farms, hiring staff. They are gambling a lot on a promise of a miracle."

"Exactly," Enzo said. "And Bertram has hidden the details of the deal from me and Myles. He signed it without letting us look at it, and he won't tell me what happens if we don't deliver."

"He told me," Gwynn said. "TenDek takes everything. And we should feel lucky they are willing to. Without their help, Dad's debtors were going to send him to prison, force me into indentured servitude until I paid off my portion of the debt, and we'd still lose everything."

"I don't understand," Enzo said. "What are you talking about?"

"Dad told me about the debt," she said, her voice cracking with emotion. "He told me why he was so desperate for the Ingrams to invest."

Enzo put his hand on the side of her face, looking deep into her eyes with all the love she never felt from her father.

"Sweet-one, your father has lied to you. He never would have gone to jail, and I would never have allowed any deal that would force you to become an indentured servant."

"He told me," she said plaintively. Enzo's brows crossed in concern.

"Your father hasn't been handling the finances," he told her. "He makes the decisions, sure—the ones we allow him to make. But we all know who your father is. Myles and I have been incredibly careful with managing the money. It's why we shut down certain farming stations, why we were looking into other, smaller investors."

"Now I don't understand," Gwynn said, taking Enzo's hand from her face and holding it tightly. "Then why are we struggling so much?"

"Your father does love to spend," Enzo said. "But we have

been countering that to the best of our ability. We weren't flush, not by a long shot, but we would have survived."

"Father said we wouldn't have lasted another lunar cycle without TenDek."

Enzo shook his head.

"He wasn't pleased with our rate of growth and recovery. He didn't like our conservative approach. He sought out TenDek, made a deal with them."

"But why? And why this deal? It doesn't make any sense."

"I think it's starting to make a lot of sense, actually. Sweetone, think. This was never about the crystals. Your father has felt trapped running the farms for a long time. He wants out. TenDek must be his way out."

"But I came back home, I left Savenel. He asked me to. He told me if I didn't...."

Enzo shook his head, sadly.

"I thought I was protecting you from all this. I hadn't realized what Bertram was filling your head with. I thought you wanted to come back, after all that happened with your cousin."

Gwynn crossed her arms across her chest and shook her head.

"Dad told you that, didn't he?" she asked. Enzo nodded.

"Then this deal...."

"They know there won't be any crystals," Enzo said. "They have to. It doesn't make sense otherwise. But, it's a pretty story. It's a way for Bertram to sell Flaxen Moons without having to admit that he wanted to, that he was voluntarily giving up his family legacy."

"He's putting the blame on me," Gwynn said, feeling the words like ice-water against her skin. "How could he do this?"

"He has never been the same since your mother died," Enzo said, reaching out a hand to fuss over Gwynn again. She pushed it away and stepped back.

"Stop making excuses for him," she said. "Stop protecting him. I'm old enough now, I need the truth. Promise me."

Enzo smoothed the front of his jacket down as if smoothing his own feelings out and nodded.

"I promise—I won't hide things from you anymore."

"We've lost it though, haven't we? The business, all the farms. Everything we fought so hard to keep."

"I think so," Enzo said. "I never would have thought it, but, yes, I think so."

He looked uncertain then in a way that Gwynn had never seen him look. She recognized the lines around his eyes, the heavy streaks of white in his short hair. He was near seventy now, probably looking at retirement in a few years. There was perhaps some part of him that would be relieved to give up the fight for Flaxen Farms, especially if what he was saying was true, that he and Myles had been fighting for it despite her father's efforts to bring it to ruin.

Gwynn patted at her hair and smoothed out her dress, composing herself.

"He'll probably insist on keeping the ball," she said. "It's the only thing he really enjoys. We should go and meet him."

Enzo looked at her with an expression Gwynn recognized

as pride. She wasn't sure she'd ever seen that look on her father's face. But then, she didn't really need to.

Enzo held out his arm for her to take and smiled while she placed her hand over it.

"You really do look marvelous," he said.

"We both do," she replied.

She kept her head high and her eyes open, while Enzo's revelations churned inside of her.

It had all been a lie.

She focused on her steps.

Two years of her life, wasted.

She kept her spine straight as they turned the corner, and Gair and Bertram greeted them.

She was never going to be able to save Flaxen Moons.

She smiled politely at Gair as he offered his arm in turn.

But inside, Gwynn wanted to scream.

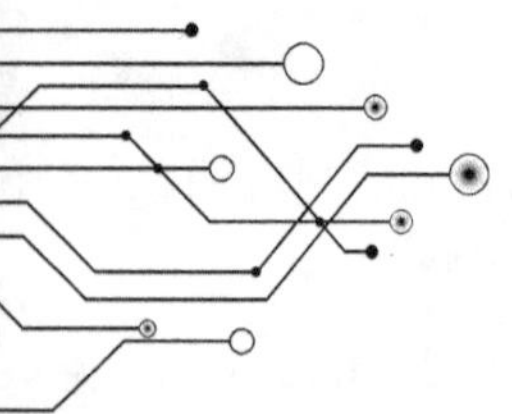

Chapter 9

THE FLAXENHART MASQUERADE

There were a lot of places in the galaxy worse than this one, Aderyn reminded herself. She yanked up the top of her dress, trying to find a happy medium between the amount of cleavage it wanted to give her and the amount she was comfortable with showing. She wasn't against showing off her breasts, per se. She'd spent a great deal of time at the nude beaches of Verbor and never gave a second thought to how much flesh she was showing. But there was something about this in-between space of fully covered and fully naked that felt more vulnerable than either of the other states. It was as if the scant amount of cloth propping her breasts up brought more attention to them than if she was wearing nothing at all, as if the promise of further nudity was more alluring than the actual reality of nakedness. She knew she was going to get a lot of attention and was already resenting it. It was going to take a lot of self-control not to pull her taze-stick from the garter belt beneath her skirt, the right pocket bottom-less just to give her access.

"Your dress has been designed to exactly fit your body and engineered to provide the ideal amount of support for your breasts," Gilda informed her. "Pulling at the top of it will not move it."

"It's a psychological tug," Aderyn replied, turning to survey the rest of her dress. Gilda was right—the thing was designed not to go anywhere, but she did a few experimental jumps to confirm that the material had a firm grip on her boobs. There was jiggling, but no slippage. The skirt only went to just below her knees and billowed out, giving her a lot of freedom of movement without too much material to negotiate if she had to defend herself.

"Do you need psychological support?" Gilda asked.

Aderyn snorted.

"I'm good for now, thanks," she said. "Have you checked on Ruby lately?"

"She is sleeping in her enclosure. Should I wake her?"

"No," Aderyn said, "Let her sleep."

Aderyn and Tuari had spent a good hour earlier playing with her pet genet, hoping that it would wear her out enough that she wouldn't cause Gilda any problems while Aderyn was on *Flaxen One*. Last time Ruby had escaped, the cat-like creature managed to type in random codes while walking across the control console of the ship before covering it all with a giant hair ball.

"Any word from the *Cardinal de Richelieu*?"

"None since the last time you asked fourteen minutes ago," Gilda informed her. Aderyn wondered if the AI got some of her sassiness from her as well.

Aderyn patted at her hair and checked the stability of the decorative pin that doubled as a thin knife that held the top part up in a twist. The rest of her hair cascaded over her right shoulder, as much of the purple exposed as possible. Gwynn may be ashamed of her heritage, but Aderyn was proud. She'd matched her dress to her hair, a reddish-purple satin, bright and shiny.

As a last touch, she brushed purple sparkles just under her eyes, bringing out the amethyst. She hoped it would give her a slightly exotic look—remind Gwynn that there was more to the galaxy than the Flaxen Moons.

"You appear to be nervous," Gilda said. "Is there something you are concerned about that I should know about?"

"I am just not a fan of big parties," Aderyn said, sighing. She wasn't sure her AI was complex enough to get the nuances of human relationships yet.

"Then why are you attending one?"

"That is a good question," Aderyn said. "And the answer is—because I have to."

"Tuari wishes to speak with you. Should I open your com?"

"Yes," Aderyn said.

"You ready?" Tuari's voice rang out, louder than Aderyn was comfortable with. She would have to look at the volume controls for her com system later.

"Coming now," she said though the speaker.

Aderyn grabbed a black mask from the top of her console on her way out, the door chiming as it closed behind her.

Tuari was waiting in the corridor wearing a black jacket over a silver vest, white shirt, and black pants, and he dangled a silver mask from his fingers. He pulled at the collar of his shirt as if trying to give his neck more room.

"I will never get used to these clothes," he said. His hair was down, and he'd braided silver and black beads into the hair on the right side of his face.

"They are traditional," she said, stepping close enough to adjust his bowtie. She caught his eyes looking down as though entranced by her cleavage and poked him.

"Watch the eyes," she said.

"Sorry!" he said, immediately looking so far up he could probably count the tiles on the ceiling.

"It's a few hours, and then we can get out of these clothes," she said, smoothing the lapel of his jacket down. His eyes flickered down to hers, and she felt heat rise up her back. "Not like that," she said, stepping away from him.

"I know," he said quietly. But for a moment, he sounded regretful, and Aderyn had to force her eyes away from his. That way was madness, she reminded herself. That way had already cost her more than she had been prepared to pay.

"We don't talk about things anymore," he said suddenly. Aderyn found herself studying his face again, noticing new lines around his eyes. "I don't tell you about my work, and you don't tell me about yours. You didn't tell me what your business was with Chianna."

"You didn't ask," she reminded him.

"I know." He looked down at his clothes, tugging at the bottom of his vest. "It just feels...."

She wished he would look up, and she was relieved when he didn't.

"Everything is different," she said softly. "Because it has to be."

Then he did lift his head and meet her eyes.

"Entering final approach," Gilda informed them. "Time to get clearance to dock. Your presence is requested on the bridge, Aderyn."

"On my way Gilda," she told her AI, still staring into Tuari's face. There was a lot she wanted to say. It felt all trapped in her throat, and she made a noise to clear it, and then chickened out. She walked past Tuari toward the bridge of the *Herald*, relieved to have something else to focus on.

Aderyn wasn't prepared for the view out of the bridge viewscreen, and stared in awe at *Flaxen One*, the largest space station of the Flaxen Moons. It hadn't been built the last time she was out this way, and she was shocked by the size of it. From this angle, she could see the large dome at the center of it, which she assumed was the infamous Hart Ballroom. She reviewed the docking procedures that had been automatically transmitted to her ship and watched as the ships ahead of her were moved away from one of dozens of airlifts by large mechanical arms and locked in place by magnetic fields in a storage area under the station. She knew the station was built for high traffic, but she hadn't been prepared for just how much traffic. It must have cost a fortune to build, and a second one to keep running.

She had a sudden pang of sympathy for her cousin, somewhere in the middle of all that, and stuck with the responsibility of keeping it all going.

Aderyn transmitted her ID information to the station and waited for clearance to approach. It was a smooth ride in, and soon her ship had a solid seal against the station's airlock.

Tuari was waiting for Aderyn down below, standing stiffly in his tuxedo. Aderyn still couldn't find anything to say, and was glad when the inner airlock door opened, giving them access to the station. They joined in with a stream of traffic all heading to the heart of the station. Aderyn tied her mask onto her face as they walked, and after a moment, Tuari did the same. The masks did little to hide their identities to anyone who knew them, but it did help Aderyn feel like part of the crowd to be one of many masked faces. She fought the urge to pull at the top of her dress, wishing she hadn't let her Aunt Leona talk her into something strapless.

Aderyn was starting to regret a great many things. She hadn't been to a Hart Ball since she and Gwynn were both at Savenel together, and she hadn't been expecting this many people. There was something about the crowd that was making her uneasy, but she couldn't name it. She also hadn't warned Gwynn she was coming.

"This is a bad idea," she said as they slowed down, caught in a choke point on the path to the ball. "She's going to freak when she sees me."

"Gwynn invited me, and I needed a ride," Tuari said, pulling down at the bottom of his vest again.

"And now we're arriving together," Aderyn said. "And how is that going to look?"

Tuari shot her a side-glance that made it clear he hadn't thought of that.

"It's fine, everything is going to be fine." But he didn't sound convinced.

Soon they were at the ballroom doors, and it was the first time that Aderyn could place what had seemed so different about the crowd—a large portion of them were wearing a familiar shade of green. She put the pieces together as she saw people in distinct green and gold uniforms scanning people's com bracelets at the door.

"TenDek," she said, her eyes instinctively looking for the nearest exits. With the push of the crowd, it would be nearly impossible for her to get to one with any speed.

"Of course," Tuari said, giving her a confused look. "Because of the merger."

"The merger?"

"TenDek is partnering with Flaxen Moons in a not-so-secret secret deal. I thought I told you. They basically are the reason why the farms are still running at this point."

Aderyn felt her mouth go dry the same time sweat began to gather at the small of her back.

"Gwynn is working with TenDek," she said, trying to wrap her mind around the idea.

"Are you all right?" Tuari asked. Aderyn felt like she wanted to stop and catch her breath, but the crowd behind them was too thick and there was no place to go. Then they were at the doors, and she was holding out her com bracelet to be scanned, and then they were through, and there was space to move again. Aderyn made her way to a low bench bookended by two large potted palms, plopped down, and wished she'd thought to bring a hand fan with her.

"Seriously, Addy, what's going on?"

Aderyn looked up to answer Tuari, and then froze.

A man in a gold mask with matching vest and short cropped hair was staring at her. Even with the mask, his face seemed familiar, as did his overall build. As if recognizing her recognizing him, he bowed to her, his blue-green eyes fixed on her face. Aderyn reached up to grab Tuari's arm before he could turn to follow her gaze.

"Get to Gwynn," she said, keeping her eyes on the man in gold. "Stay with her. Right by her side. Do not leave her alone. I'll tell you why later."

The man waved and turned, moving further into the crowd. Aderyn shot up, pushing past Tuari to follow.

"Aderyn!" he said, grabbing her arm. She turned and shrugged him off.

"There's no time! Get to Gwynn!"

She marched into the crowd, trying to track one figure in the sea of bodies. For a moment panic rose in her, and she took a slow breath. Think, she told herself. Don't look at the masks, look for the way the people move. She let herself get carried into the current of things and stopped seeing the crowd as a mass of individuals and saw them as sets of patterns: some were swaying to music, some clustered in conversation, and some on the move. Her eyes searched out the anomaly, the body that would seem slightly off among all the finery, the movements both more graceful and less refined, the figure that would move with intention, expertly avoiding the people around him.

There. She let her eyes trace his trail to a likely destination, and aimed herself at the same end point, moving with the ebb and flow of the revelers around her. Finally, she broke free from the general mass of bodies and landed near a doorway that led to a room filled with low couches and hanging curtains. The light was lower here, allowing the occupants even more privacy as they paired off, and it made it harder for Aderyn to find the man in the gold mask.

Finally, she spotted him in a corner, and hurried to it, determined not to lose him again.

"Hi, Aderyn," he said as she approached. "Or do you prefer Addy?"

"Warren Frey," she said. "What in the hells are you doing here?"

"It's a party," he said, gesturing at her with a napkin that appeared to have a half-eaten roll in it. "I like parties. They serve small food."

She knocked the roll out of his hand and pinned him against the wall, her forearm against his neck, and her free hand pressing the still-dormant taze-stick against his lower stomach.

"Don't test me," she said. "I want answers."

"You agreed not to ask any questions," he said, seemingly unperturbed by his predicament. "You aren't going to break your word, are you?"

"This is different," she said. "The Flaxenharts have nothing to do with...before."

"Are you sure?"

Aderyn faltered for a moment. It was all the opportunity he needed, and he pinned her lower hand back against her body, twisting her wrist until she let go of the taze-stick. Then he spun her with his other arm so that her back was pressed against his chest, his arms wrapped around her, one holding the taze-stick against her belly, the other around her neck. He held her firmly, and his arms felt like iron around her, unbendable and unmovable.

She struggled anyway, but he didn't actually seem intent on hurting her.

"I understand that you have family here," he said into her ear as she stared out at the rest of the room, realizing that their pose would look romantic and not like they were fighting. No help was going to come that way. "But I promise you, they aren't in danger. And I also promise you that you don't want to get involved in this. You're bright, you've got a good thing going with your information trade. Stick with what you know."

He let her go then, moving quickly out from behind her and turning to face her.

"All these people in all these masks, and you still recognized me," he said, grinning. "Gotta say, I'm flattered."

"I'll call security," she said, trying to watch him and look past him for potential help at the same time. He pulled back a flap of his jacket to reveal the gold and green logo of TenDek.

"I am security. Which is why I have to confiscate this." He made a show of slipping her taze-stick into an inside pocket of his suit jacket and continued to back away from her. Aderyn felt paralyzed with indecision.

"I can't trust you," she said.

"You don't have a choice," he retorted. "Not unless you want to tell everyone how you know me. You wouldn't just break your word, you'd be admitting to breaking the law."

Aderyn hesitated. He was right, but she didn't want to admit it.

"I want my taze-stick back," she said. He tilted his head as if contemplating her request, then pulled it out of his pocket and tossed it at her. She almost missed catching it, surprised by the gesture.

"A symbol of good will," he said. "Find your cousin, keep her close if you're so worried. I promise—she's safe."

After a moment, Aderyn slipped the taze-stick back into its place in her garter, keeping a wary eye on Warren.

"What now?" she asked. He shrugged.

"I'm on duty," he said. "I really am security. I'm going to go back to doing my job, patrolling the perimeter. You should probably go do ball things."

"Ball things?"

"Dancing, drinking, looking gorgeous in that dress. Ball things."

Aderyn scowled and fought the urge to pull up her neckline again.

"I hate this thing," she said.

"You're right. It's terrible. Horrible dress. If you need help taking it off...."

"Stop!" she said, putting up a hand palm out.

"I'm not sure I can," he responded. "It's the mask. It makes me impetuous." He tilted his head to the side again, this time looking like he was listening to something. "Some folks are trying to take an unguided tour of the station. Duty calls."

He hesitated as if waiting for her permission. Aderyn shrugged helplessly.

"Fine, go."

"Really though, purple is definitely your color," he said, grinning. Then he turned and made his way back to the main ballroom, weaving around what were likely trysting couples. Aderyn stared after him for a long beat before making her own way back to the domed room.

She was going to have to find Gwynn and come up with some sort of explanation for Tuari, and neither of those seemed like fun things to do. She snagged a glass of sparkling wine from a tray as she passed it and downed the wine quickly, putting the empty glass on another tray.

"Ball things," she said, chuckling. She added a sway to her movements and danced her way through the crowd.

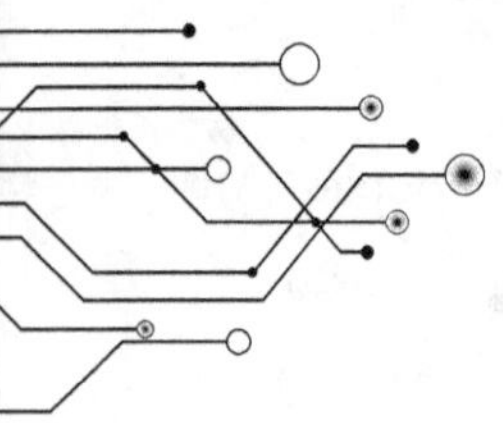

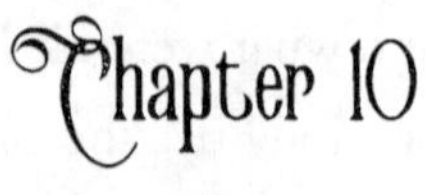

Chapter 10

THE INVISIBLE CHASE

Aderyn couldn't find Tuari and had just opted to try calling him on her com bracelet when she spotted Elidor Ingram standing alone at the edge of the crowd.

She approached him slowly, unsure what she might say, unsure if she should say anything at all.

"Elidor Ingram," she said, deciding the direct approach would be best. He turned sharply at his name, disturbing the glass in his hand and dripping something bubbly onto his shoe. He looked down at the shoe and then back up at Aderyn.

"Ms. Ryder," he said, and sounded surprised.

"It's a lovely gathering, don't you think Mr. Ingram?" she said as she got closer, offering him a polite smile.

"Lovely," he echoed, standing awkwardly beside her.

Aderyn was glad that her taze-stick was on the opposite side. Her hand slipped into her pocket.

"I assume your work has been going well," he said in a forced calm and casual tone.

"Very well," Aderyn said, keeping her own voice neutral. "I saw Warren," she added. "Said hi."

"Mr. Frey was pleased by that, I'm sure." He was staring out into the crowd and tried not to demonstrate distress at her words.

"You have known him long then?"

"Long enough," he replied.

"So, I hear your family is doing business with mine," Aderyn said, trying a new line of inquiry.

"Yes, a wonderful opportunity for both sides," Elidor said. It sounded like a well-practiced line. "I have had the opportunity to meet with your cousin, Gwynn," he added, his voice shifting slightly. "She is a very bright and talented young woman."

Aderyn nodded.

"Yeah, Gwynn's great. Bertram as well, though he is not, perhaps, as bright."

Elidor made no comment to this.

"It's just that—they're family," Aderyn said. "And I have certain rules in my profession, but this—this feels like one of the rare times it might be prudent to break them."

"And what would you say to them?" Elidor asked, turning toward her. "What have I done that would make you believe they are in any way in danger?"

"What have you done?" Aderyn asked, incredulous. "You are not being honest. What happened at TenDek Research and Development…."

Elidor put up his hand.

"We agreed not to speak of such things."

"Such things are the very reason why I don't trust you."

"I understand," Elidor said. "But I think perhaps you don't have all the information to make that determination."

Aderyn snorted in frustration. "You could maybe fill me in. Give me one good reason why I shouldn't march up to my uncle and tell him everything."

"Because it's too late," Elidor said. "Your uncle entered into an agreement with my brother that is legally binding, the terms of which are unbreakable."

"And just what exactly are those terms?"

"If Flaxen Moons doesn't produce tuotarium crystals—actually produce, here on the station—then TenDek takes everything."

Aderyn scoffed.

"That's a ridiculous deal—no one would make that deal."

"Bertram Flaxenhart did."

"Bertram has no idea how to make crystals, no one does. It's a fool's errand. No one in their right mind could even think...." Then Aderyn stopped and closed her eyes. "Gwynn," she said.

"Yes, your cousin does seem to be under the impression that it's possible. More than that, she seems to be unaware that anyone else thinks otherwise. Apparently, she has been working the problem for over two years."

"That's what she came back here to do? Make crystals?"

"And save her family's legacy."

"But she's just a kid. A brilliant mind, sure, but she doesn't have the training for something like that. She had three years at Savenel. She'd need a doctorate in the subject to even get close, and an entire team of researchers to work with, and at least a decade."

"She has until tomorrow at midday," Elidor said.

Aderyn stared at him in shock.

"I did not make this deal," he added, as her shock turned to anger. "This was done between my brother and Mr. Flaxenhart."

"They're going to lose everything," Aderyn said. "And worse, she's going to think it's her fault."

"Perhaps," Elidor said, though Aderyn couldn't tell which part he doubted. But he didn't know her cousin, didn't know how Gwynn took things on, and blamed herself. Her younger cousin was plagued with doubts, always worrying about not being good enough.

This was at least partly Aderyn's fault, she knew. She let Gwynn have the space she asked for, never came by to see how she and Bertram were really doing. The Ryders assumed that Bertram had at least some of his family's business acumen. And they were also grieving the loss of Cora. Aderyn had been eight, and she still felt the pain of it—Cora had been her favorite aunt.

Gwynn had only been three and never really got to know her mother. And she was so determined to be a Flaxenhart, continue the legacy. What wouldn't Gwynn do for her family?

"She's going to be devastated," she said at last.

"I think you underestimate your cousin," Elidor said. "She is made of stronger stuff than you think."

Aderyn hoped that was true. She gave Elidor an assessing look.

"And you had no idea this deal was happening?"

"As you yourself have said—my brother doesn't share as much with me as I'd like."

Aderyn looked at him with new appreciation. She knew then that she didn't want to know why Elidor felt the need to steal from his own company. But she felt a perverse satisfaction knowing that Gair was hurt by something she had a hand in. He was taking advantage of the Flaxenharts and putting Gwynn in an impossible position.

"I need to find a way to protect her," Aderyn said.

"I think you will find that she has the ability to take care of herself," he said.

"Not from what she doesn't know," Aderyn said. "If you'll excuse me." Her eyes scanned the room, looking for Tuari again.

"Ms. Ryder, if I may."

Aderyn turned back toward him, feeling anxious and impatient.

"You might not be the right person for her to hear it from."

Aderyn tried to connect with his eyes under his mask and wished she could see more of his face.

"You care about her," she said.

"She is easy to care about," he responded. "She tries so very hard."

Aderyn smiled.

"Thank you, Elidor," she said.

"You're welcome, Ms. Ryder."

Aderyn bowed respectfully toward him before turning to head back into the crowd. That conversation had not been what she expected—not that she had ever expected to have a conversation with Elidor Ingram after their encounter in the Dekken system. But she was beginning to find the younger Ingram very interesting.

Unfortunately, she had more urgent things to think about and had to put whatever analysis she might make of Elidor off for another time.

Aderyn let the movement of the revelers carry her as her eyes floated over the faces and bodies around her. People were dressed in bright jewel colors, silver and gold draped around necks, bright gems dangling from ears and woven into hair, and masks both simple and elaborate obscuring faces and framing smiles. Tuari would be harder to spot than Warren was, being both shorter and slighter than the older man. She contemplated calling again, but Aderyn also realized that any communication in the crowd would be impossible to hear.

There was another way, and Aderyn felt only slightly guilty as she took refuge in the lee of a pillar so that she could focus on her com bracelet.

It was short work to get into the station's network, and only slightly harder to gain access to the internal sensor system. Aderyn made a mental note to help the Flaxenharts upgrade their security.

Everyone had to keep their ID chips with them at all times, as the security types at the main entrances of the ball had demonstrated. Aderyn searched for Tuari's ID, and then ran a second search to find his location in the ballroom. The first went fine—a pic of his face popped up with a string of identifying numbers. However, the second came up empty. She expanded her search to include the entire compound, wondering if maybe he was looking for Gwynn in her quarters or elsewhere on the station. Again, nothing came up.

Aderyn ran a search for her cousin, and then her uncle, easily finding both in a room just off the main hallway that had significantly fewer bodies in it than other similar rooms. She guessed this one had been set aside just for the family for security purposes. But again, no Tuari. She reversed her search and brought up the name of everyone in the room with her cousin, which included Gair Ingram, Enzo Drystan, and several nameless security officers. No one in the room was unidentified.

Aderyn's mind began to build scenarios ranging from Tuari turning his ID badge off for some innocuous reason, to him being kidnapped from the station. None of the scenarios made any sense. She ran a query to see where he had been, and his last registered location was in the middle of the ballroom, which didn't help her at all and made her lean toward him intentionally shutting off his tracking chip.

Aderyn ran another search, bringing up Warren Frey's face and ID number. She ran the ID through the sensor system.

Nothing. Now Aderyn was really getting frustrated. His last location was also in the ballroom. She searched for herself and found the little dot that represented her in the midst of lots of other dots and could click on the ID tags around her to see the names of the people in her vicinity. A visual comparison seemed to line up with the names she was reading, though she only vaguely recognized a few of them.

Warren and Tuari both not showing up on the sensors felt wrong, and Aderyn was frustrated that she couldn't think of any good reason for it. There had been too many weird things happening lately, most of it involving tech. She reached for any good explanation—maybe her com just didn't have the capacity to process the information she was looking for, and somehow this was a user error. She wanted to rule that out and pulled up a general map of the area, looking for a workstation.

The nearest one was in the Flaxenhart Museum, which was

closed off to the public. Aderyn modified her own ID chip to designate her as part of the station staff and headed for the nearest exit. The guard there didn't look twice at her or his screen as he scanned her ID, so at least that much was working.

She relied on the map to help her get to the museum and marveled at the new and improved design. Everything looked so shiny! She wished she had time to explore, but her concern for Tuari and suspicion of Warren was growing. Aderyn slipped behind the customer service counter and logged into the workstation, bringing up the same security sensor logs on the monitor there. She cross-referenced that with the general sensor logs, those that tracked any and all things happening in the station, from what lights were on to which bathroom was being used. She layered both sets of information into a single map of the station.

It took time, more time than Aderyn wanted to spend on it, but she finally saw what she was looking for—doors that were registering as opening and closing that weren't showing any people near them. Aderyn looked for markers around the doors that were being triggered. They led to and from a part of the station that only housed two things: the station science lab, and Gwynn's living quarters.

That could possibly be Tuari, she thought, looking for her cousin. Though it could also possibly be Warren, stealing information from the lab. In fact, it could really be anyone who had managed to make themselves blind to the security sensors. She checked the logs of the workstations near the last doors she saw open and close, and none of them had been active in the last half hour. Maybe they hadn't used any of them. Or maybe they were really good at hiding their tracks.

Aderyn transferred her map to her com bracelet and took off at a light jog, watching to see which doors were being activated as she went. It was difficult to predict which path the invisible person was going to take, as the station was essentially a large donut-shape surrounding the ballroom in the middle, with many ways around it.

Aderyn cursed as it seemed clear that the invisible visitor was heading back to the ballroom—on the far end of the station. If she kept trying to go this direction, they'd be back to the ballroom and disappear into the crowd before she could catch up to them.

Then again, if she tried to cut through the ballroom, she could get held up in any number of ways and still miss them. She searched through the sensor logs, looking for another way across.

There: worker access tunnels that ran under the ballroom and across the station, a direct line from one side to the other. It took a moment to find an access point, but then Aderyn was in the tunnels, feeling more than overdressed for the exposed pipes and wiring conduits, all the inner workings of a large station that people didn't want others to see. Her journey was not quite as fast as she hoped it would be as she had to duck under and climb over more things than she had pictured, and there were many tunnel hubs that made her bring up her map to make sure she took the right branch.

Finally, Aderyn emerged from the tunnel system via an access point close to the entrance of the ballroom and watched her com bracelet for signs that she hadn't missed her mark.

Nothing, nothing, nothing.

There!

She spotted a door opening not far from her, no ID indication on the other map. Aderyn headed in that direction.

A hand grabbed her arm, and she whirled, shaking the hand off, caught completely by surprise. She had been too focused on her screen, hadn't been paying enough attention to the dots moving toward her.

"Ms. Ryder?" a man asked, confused, his hands up as if afraid she might attack him. It took Aderyn a second to recognize him in his tuxedo and yellow vest.

"Mr. Drystan?" she asked. Myles Drystan—Enzo's husband.

"Please, call me Myles," he said, grinning. He was shorter and rounder than Enzo, and his silver hair was long and wild on top of his head, poking out in various directions. Aderyn looked back over her shoulder and snuck a glance down at her com bracelet before clearing the screen.

"If you're looking for your cousin, I can take you to her," Myles said. "They haven't started the speeches yet."

Aderyn looked again back toward the door that led out of the room, away from the ballroom.

"Do you know what's in that direction?" she asked Myles.

"One of the kitchens," he said. "Are you looking for something in particular?"

"And is there more than one way from that kitchen to the ballroom? Another way besides coming through here, that is?"

"Oh, let me think," Myles said. "At least three, I believe. But there is no one using that particular kitchen tonight—one of the pipes burst and the water to that section had to be shut off."

Aderyn's shoulders slumped, and she sighed. It had been long enough—if the person she had been tracking was going to come this way, they would have.

"Actually Myles, I would very much appreciate it if you could take me to my cousin," she said. "I have a lot to tell her."

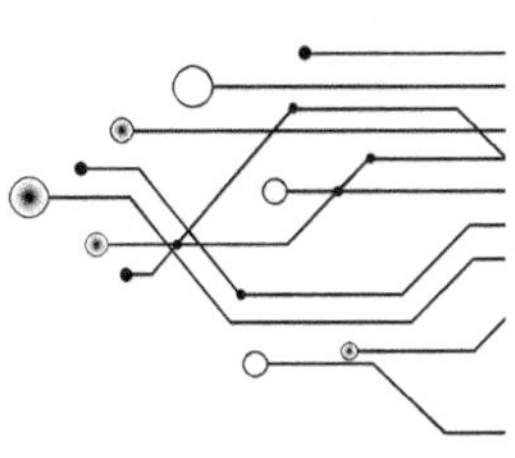

Chapter 11

THE PUBLIC PROPOSAL

Gwynn stared down at her com bracelet and almost couldn't believe the message she was reading.

IT IS DONE.

There was no way to verify that, not now. She had never resented her status at Flaxen Moons more than being stuck in a roped-off section of the ballroom behind the center of the dome with Gair and several top TenDek shareholders and no way to discreetly sign on to the AltFeed or run off and check her quarters. Technically, the crystals weren't due to TenDek until tomorrow, but she was certain no one believed that she would deliver.

No one seemed very upset by that either.

Gair tried to regale her with stories of his travels around the galaxy as Gwynn struggled to give him the attention he was used to getting from her. She didn't want to him to think anything was wrong.

"Are you well?" he asked as her attention drifted back to her bracelet again.

"Just nervous," she said. "I hate getting up on the dais."

"The heights or the attention?"

"Both," she said, giving him her best shy maiden smile. He smiled back.

"And there is nothing else that is bothering you?"

"What do you mean?"

"The crystals," he said. "You haven't spoken of them in some time, and I know your father shared details of our deal with you."

Gwynn nodded. "That if we don't deliver proof of concept to TenDek tomorrow, then the corporation takes over the farms."

"For a price!" Gair said. "We will pay for the honor. And it is an honor. I promise you Gwynn; it is my intention only to build on the legacy of your family, not erase it."

"Why do you want Flaxen Moons?" she asked. It was clear to her that he did, that he had coveted the farm for possibly quite some time.

"TenDek is a young corporation. We have money and resources, but we don't have the same gravitas of an institution such as Flaxen Farms. You can trace the farms back to the colony ships, your ancestor building the first station around the moon before anyone even contemplated the Planetary Alliance. Everyone in the galaxy knows the three-moons logo."

Gwynn wasn't sure about that.

"At least this part of it," she said, "But why not just buy the farms? Why this deal with the crystals?"

"Your father wouldn't sell," he said simply. "This was the deal he made."

Gwynn shook her head.

"He has a lot of faith in you," Gair added, looking solemn.

Gwynn wondered then if maybe Gair actually believed her father when he made the deal, really believed that she could make crystals.

But no one was that dumb, except maybe her. She couldn't

think of Gair as an ally, not now. She couldn't think of anyone as an ally, had to be smarter, plan steps ahead.

Like Aderyn, she realized, who personified the Ryder motto: adapt, and survive. Gwynn hoped she had inherited more than purple hair from her mother's family—she was going to need some of their cleverness too.

"I appreciate what you're saying," she said to Gair, careful to keep her tone and words neutral and vaguely positive. "You have become a dear friend to me and my family. I hope that friendship can continue in the future."

Gwynn wished she had any knack with flirting and tried gently touching Gair's arm to make the moment seem more intimate.

"I have no reason to think it will not," he said, placing his hand over hers. That seemed to work, she thought.

She turned then to look out over the revelers filling the ballroom, trying to find a clue as to what to say or do next. Could she get away, get back to her quarters before her father's speech? Would she be able to easily get away after?

Gwynn shook her head to clear it, trying to track the last thing she saw. It took her much longer than she would have thought to identify the woman in the purple dress and black mask making her steady way toward the roped-off section. But the bright purple hair was unmistakable, and for a moment Gwynn forgot all about IMP and the tuotarium crystals. She took several steps away from Gair before realizing she'd done so.

"Is everything all right?" he asked. She looked back at him, still feeling too shocked to pretend.

"My cousin, who I haven't seen in eons—she's here."

"Good news then?"

Gwynn watched as Aderyn pushed past a rather loud group and glanced up. For a second, their eyes met, amethyst to amethyst, and a wave of emotion washed over Gwynn. She adored her cousin. She hated her cousin. She felt lost without her. She was better off without her.

Finally, her emotions landed on a theme: what the hells was Aderyn doing here?

Aderyn seemed to see something in her face and looked down sadly, pushing forward again.

"I...." Gwynn didn't know how to respond. She smoothed her hands over her dress and tried to think of what to say.

Her older cousin ducked under the otherwise watchful gaze of the guards posted around the roped-off corner Gair and his brother insisted on having and made her way directly to Gwynn, Myles trailing after her.

"Hi," she said breathlessly.

"Hi," Gwynn said back. Gair became a strong presence at her side then.

"I found Aderyn," Myles said, his breath noticeably labored. "She was most anxious to see you," he added, not sure how to read Gwynn's response.

"Thank you, Myles," Gwynn said, because he hadn't been the one to do anything wrong.

"I don't believe we've met," Gair said, filling up the silence that Gwynn had left. "Gair Ingram of TenDek Corporation." Aderyn smiled warmly and grasped his outstretched hand by the wrist, the traditional hand-shake of the Dekken Solar System. Gwynn wasn't the least surprised that Aderyn knew the custom.

"Aderyn Ryder," she said. "I'm Gwynn's cousin on her mother's side."

"Ah yes, the Ryder clan," Gair said, clasping her arm warmly. "Where Gwynn gets that lovely violet stripe of hers."

"Indeed," Aderyn said. She seemed to notice something interesting on the other side of the small roped-in area, and Gwynn tried to follow her cousin's eye-line, but only saw Elidor and a few other Dekkens standing in a group and talking.

"And you got here when?" Gwynn asked, still trying to process the appearance of her cousin.

"Just tonight," Aderyn said. "Have you seen Tuari?"

"He's here? He hadn't confirmed, said he was having trouble getting a ride. His family is in a critical place on Spres—they couldn't spare any shuttles."

"I was his ride," Aderyn said, ducking her head slightly as if embarrassed to admit it. Or maybe more like guilty. "I happened to be going through the area."

Gwynn felt the usual bud of jealousy bloom inside of her at the thought of Tuari and Aderyn doing anything together and clenched her jaw tight to keep her feelings off her face.

"I haven't seen him," she said.

Aderyn made a face, obviously unhappy with that news.

"I thought," she began, and then shook her head. Her eyes were on Elidor again, and Gwynn wondered suddenly if her cousin knew Gair's younger brother.

"This is quite the surprise," Gwynn said. "If I had known you were coming, I would have sent an escort to the airlifts. You could have come here directly."

Aderyn smiled at that.

"The proper royal treatment," she said. "That's a lovely thought. But I quite enjoyed being among the revelers. There's magnificent energy out there tonight."

"People are excited that the farms are doing so well," Gwynn said.

"There has been much to celebrate," Gair added. "I'm sure you've heard."

"About the merger," Aderyn said, nodding. "Yes, I did."

She opened her mouth as if to ask questions, and then shut it as she noticed Elidor coming up to their group. Gwynn was puzzled by her cousin's reaction.

"Elidor, we've had a wonderful surprise," Gair said. "Gwynn's lovely cousin, Aderyn Ryder, has joined our festivities."

Elidor in turn bowed at Aderyn in his usual formal way, matching his welcoming gesture to the culture of the person he was greeting.

"Ms. Ryder," he said. "A pleasure to see another of Gwynn's family."

"We have met several of the Flaxenharts, but you are the only Ryder I think to have made it tonight," Gair added.

"We're a busy group," Aderyn said. "Our cousin Treasa is pregnant, and most of the family is traveling with her back to Oster for the birth."

"Please pass on our congratulations," Gair said. "That is wonderful news."

"I didn't know," Gwynn said, feeling guilty. She didn't know Treasa nearly as well as she knew Aderyn, but she'd always liked her.

"We should talk more," Aderyn said. "In fact, if you have a moment—"

"I'm sad to say that she does not," Gair said, "as the speeches are about to begin. But I'm sure we can give you two space to catch up later."

He grinned widely and pleasantly, but Aderyn frowned in response, and Gwynn wondered what that was about.

"I can be brief," Aderyn said, staring hard at Gwynn as if trying to get a message to her.

"Perhaps the speeches can have a small delay," Elidor offered. "Surely family comes first."

He and Gair exchanged a look that Gwynn couldn't read. It was getting really hard to track things, and Gwynn couldn't help but wonder if everyone else knew something she didn't—besides the obvious, that the merger with TenDek was a sham and her father a liar.

"I'm afraid the schedule is quite tight," Myles said, frowning. "If I had known Aderyn was coming...."

"All is well," Gwynn said, still struggling to get her myriad emotions under control. "Addy and I can talk later."

"Will you join us on the dais, Ms. Ryder?" Elidor asked.

Aderyn shook her head.

"After," she said. "I'm not one for attention."

"And yet you wear such bold colors," Gair said, still smiling. Gwynn watched Aderyn's face freeze, uncertain how to take what Gair said. Gwynn herself wasn't sure if Gair was insulting or complimenting her cousin.

"I was born with a bold color," Aderyn said, running a hand down the purple strands of her not-hair, blatantly displayed. "It gives me as much attention as I could ever desire."

Gwynn couldn't help but frown. It wasn't true, she wanted to say. You want all the attention, from all the people, all the time. But that was Old Gwynn, the Gwynn of this morning who had time and energy to think such petty thoughts. New Gwynn, as she thought of herself, could afford to be more gracious. In fact, she probably needed to be.

"I can relate," she said to her cousin.

Aderyn gave her a wry smile in return, her eyes wide with surprise.

"I'm sure you understand more than most," she said. "I at least was raised with others sporting the same look."

It was Gwynn's turn to be surprised by Aderyn, though she knew that once upon a time this sort of exchange had been normal between them. Spending time with Aderyn at Savenel had been life-changing. Her older cousin had taken her under her wing, stood up for her, introduced her to wonderful new things, and helped her understand and even appreciate her Ryder heritage.

That was, of course, before Gwynn caught Aderyn and Tuari together in bed, her best friend and her cousin keeping secrets from her.

"Your father is waiting," Gair said, pointing to Bertram standing on the platform that would rise above the crowd for his speech. Gwynn nodded.

"After," she told Aderyn. "We'll have to get caught up."

"I do hope you watch the speech," Gair said, putting out his arm so that Gwynn could take it. "I have a feeling you are going to want to hear this."

Aderyn just smiled back, and even Gwynn had to wonder what Gair was alluding to. Still, she took his arm and walked with him up to the dais, Elidor following them close behind. She couldn't help but feel her heartbeat speed up as she looked out over the crowd, and she wondered if Tuari was down there, if he saw her with Gair by her side.

Her father greeted her warmly at the top, pulling her close and kissing each cheek. He gave similarly friendly greetings to Gair and Elidor, and Gwynn had to struggle to keep her composure, wanting to scream at all of them that they were liars.

Instead she smiled back, the dutiful daughter, and waited while her father turned to stand in front of a set of voice amplifiers, his image broadcast on a large screen behind him. The platform hummed as it rose up above the crowd, voices below them quieting in response.

"Good evening fair folk, and welcome to the Hart Ball!" her father said. Thunderous applause echoed around the room, and he waited for it to die down before continuing. "I am so very pleased to see so many old friends here tonight, and, as you can tell, quite a few new ones as well." More yelling and clapping greeted him, mostly coming from folks wearing Dekken colors. "While every year is a celebration, this year feels particularly special. This year, Flaxen Moons is proud to share that we have joined forces with TenDek Corporation." The cheers were almost deafening now, and Gwynn struggled not to wince at the noise. "Now I know you all look forward to a speech from me every year, but this year, I thought I might hand things over to my new partner, Gair Ingram, who I believe has something very important he'd like to say."

Bertram stood back, clapping his own hands as Gair stepped toward the center of the platform, his image filling the screen behind the dais. Gwynn couldn't help but notice how much more regal he looked than her father, how much more elegant the cut of his clothes, how bright his chains. He reminded Gwynn of her grandfather, who had that same ability to look noble in every setting.

"My dear Flaxen workers, TenDek workers, friends, and guests, I am very honored to be here," he began. "Just as I am honored to combine the efforts of father's business with the grand and long legacy of the Flaxen Moons. I have learned much in my time here about the history of these farms and the role they played in the expansion of the colonies and the building of the Alliance. Even when war came to the galaxy, Flaxen Moons stood tall, supplying our troops and ensuring a Progressive victory."

This line got more raucous cheering.

"We are not here tonight just to celebrate the past, but also to look forward to the future. And in that spirit, I would like to ask Gwynn Flaxenhart to join me." He turned then and reached a hand in Gwynn's direction.

She felt her face grow hot and her palms grow clammy. Surely he wasn't going to announce their effort to make crystals? Why share the big lie? Was he just trying to humiliate her?

But as he was beckoning her, she had no way of turning him down. All eyes were on her, whether she wanted them there or not. The thought gave her the boost she needed to walk confidently to Gair's side, plastering a smile on her face for the benefit of the vid-feed.

"As Bertram represents the rich history of Flaxen Moons, Gwynn represents the promise of its glorious future. And to ensure that future is as bright as it can be both for Flaxen Moons and TenDek, there is something I want to ask her."

Here he turned to Gwynn, and to her utter confusion, lowered himself on one knee. The crowd became a roaring din, others recognizing something in his posture that Gwynn herself did not. She watched perplexed as Gair pulled a small box from his pocket, opened it, and presented its contents to Gwynn. Inside was a gold ring with a small purple tuotarium crystal embedded on the top.

"Gwynn Flaxenhart, I have only been acquainted with you for a short while, but in that time have come to know you as a brilliant, dedicated, and compassionate person. I have been dazzled by your creativity and enamored of your beauty. It would be my greatest honor if you would agree to take my hand in marriage."

Gwynn clasped her hands to her mouth and looked at the ring, at Gair's smiling face, at the crowd going crazy below them, and finally up at her father, who was smiling and nodding, making small shooing gestures at her with his hands, encouraging her to take the ring. He knew. He wasn't at all surprised by this turn of events. She wondered then if this had been the plan all along, the final part of the deal between TenDek and Flaxen Moons—a merger sealed with a marriage.

Suddenly Gwynn understood all Gair's compliments and all his attentiveness. She had a choice now to accept or reject his offer, knowing what she knew about the deal and the crystals, knowing who she would actually be marrying. Her father put her in this position, set her up for this moment. Maybe some part of him thought she would be excited. He still thought of her as a little girl, she knew. Naïve. Simple. Moldable.

But Gwynn had grown up very fast in the past few hours, years of delusions stripped away from her. And there was only one sure way left to save Flaxen Moons.

Gwynn swallowed hard and forced her hands away from her face, painting a smile on befitting the occasion.

"Of course!" she said, taking Gair's hand. "Oh, of course I'll marry you!"

Gair stood then and pulled her into a chaste embrace before making a show of sliding the ring onto her finger. Then he pulled her hand to his lips, kissing the top of it, his eyes meeting hers all the while. Old Gwynn would have thought it heartbreakingly romantic.

He turned to the crowd then, holding her ringed hand up, his fingers entangled with hers.

"To our future!" he yelled to the crowd. "Flaxen Moons and TenDek Corporation! Two great companies, one amazing union!"

Gwynn waited until the crowd seemed just about screamed out, and then stepped forward, pulling Gair behind her.

"And to add to the joy of this momentous occasion," she said,

"I feel the time is right for all of you to know—for many years I have toiled on a single project, hoping that it might bring glory to Flaxen Moons, and to my family. And tonight, I am proud to announce to you my success: Flaxen Moons has found a way to turn algae into tuotarium crystals!"

There seemed to be a collective gasp from the people below them, and Gwynn felt Gair go still behind her.

Then the place erupted in cheering louder and more enthusiastic than any heard before. This time it was the folks in yellow and white cheering loudest, and Gwynn beamed at them.

She hoped that she was right to put her faith in IMP, and that she hadn't just made herself the biggest fool in the galaxy. She hoped that maybe, just once, she might have the upper hand.

PART 3: A Change in Fortune

And when the king came in the morning, and found all as he had wished, he took her in marriage, and the pretty miller's daughter became a queen.

Jacob and Wilhelm Grimm, Rumpelstiltskin

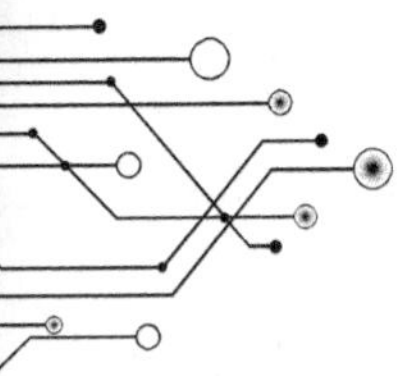

Chapter 12

THE BITTER STING

Aderyn rushed toward Gwynn as soon as the dais lowered, shoving past several TenDek shareholders in the process. Elidor spotted her and made space for her next to her cousin, and Aderyn grabbed Gwynn's hand, pulling her close to whisper in her ear: "What in hells are you thinking?"

Gwynn pulled back from Aderyn and glared at her, a look Aderyn had come to know in their time at Savenel together.

"Aderyn!" Gair exclaimed from the other side of Gwynn. "Wasn't I right? That was not to be missed!" His eyes were bright and he was smiling, but there was sweat beading at his hairline, and Aderyn suspected that the head of TenDek was feeling a lot more than he was willing to let on.

"It was something I will never forget," Aderyn said honestly.

Bertram bustled past Aderyn to get closer to his daughter, kissing her cheeks before holding her face in his hands.

"You did it, you really did it! I always had faith, always knew!" His eyes were bright with tears and Aderyn wondered for a moment if she had her uncle all wrong—maybe he hadn't set his daughter up after all.

"I am so pleased I could deliver on the faith you placed in me," Gwynn said, her voice sugary-sweet. There was an edge to it that Aderyn could read, and she doubted that Bertram would miss it. She assumed Gwynn didn't want him to. "All I ever wanted was to make you proud."

Some truths sting, and Bertram's hands floated back to his sides, though his smile never faltered.

"I am very proud," he said quietly. The whole thing read like a touching moment, if Aderyn didn't know the subtext.

"But we must see this," Gair said, reclaiming Gwynn and putting a possessive arm around her. "We must see what you have achieved with our own eyes."

His voice was full of enthusiasm, and he was putting on a very good show of faith and support toward his new fiancé.

"Of course," Gwynn said. "You'll join us, won't you cousin?"

Aderyn didn't appreciate having Gwynn's false sweetness directed at her but nodded anyway. She definitely didn't want to miss this.

"Addy!"

Aderyn turned to see Tuari standing by Myles near the roped-off area. He waved at her and she waved back, tension she hadn't even been aware of holding draining from her shoulders. Then she watched as he took in the sight of Gwynn in her impossibly gorgeous green dress and her impossibly handsome and rich fiancé, and her spirits faltered. Aderyn couldn't help herself from taking in Gwynn's returned look of joy mixed with sadness, the look she always seemed to give Tuari. New tension crept up Aderyn's body, and she did her best to ignore it.

Soon the little group from the dais was back in the roped-off area, and introductions were made quickly.

"We need to go to my quarters," Gwynn told the group. "I've been working out of there. You're coming too, right Tuari?"

He looked at Aderyn, clearly lost as to the purpose of this little field jaunt.

"To see the crystal that Gwynn made," Aderyn filled in and took some small pleasure in the creases between Tuari's eyes increasing with still more confusion.

"You did see the speeches?" Gwynn asked.

"Just," Tuari said, and Aderyn had questions as to why, and why he wasn't on the sensor logs, and why he seemed to look to so hurt by Gair's constant touching of Gwynn.

"Then let us go see this marvel of ingenuity and begin our celebrations properly!" Gair said.

Myles and Enzo joined the group as they walked, two and three across, out of the ballroom and back toward the kitchen Aderyn had come in through when chasing the invisible guest. She tried to get close to Gwynn to warn her that things might not be as Gwynn expected them to be, but Gwynn was sandwiched between Gair and her father, Tuari walking with Myles and Enzo, and Aderyn found a walking partner in Elidor.

"Is everything well?" he asked her discreetly.

"I very highly doubt it," Aderyn said, but she didn't feel comfortable saying anything else.

There were a lot of doors between the ballroom and the part of the station that housed Gwynn's quarters, and Aderyn realized that her path through the service passages earlier had been the right choice. Finally, they got to their destination.

"One moment," Gwynn said, untangling herself from Gair's constant embrace. "I want to make sure it's tidied before you all come in."

She disappeared into the room for a long moment, and Aderyn grew nervous, picturing any number of outcomes. The group shifted their feet but stayed silent.

When Gwynn finally re-emerged, she had a huge and genuine smile on her face.

"Come in," she said, gesturing invitingly.

Gair entered first, his careful composure slipping as he rushed, and Bertram was his shadow. Aderyn waited for Enzo, Myles, and Tuari to enter before taking a moment to talk to Elidor.

"Do you know anything about this?" she asked.

"I don't know how I could have," he replied. "Gair didn't tell me about the proposal," he added. "I have been as surprised by these turns of events as you have."

He bowed politely, indicating that she should go first through the door, and Aderyn obliged, finding a spot in the semi-circle that had formed around Gwynn's workstation.

A tuotarium converter stood in the corner, a series of lights attached to the outside of it, and a pale green crystal in the center of it.

"A demonstration," she said. Gwynn typed a command code into the chamber, and within seconds, the lights began to glow brightly.

Aderyn held her breath. The lights continued to glow. And then continued glowing even more.

"How long?" Tuari asked, and she could see the wheels whirling in his head. They learned at Savenel that most crystals folks made could only withstand being inside a tuotarium converter for less than a minute before shattering. Only the real deal lasted longer, and it was a common test to run the crystals for a minimum of two minutes during sales in order to separate out the authentic crystals from the counterfeit.

"One minute, forty-five seconds," Gair said, staring down at his com bracelet.

"Two minutes," Bertram chimed in a few seconds later.

"And counting," Enzo added, grinning. He clapped his hands together and pulled Gwynn into a tight embrace, and she returned his hug, laughing at him.

Myles and Tuari also burst out into laughter, hugging each other, while Bertram bent forward, hands on his knees, shaking his head in disbelief.

"But this was made, here? On this station?" Gair stared at the crystal and the glowing lights.

"The research is all here," Gwynn said, showing data displayed on her work console's monitor. "And of course I'll expect the other scientists to do whatever tests they need to do to verify—for publication."

"Of course," Gair said, leaning over the monitor and scrolling through the information there. "You really did it." He turned and stared up at Gwynn, genuine awe on his face.

Aderyn shook herself out of her shock and looked around the room, trying to spot any sign that someone else had been there. It was a large area, with one whole section of it dedicated to Gwynn's work space. Evidence of past experiments littered the top of her console, including pieces of failed crystals, various data pads, and tubes filled with what Aderyn assumed were different solutions.

The rest of the room was tidy, the bed made, and clothes put away, trinkets and such placed neatly on tables and shelves. The space looked lived in, well used.

And yet, something about it all felt wrong. Aderyn could feel it in the prickling of her scalp, some ancient instinct warning her of an unseen danger.

As she watched the dance of celebration happening in front of her, Aderyn also realized her chance to talk to Gwynn about her worries was slipping away. Gair was being possessive of her cousin's attention, and her father was chatting about all the people he wanted her to talk to back at the ball, while Myles was trying to convince Enzo and Elidor to start planning Gwynn's wedding. Tuari was going over the data on Gwynn's monitor, grinning as he read.

Aderyn needed a way to clear everyone out, get her cousin alone. She flipped through various possibilities in her head and landed on one that had the greatest likelihood of working—and of going horribly wrong.

Aderyn slipped her hand into the pocket of her dress, reaching past the bottom of it to her taze-stick, extending the rod. She took a deep breath and let it out slowly as she flicked the stick on and off as quickly as possible, feeling a tingling heat hit her thigh, travel up toward her hip, and slowly spread out over her torso and limbs, momentarily paralyzing her. Then all her muscles released at once.

She let out an involuntary gasp at the pain, and Elidor turned toward the noise, dashing toward her as she felt her body begin to fall.

"Aderyn!" he shouted. This made the others jump into action, Enzo practically leaping to Aderyn's side, helping catch her before she reached the floor. He picked her up easily in his arms and carried her to Gwynn's bed.

"There's a med kit in the lab next store," he told Elidor, who sprinted away to get it. Myles traded spots with Enzo, reading her vitals on her com bracelet, and then taking her pulse the old-fashioned way. He'd been a medic in the war, Aderyn remembered, and she was glad that he was there. She was afraid that she got more of a charge than she planned on.

"She seems to have had some sort of shock to her system," Myles reported. "But her vitals are stabilizing."

"Addy, dear, are you all right?" Bertram asked, hovering behind the others and broadcasting his concern on his face. Aderyn wanted to tell him that obviously, no, she wasn't. Even her com bracelet was telling everyone that. She tried to speak and reassure him, but her stomach roiled, and she leaned over the edge of the bed. Tuari got some sort of container under her just in time as she emptied her stomach.

Elidor arrived then with the med kit, and Myles pulled out a more advanced scanning device than her com bracelet, waving it slowly over her body.

"These readings don't make any sense," Myles said. "It's as if her body was shocked by something." He pulled some sort of hypospray from the kit and pressed it against her neck.

"For the nausea," he told her.

"Should we call security? Get a doctor?" Bertram asked.

Gair took a protective posture in front of Gwynn.

"If someone is attacking people at this station...."

None of this was going according to Aderyn's plan, and she struggled to sit up so that she could tell them all that it was fine, she'd just accidentally tazed herself with her own home-made weapon that she always kept hidden on her person.

Aderyn closed her mouth and laid back down.

"You need to stay in bed," Myles said, helping ease her head onto the pillow.

He turned to the others.

"It doesn't appear to be fatal, and there's no indication of any foreign substance in her system. I think she just needs some time to rest and recover."

"Everyone out," Enzo said.

"Gwynn!" Aderyn managed, reaching her hand out toward her cousin.

"Everyone but Gwynn," Enzo amended.

"Yes, Gwynn should stay with her," Bertram said, sounding relieved to be leaving. "At least for a little while. Gair, Elidor, and I should go back and tend to the guests. I'm sure we are all being missed."

Elidor looked doubtful, though Aderyn couldn't tell if that was because he didn't think they were being missed or if he didn't want to leave.

"Gwynn, dear-heart, you should stay, tend to your cousin," Gair said. He clamped a heavy hand on Tuari's shoulder, pulling him toward the door. "The rest of us will give you space."

Tuari looked like he wanted to object, but Enzo followed behind, making shooing motions with his hands.

Then it was just Myles, Gwynn, and Aderyn. Almost as if she

had planned it, Aderyn thought wryly, swallowing against another wave of nausea.

"I want to go get a better scanner," Myles said, still frowning at his readouts. "Will you be all right to stay with her?" he asked Gwynn.

"Of course," she said, genuine concern on her face.

Aderyn felt a small stirring of triumph before bending over the container again and hurling. She was going to have to get Warren to get her some of those healing nanites he'd talked about.

"Addy, what happened?" Gwynn asked, bending over her and putting her hand against her forehead, as if doing so would tell her anything.

"I needed to get you alone is what happened," Aderyn said. She pushed herself into a sitting position, breathing out through her nose as she fought back the urge to vomit again. "Gwynn, what is going on?"

"I don't understand," Gwynn said, shaking her head. "You did this to yourself?"

"The crystal, where did it come from?" Aderyn was having a hard time concentrating, her stomach trying to take all her attention.

"I made it," Gwynn snapped, pulling away from her cousin.

Aderyn shook her head. Wrong tack, she told herself.

"There was someone in your room, before," she said, trying again.

"Lots of people were in here before."

"No, earlier. Before we all came back here." Aderyn took slow deep breaths, trying to will her body to listen to her instead of rebel against her.

"Enzo saw me off before the ball," Gwynn said, clearly confused. "What are you trying to get at?"

"I'm not saying this right," Aderyn said, holding her stomach. "This will pass, I swear, and then we need to talk."

"You know what's wrong with you," Gwynn said, her voice getting angry. "You somehow did this, didn't you? Why? To get me alone? For what?"

"I know something is wrong," Aderyn said. "Something doesn't add up."

Gwynn stood up then and began pacing around the room.

"Of course you'd think something was wrong. You couldn't just believe in me," she said. "Not little Gwynnie. There's no way I'd be able to accomplish this on my own, right?"

Aderyn shook her head.

"That's not what I'm saying."

"No, but you're suspicious. 'Something is wrong'. Of course you'd have to think that. All the good things are happening to me for once."

Aderyn dragged herself to the edge of the bed and tried to stand. She was still dizzy though and fell back hard on her ass.

"Gwynn, I think you're in danger." Aderyn didn't know how to say it any plainer than that.

"I can take care of myself." Gwynn's face was the perfect picture of resentment and rage. "I'm going to go celebrate my major scientific discovery with my fiancé, the CEO," she said. "Don't be here when I get back." She turned and huffed out of the room.

In the corner, the string of lights on the outside of the tuotarium converter continued to glow.

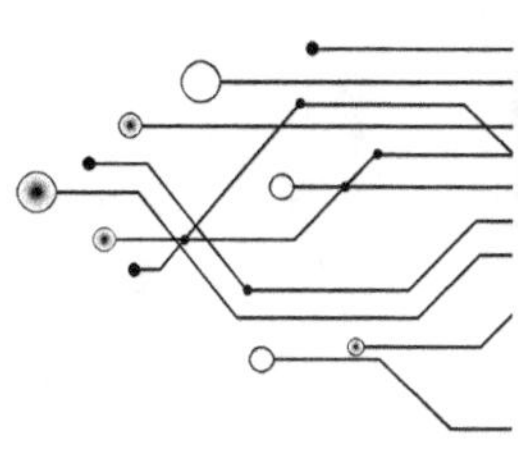

Chapter 13

THE ABJECT RETREAT

Aderyn had lost all sense of time. She was surrounded by people, overwhelmed by the press of their bodies, the smell of their perfume. Tuari was her anchor and she clung to his hand, afraid that if she let it go one of them would be lost in a sea of bodies.

Gwynn was somewhere else, shaking hands and showing off an engagement ring and reassuring people that yes, she really had made a tuotarium crystal, it really was all real.

It wasn't all really real, Aderyn knew. She had no proof of it of course, but she knew it anyway. And knowing had gotten her kicked out of her cousin's room, forced to limp along as she recovered from a self-inflicted tazing, until she found Tuari.

And then they both found alcohol.

"It's not real," she said into Tuari's ear. "Can it be real?"

"Gwynn, engaged?" he said back, incredulous. Aderyn noted that they seemed to be impacted by very different parts of the evening and shifted her hold from his hand to his arm.

"We're never going to get to her through all of this," Aderyn said.

"We can't leave," Tuari said back. "Gwynn is here. She needs us."

"Gwynn isn't speaking to us," Aderyn said.

"She isn't speaking to *you*," Tuari corrected. "And she hardly got a chance to speak to me. We need to find her."

"We need to get out of here."

Tuari shook his head.

"Just the ballroom," Aderyn responded, pulling him back toward one of the exits.

"We need to find Gwynn!" he said adamantly, standing his ground.

"I can track her," Aderyn said, lifting her wrist to wave her com bracelet at him. "Let's get some place easier to breathe. And think. And look for her." She pulled harder on his arm, and he finally started to move in the direction she wanted.

"What do you mean you can track her?" he asked.

"Through the station's security sensors," she responded over her shoulder, weaving them through two bunches of people. He pulled back hard, stopping Aderyn in her tracks.

"You hacked the station?" he asked. His brows were furrowed in anger.

"You're just mad because you didn't think of it first," she said. She tried to pull him again, but he was solidly planted and glaring at her. "Do you want to find her or not?" she asked after a moment.

He snorted out a breath as if he was trying to release some pent-up emotion. Then he walked past Aderyn, taking the lead through the crowd and dragging her roughly behind him.

She liked it better when she was leading—she was better at navigating. And gentler on his arm, she noted, sure he was leaving a bruise with his grip.

At last they found a spot relatively free of others, and Tuari whirled around, pulling Aderyn close to him.

"What the hells are you thinking?" he growled. "Do you have any respect for anyone else's privacy?"

Aderyn yanked her hand back, freeing herself from his grip.

"Are you forgetting who I am?" she asked. "What I am? Because you and your family have definitely benefited from that before."

"Leave my family out of it," he said. "We're talking about you. How you find a way of betraying Gwynn over and over again."

"I'm not betraying her, I'm tracking her!"

"She kicked you out of her room for a reason," Tuari said. "What did you say to her?"

"That's it's not real," she said.

"Her engagement?"

"The crystal," Aderyn said, her own anger flaring up. Tuari really needed to focus.

"You saw it with your own eyes, and you're still doubting her?"

"There's things happening," Aderyn said. "It didn't go well when I tried to tell Gwynn either." She brushed hair out of her face, a thick purple strand sticking to her cheek.

"What's happening is that once again you have selfishly chosen yourself over your cousin," Tuari said. "Why can't you ever just believe in her?"

"I'm not doing this again," Aderyn said, and tried to head back into the crowd. Tuari stepped in front of her, blocking her way.

"You never even went to see Gwynn after."

"She didn't want me to," Aderyn said, frustration making her gesture wildly. “And you didn’t want me to, either. It would have been a lot harder to salvage your friendship with her with me hanging about, and you know it. So I made a choice. For her. For you. I made myself scarce. And it worked. Gods help me, it worked.”

Aderyn felt tears forming and pressed the palms of her hands against her eyes, willing them away. She hadn’t realized how much of this old hurt she was still holding.

“I messed up,” she said, lowering her hands. “But you messed up worse. You never told her how you felt. Hells, you never told me either. There were two of us in that bed, and somehow I’m the one that gets all the blame.”

“Because you’re the one that seduced me,” Tuari said. “I never would have been with you otherwise.”

“Is that what you tell Gwynn? Is that what you tell your family, so they understand why you took a risk sleeping with a modified girl? And kept sleeping with her? Just how seductive am I?”

“You don’t get it,” Tuari said. “You wander around with your purple hair hanging down, daring the whole galaxy to say something. You want the fight. You use it to justify who you are, how you act, so you never have to be blamed for the consequences of your actions.”

“What are you even talking about?” Aderyn asked, genuinely confused. “You have no idea what I go through. Remember the war? Remember when terrorists like The Thirteen started it all off by systemically hunting down modified folks like me and killing them ‘to preserve the bloodlines’? Remember that? Do you think that just went away, that I don't live every day knowing that I may encounter someone who wants to kill me for who I am?"

"Look who you're talking to," Tuari said.

"And you'd really think that would help you understand." Aderyn shook her head.

"My family stayed neutral in the war."

"And your family would disown you if you married me," Aderyn said. "Or Gwynn. She faces the same prejudice I do."

"At least she doesn't flaunt what she is."

"Spoken like a true Naturalist," Aderyn said. "No, your family didn't fight in the war. But don't think for one second that means they aren't still filled with hatred toward modified folk like me."

"No one in my family hates you," he said, shaking his head.

"They just refuse to be like me," Aderyn said. "They won't even make simple modifications, things that would help them with their work cleaning up war damage."

"You really don't understand," Tuari said his voice filled with quiet anger. "My family has fought to preserve who we are since before the colony ships left Earth. We are fighting to hold on to a culture that other civilizations tried to wipe out. Fighting for who we are is part of us, just as fighting for the preservation and restoration of nature is, so that war-torn planets don't go the way of Earth, with species after species wiped out. We fight to live in harmony, in balance. What do you fight for?"

"Survival," Aderyn said, her voice a blade. "The family motto: adapt, and survive."

"Sounds an awful lot like assimilation to me," Tuari said.

"Becoming something new isn't assimilating," she said, struggling to find the right words. "It's evolution."

"You really just don't get it," Tuari said, his hands in fists at his sides. "Your people were never forced to change."

Aderyn didn't have an answer to that. She wanted to, wanted to tell Tuari about how she didn't have a choice being born the way she was, with weird purple hair that marked her as a modified human everywhere she went. That survival at any cost was drummed into her brain for as long as she could remember, and that sometimes the cost felt much too high. That she had struggled to be proud of her heritage, just the same as Tuari did. That she had finally made peace with being different in a galaxy where half the people treated her as less-than-human because of it. That she wasn't willing to give that peace up for anyone.

But he was too locked into his own pain to listen to hers.

"This galaxy has screwed us all," she said. "I don't understand why we aren't on the same side."

"Because the only side you care about is yours," Tuari said. "You'll do anything for your own benefit, damn the consequences."

"Keep blaming me if you want to, but I have the same memories you have, and I know how you truly feel."

"You really don't," he said, his voice cold. "After Gwynn found out about us, I felt so lost. You helped me find myself. But I never felt the same way you did."

Aderyn felt her history being rewritten in front of her, and suddenly the room was too warm, the air too thin. Everything around her felt wrong, wrong, wrong.

She turned blindly and started walking.

Tuari grabbed her arm.

"Wait Addy, I didn't mean...."

She shoved his hand off her and kept walking.

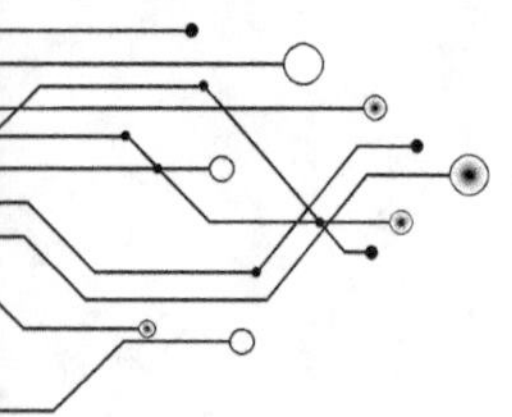

Chapter 14

THE DEAD END

Aderyn was lost in the mass of bodies in the ballroom, taking random drinks from trays that she passed and downing them as fast as she could. When the crowd suddenly cleared out in front of her, she stumbled, suddenly realizing how hard it was to walk without other people around her propping her up. She was dizzy, and things were looking blurry, and Tuari had never loved her.

There were men in front of her eyeing her cleavage, noting her hair. Two of them came toward her, one slapping the shoulder of the other as they both grinned, clearly egging each other on. Aderyn reached for her taze-stick at her side, pulling it out just in case.

"You're one of those mod freaks!" one of the men said. He was tall and wide, and he was circling around as though to get behind her while his friend stayed in front. "That purple only on your head?"

His buddy laughed and reached out toward Aderyn as though to grab her. She swung her taze-stick out and whacked him on the arm, watching in satisfaction as he grew stiff as the current went through his body. Aderyn whirled then, kicking in the knee of the man behind her, and knocked the pommel of the taze-stick against his temple as he went down. There was only so much juice in the taze-stick, and she didn't want to bother draining it on this man.

"What the hells?" another said, running forward. "What did you do to my friends, you freak!"

Aderyn lit up her taze-stick again, feeling the slight hum as electricity crackled along its edge. The man stopped short, his friends behind him watching Aderyn and her taze-stick warily.

"I'll show you who's the freak!" she shouted, squaring off with the men, ready to take her anger out on the lot of them. Even if there were rather a lot of them. She ignored the warning voice in her head that this might not be such a good idea.

Suddenly strong arms were around her, and the taze-stick was twisted out of her hand, and deactivated.

"I kinda thought giving that back to you was a bad idea," Warren said from behind her.

She twisted out of his arms and turned to face him.

"No mask," she noted.

"You seem to have lost yours as well."

Aderyn patted her face and felt only skin.

"Apparen-tal-ly," she said, unintentionally dragging the word out and trying to keep an eye on him and the group of angry men behind her at the same time.

"We should probably leave now," he said. "You are *appar-en-tal-ly* too drunk to be good in a fight."

"I'm just the right amount of drunk to be good in a fight," she countered, and turned back to the other men. She could take on...she counted...six guys. Probably.

Warren stepped forward, holding his security badge out to the men who were watching with increased reluctance to engage, shuffling their feet and looking anxiously at the men Aderyn already took out.

"Security," he said. "I got her." The men seemed to be satisfied with this and kept their distance.

"You don't have me!" Aderyn said.

"It's probably best if you don't beat up more people," he said back, motioning to the still frozen man and his friend on the floor. "Also, it's going to be very un-pretty once that paralysis wears off."

"Oh, I know," Aderyn said, nodding.

"And this is your family's celebration—maybe you don't want to make a spectacle?"

Aderyn felt the room spinning and considered. She looked back at the other six...no five...no six. Oh hells, she was drunk.

"Fine," she said, walking toward Warren and letting him lead her away. He aimed her toward one of the exits out of the ballroom, which Aderyn thought was probably a good idea.

"My cousin is engaged," she announced.

"I saw."

"And it's all a sham."

"Most corporate marriages tend to be."

"And Tuari doesn't love me. Never did."

Warren shook his head.

"Now that doesn't make any sense at all. Tuari is a stupid-head."

Aderyn started to giggle. And once she started her laughter seemed to take over, turning at some point into sobs before she could catch her breath and control herself again.

"I don't feel good."

"You've had a rough night," Warren said. "How about I take you someplace where you can rest?"

"Rest sounds restful."

"Right," he said, guiding her away. But then the floor seemed to be sliding out from under her, and she grabbed onto Warren's arm, looking up at him with surprise.

"Has the gravity gone wonky?"

"Only for you," he said, reassuring her. But her knees didn't seem to want to support her, and she began to slide down again. Warren solved the problem by picking her up.

"No more floor," she said.

"It wasn't working out too well for you."

She nuzzled up into him, her eyes closed.

"Not many things are," she said into his neck, and then she fell asleep.

When Aderyn tried to open her eyes again, they felt crusty and sticky. She wiped at them with her fingers, freeing her lashes so that she could peek out from under them. Her fingers were purple, and she stared at them for a long moment, trying to understand why.

"Sparkles!" she said at last.

"You seem to be a fan," a voice said to her right, and she turned her head carefully to look at who it was.

"Warren Frey," she said.

"Are you just going to go around naming things?"

"Hangover," Aderyn said in response.

"A pretty epic one, I'd imagine. I could help you with that, if you want."

He held up a glass full of a thick green substance. Aderyn made a face. Then she reached out for it, propping herself up on one elbow. It took her three large sips to swallow it all down, and she struggled against a desire to retch. She handed the glass back to Warren and put her head down, closing her eyes.

Soon the sensation of spinning abated, and the pounding at her temples eased up, and her stomach stopped threatening to violently empty itself.

She sat up fully then, taking her time and getting her bearings as she did so. She was on a bed tucked under a sloping bulk-head, and the space around her was compact, but tidy—a dressing area just past the head of the bed and a low couch opposite it, and a small table in front of the couch. A workstation up by the door that presumably led to the rest of the ship rounded out the room, with a few odds and ends strapped to the walls. One of those was a wicked looking curved sword. Aderyn stared at it for a long moment before letting her gaze take in other details as Warren's hangover elixir continued to work. He had a blanket on the couch the same material as the one she was under. There was a coffee cup on the table in front of it, and....

"Is that a book?" she asked, incredulous. She swung her legs over the edge of the bed, but her attempt to stand up made her drop back down to the mattress with a small grunt.

"Easy," Warren said, reaching out to take her arms and help steady her. "My hangover cure is good, but not that good. You need to take it easy."

Aderyn looked down at herself and noticed a man's shirt. She yanked her hands free from Warren, and patted down the front of the shirt, pushing back the blanket to reveal a crumpled purple skirt underneath. She lifted the shirt to see the bodice of her dress covering her. She looked up at Warren, confused.

"It was too much cleavage to sleep in," he said straight faced.

Aderyn burst out laughing, and then immediately reached up to cradle her head.

"Don't make me laugh," she said.

"I'm not very good at stoic," he said, squatting down in front of her. She was grateful—it was easier to look down than up.

"How long?"

"Twelve hours," he said.

"Anyone come looking?"

"Your com bracelet has been very active," he said, gesturing to it with a nod of his head.

Aderyn pressed the surface and saw a half a dozen messages flash at her. Two were from Myles. Three were from Treasa. One was from a business contact looking to hire her.

None were from Tuari.

"Why did you help me?" she asked, looking back down at Warren.

"You needed the help, and I had the ability to give it." He shrugged. "It's really not any more complicated than that."

"You could have left me with my cousin," she said. "Or one of her people."

"I had reason to believe that might not be a good idea," he said. Aderyn wondered where he got his information from. He obviously had good sources.

"I should let my people know I'm safe."

"I sent word," Warren said.

Aderyn shot him a sharp look, then went back through her messages again, noting the time stamps on each. She read the most recent one first, from Treasa.

Glenda did a check and approves. I checked out his pic, and I do too. And you said you had no young man. Com when you wake up.

"You contacted my family," Aderyn said, putting things together.

"Just the ones that reached out to you."

"This com bracelet is bio-locked."

"Unconscious people still have fingerprints."

"And there's a password."

"I'm a good guesser."

"I need to get back to my ship," she said at last.

"We're locked in synchronous orbit—you just have to walk through an airlock."

"Is there anything you didn't think of?" Aderyn asked.

"Not that I can think of," he said.

Aderyn chuckled.

She stood up slowly, smoothing her skirt down over her legs in a vain attempt to take the wrinkles out of the material.

"Help or no help?" Warren asked as Aderyn contemplated taking her first step.

"Help," she said after a moment, and he reached out a strong, steady arm. He was wearing a dark gray tank-top, and Aderyn noticed a blue band around his upper arm. Lots of things about him suddenly made more sense, including the expert training and excellent health care. The Blue Band was essentially a corporate army created to fill in the gaps the Planetary Alliance had in their security coverage after the Genome War. Funded by a joint commission of all the large corporations, their mission was to keep peace in the galaxy, especially along trade routes. As the Alliance withdrew from more systems, the Blue Band and the corporations were facing more and more pressure to make the arrangement permanent. Aderyn had to wonder if Warren was still actively Blue Band, or only working for TenDek, or possibly freelancing. Her head felt too fuzzy to consider all the options and what they might mean.

It was hard for her to focus on walking and conversation, and she was grateful when Warren seemed comfortable with silence as he helped her move through his quarters and down the external corridor. She got the sense that his ship was smaller than the *Herald*, and it had a more polished, uniform look to it, like he didn't have a hand in designing it himself. If he was Blue Band, that tracked—they would have given him a ship.

Soon they were at the airlock.

His airlock door opened, and they stepped in front of hers. Aderyn used her com bracelet to contact Gilda.

"I'm outside," she told the AI.

"Are you feeling better?" Gilda asked. "Warren thought it would be better for you to have human monitoring, and not just AI."

"You're on a first-name basis with my AI?" Aderyn asked.

"I'm a friendly guy," he said. "And Gilda is an amazing program."

"Thank you, Warren," Gilda said.

"You are most welcome," Warren replied, grinning. He helped Aderyn down her own hallway and to her kitchen, lowering her into a chair next to a small round table. Then he looked around, and Aderyn felt nervous about how things looked from his perspective. She thought the *Herald* was homey, with bright colors and woven textiles, artwork secured to the wall, and real ceramic dishes from Oster latched down carefully in the rack above her sink. But maybe he thought it was too busy, or impractical.

And maybe she shouldn't be worrying about what he thought.

"Great ship," he said, sitting down in the chair opposite her. "Love the chair cushions."

"They are secured," Aderyn said, in case he thought she was frivolous.

"I've no doubt," he said. "You managed to find a great balance between space-flight safety and homey comfort." He seemed sincere, and Aderyn smiled at the compliment.

"So now what?" he asked.

"Shower? More sleep? I'm not really in a planning space right now."

"I mean, now what with us? Though I'm not opposed to sharing either a shower or a nap. Thought we might try dinner first."

Aderyn felt caught off guard. Yes, there had been flirting, but Warren was a bad guy, or worked for a bad guy, or at least was suspicious.

But he was also good looking, gregarious, helpful, and direct. And somewhere along the line she had stopped thinking of both him and Elidor as people on her "bad" list.

"Can I get back to you on that?" she asked. "My head is foggy and I'm not sure I can trust my decisions right now."

"You have concerns."

"You pulled a gun on me. Twice."

"And you left me paralyzed in front of a lift." He shrugged. "It was kind of hot, actually."

Aderyn laughed.

"Go back to your ship. Let me hydrate, clean up, clear my head."

"Sure," Warren said, standing up. "And then maybe dinner after that. I'll keep our ships connected for now, just in case."

Aderyn grinned.

"And I'm keeping your shirt," she added.

"I was going to insist," he said. He winked at her and headed back toward the airlock. "I'll bring the wine," he shouted back.

Aderyn wanted to yell that she could probably do without wine, but yelling would hurt her head.

"Gilda, please tell me when Warren is off ship," she said.

"Warren is off ship," Gilda said after a moment.

"Can you summarize my messages for me? My head hurts too much to read."

"Treasa's first message said that they made it to Oster, and that the baby still has not come. Her second message stated that Glenda completed her search of the AltFeed and only found two mentions of IMP in any chat feeds, both praise for IMP's help and support, and none anywhere else. Glenda got pushback on her search and multiple attacks against her firewalls while running it."

"Is she all right?"

"She reported that the attacks were powerful, but that she was stronger. She is fine. Treasa's third message is marked as read. Would you like me to summarize?"

"No need," Aderyn said.

"Two messages from Myles Drystan ask you if you have recovered and if you could please check in when you get a chance."

"Send a reply saying that I'm fine, and back on my ship. Thank him profusely for his help and his concern."

"The final message is about business. Shall I save that for when you are feeling better?"

"Definitely," Aderyn said. "Thanks Gilda."

She pulled herself up and dragged herself to the sink for a glass of water, drinking it all down and then refilling the glass, downing that one as well. She figured she would need at least half a dozen more before she felt close to normal again.

"So that's it then," Aderyn said. "IMP is impossible to find."

"I am glad you did not let me search the AltFeed," Gilda said.

"Me too," Aderyn said. "I've lost enough friends lately. I don't think I could handle losing you."

"Who did you lose?" Gilda asked.

Aderyn swallowed hard.

"Just…friends," she said.

"Then it is a good thing that you have made a new one," Gilda said.

Aderyn laughed.

"Yeah, that probably is a good thing."

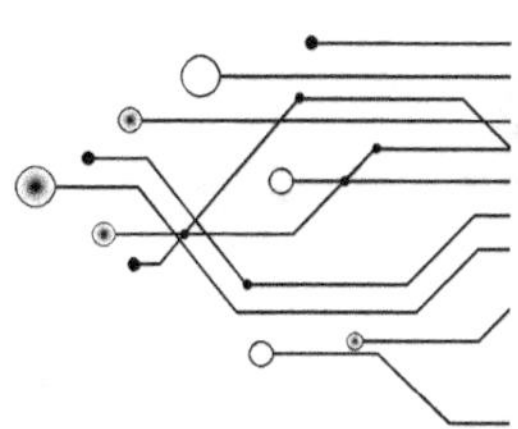

Chapter 15

THE GLORIOUS RISE

The table was green stone, a solid singular chunk roughly hewn and polished down, leaving the edges uneven and the surface flat. It was an extravagant display of wealth, Gwynn thought, clearly designed to intimidate people.

She had to admit that she felt a little intimidated.

Gair had continued to be complementary and attentive to her the entire duration of the ball. And while he had walked her back to her rooms, he remained polite and appropriately distant, calling her dear-heart and sending her to bed with a chaste kiss.

It had almost been romantic.

But he'd also peppered her with questions about the tuotarium crystal powering lights in her quarters: when did she discover the right formula? How long ago was her first test? Why hadn't she shared the news right away?

She didn't have answers to any of these questions, but over the course of the night she had learned a lot about how to play the corporate game, and countered with questions of her own: when did he first know he loved her? When did he ask her father for her hand? When did he get the ring? Why did he wait to propose at the ball? What would he have done if she said no? She giggled after that last one, a specific giggle she was developing that was an effective way to get around a lot of uncomfortable questions.

It helped that over the course of the evening they were almost never alone. Bertram was their most consistent companion, but the few times he had been lured off by food or drink, Enzo or Elidor could be relied upon to take his place. There were others, of course, shareholders of TenDek, other high-level folks from other corporations, even a couple of low-level heirs from those planets that were still ruled by a monarchy. They all fussed over Gwynn's ring and marveled at the whirl-wind romance, and Gwynn played the part of the besotted bride-to-be to the best of her ability.

She hoped she had done enough, convinced Gair that she could play the corporate game well enough to suit his needs.

Sham or not, she fully intended to go along with this marriage.

"They are certainly taking their time," Myles said, two chairs down from Gwynn. He happened to be stuck at a part of the table that jutted out just slightly, a rock protrusion poking his stomach.

"It's a tactic, isn't it?" she asked Enzo. "Like the table. Keep us waiting, make us uncomfortable. It helps them have the upper hand."

"You're catching on," he said, patting her arm.

"It seems pretty obvious," Gwynn replied, frowning. "Does it actually work on anyone?"

"And you'd think they could leave more than water in the room," Myles said, leaning awkwardly over the table to reach the pitcher of water and refill his glass. "They have so much money, you'd think they could afford some snacks."

"It works," Enzo said to Gwynn, winking at her.

Gwynn chuckled.

At long last, the two large doors behind the head of the table opened and Gair strode into the room, trailed by Elidor and a handful of others, all of whom fanned out to take their places at the table. Enzo stood when Gair entered, and Myles followed suit, but Gwynn stayed stubbornly seated. Gair shot her a smile and took his own seat. Everyone who had been standing followed after him.

"I hope you haven't been waiting long," he said. "I thought some refreshments might make up for the wait."

The other set of double-wide doors opened then and robotic workers in green and gold rolled into the room with trays loaded over with bite-sized delicacies, both sweet and savory. The bots placed the trays in the middle of the table, offering each guest a small plate to put items on, and refilled any empty water glass.

"Can I offer you any other refreshment?"

"Water is fine," Gwynn said.

"Your father is not joining us?" Gair asked.

"I didn't think it was necessary," Gwynn said. "The deal that TenDek had with Flaxen Moons through him is complete. Myles has a record of all the things you paid for on our behalf. All that you invested will be returned to you in the form of tuotarium crystals, as per your agreement with my father. The second part of the deal—where it detailed what would happen if Flaxen Moons couldn't deliver a formula for tuotarium crystals made from algae and a proof of concept—has been made null by my demonstration last night."

She signaled Enzo, who placed a small yellow box on the table.

"The crystal," she said. "It was removed from the converter by your own staff this morning, its movements carefully tracked every moment of its journey here, to you."

Enzo pressed his fingers into the side of the box and bent down to breath on a sensor on top. The box opened, and the tuotarium crystal inside rested on a bed of fine yellow silk.

"So many precautions," Gair said, smiling at Gwynn. "Do you think I mistrust you, dear-heart?"

"Not at all," Gwynn said, leaning forward on the table and stretching her hand out toward Gair, close enough for him to touch. "But this crystal is very dear to me. The work I did to create it, with your help and support, not only changed the fate of my entire family, but it also brought you into my life."

Gair reached out his own hand, resting it on hers lightly.

"It is very dear to me, too," he said.

Gwynn smiled sweetly at him for a beat, and then casually slid her hand out from under his.

"What I want to discuss today is the terms of our marriage."

"Terms?" Gair asked.

"Please don't think me unromantic, but when someone as rich and powerful as you marries, I know there have to be...discussions. Marriage, in its simplest form, is a contract. An emotional contract, of course, to love and honor one another for the rest of our years. But also a financial one."

She looked around the table to make sure that she had the attention of the rest of Gair's people. "You, of course, have the assets that you bring to the table. And I have mine."

"Your assets," Gair said, repeating her words.

"The algae farms of course," Gwynn said, smiling widely.

"Of course!" Gair said. "Flaxen Moons."

"Yes, which as you have always been so kind to say, has a very long and tremendous history."

"Yes, we have talked of it often while visiting the museum."

"I have to say, those visits were most inspiring," Gwynn said. "I can honestly say that we wouldn't be here today—not exactly here, at this table, with that crystal—if it wasn't for those visits."

"Oh?" Gair asked.

"Do you know what algae finally was the one that worked?"

"No, I don't."

"*Umbraulva kuaweuweu*," Gwynn said. "It has a fascinating history. It's a deep-sea algae that was discovered in the early twenty-first century, unusual for being found between two hundred and four hundred feet below the surface. It was named in part after a god of the Earth Hawaiian people—the god of prosperity, if you can believe that. It was worn decoratively as well as eaten. But as the ocean temperatures continued to die off, this particular species became endangered. It wasn't long until it only existed in scientists' labs. One enterprising young woman decided it would be a good algae to bring on the colony ships, since it required low-light to grow and did well under the pressure of up to four hundred feet of water."

"That is fascinating," Gair said. Myles struggled to keep a straight face as Gwynn beamed at her fiancé.

"Isn't it? The thing is, this scientist was the only one interested in *Umbraulva kuaweuweu*, and when the early colonists voted to allow people to patent their bio samples—essentially claiming ownership of certain DNA—she claimed it. And do you know who that woman was?"

"I can hardly wait to find out," Gair said.

"My great great...well, many greats grandmother, Eleanor Flaxenhart."

"Who patented the DNA of—"

"*Umbraulva kuaweuweu*," Elidor supplied. Gair shot his brother a look.

"Right. Who patented the very strain of algae that you used to make the tuotarium crystal."

"The very one," Gwynn said.

"And you have inherited that patent."

"I will—on my coming of age day next month."

"So your father owns that patent now?"

"Actually, no," Enzo said, shooting Gwynn a conspiratorial look as he leaned over the green stone table. "Eleanor is what folks in the twenty-first used to call a feminist. She believed that passing things down through the maternal line was one of the ways to ensure gender equality."

"So, right now, no one owns the algae, though of course Flaxen Moons has license to use it. We make a fine line of soaps with it, actually."

"But you will own it...."

"On my birthday, next month."

Gwynn leaned back in her chair.

"And to think, I never would have thought of using it, if it wasn't for all those walks we took in the museum."

"So when you say you want to discuss the assets we bring to our marriage...."

"I have advised Gwynn that a prenuptial agreement, protecting the respective pre-marriage assets of each party, would be in the best interest of everyone," Enzo said.

"I've got the formula," Gair said.

"Thanks to my father," Gwynn interjected.

"And you've got the algae."

"Doesn't it just feel meant to be?"

Gair steepled his fingers together under his chin and contemplated Gwynn from across the table.

"Clear the room," he said in a commanding tone of voice Gwynn had never heard him use before. "I would like to speak with my fiancé alone."

Enzo shot Gwynn a curious glance, and she shook her head in response. No, she didn't need him to stay.

Once everyone else was out, Gair stood up, walking to Gwynn's side of the table and taking the chair one away from her. He picked the crystal up from the box, twirling it lightly between his fingers.

"I feel I may have formed the wrong impression of you," he said after a long moment. "Your father, while of course a very proud and doting parent, has not been able to recognize all the ways that you have grown up."

"The truth is, he was probably seeing me more accurately than you think," Gwynn said. "I feel like almost all of my growing up has happened in the last few days."

Gair looked at her sharply.

"What changed?"

"I found out that no one—not you, and certainly not my father—ever thought I would actually be able to make a tuotarium crystal. The deal was a lie, a cover story for my father to sell his family legacy without taking the blame for it."

"But you surprised us all, didn't you," Gair said, placing the crystal carefully back in its box. "You went and pulled off a miracle."

"And it still wouldn't have saved Flaxen Moons," Gwynn said. "Not with the deal my father made. He promised you the formula—full ownership."

"Which I can lease out to whoever I want," Gair said.

"Which wouldn't do you or anyone else a lot of good without the right base ingredient."

"That Hawaiian algae—I'm guessing it's rare?"

"Flaxen Moons owns the only known supply in the entire galaxy," she said. "Trust me, I looked."

"I bet you did," Gair said, chuckling. "Now, tell me honestly—do you still want to get married?"

Gwynn sighed.

"Partly yes, partly no."

"Which part is which?" he asked with a grin, waving his hand over her body. She laughed.

"The Flaxenhart part of me," she said, putting her hand over her heart, "only wants to marry for love. But the Ryder part of me...." She put her hand over the purple streak in her hair. "The Ryder part of me wants to be smart."

"And you think this marriage is smart?"

"Don't you?"

"Oh, very much so," Gair said. "I wouldn't have proposed otherwise. It's just that, before, when I thought you were a besotted young farmer's daughter, it was easy to pretend to be some sort of heroic type. I was going to sweep in and save you, your home, and your legacy. I was counting on your eternal gratitude to make our marriage easy."

Gwynn laughed again.

"And now?"

"Now you see me for who and what I am—a boring old business man."

"A very successful one," Gwynn said.

"My parents were the successful ones." He gestured around the room dismissively. "I didn't build this—I just run it."

Gwynn leaned forward and took his hand.

"Then maybe we can think of something we can build together."

Gair's eyes met hers, and she felt like she was seeing him for the very first time.

"I would like that very much," he said. "And maybe in time you won't have to choose between the two parts of you."

Gwynn smiled. He leaned toward her then, caressing her cheek with his hand and tilting her head up toward him to kiss her lips. This kiss was not like any of the others—there was nothing chaste or forced about it. And while it was not free from spark, it was not the deep kiss of being in love.

But it was satisfying nonetheless.

Gair pulled back and looked deep into Gwynn's eyes.

"I think I'm getting the better deal," he said, smiling. Gwynn brushed his face with her fingertips, running her thumb over the lips that had just been pressed against hers.

"I guess we'll have to wait and see," she said.

PART 4: A Dangerous Search

A year after, she brought a beautiful child into the world, and she never gave a thought to the manikin. But suddenly he came into her room, and said, "Now give me what you promised."

The queen was horror-struck, and offered the manikin all the riches of the kingdom if he would leave her the child. But the manikin said, "No, something alive is dearer to me than all the treasures in the world."

Then the queen began to lament and cry, so that the manikin pitied her.

"I will give you three days, time," said he, "if by that time you find out my name, then shall you keep your child."

Jacob and Wilhelm Grimm, Rumpelstiltskin

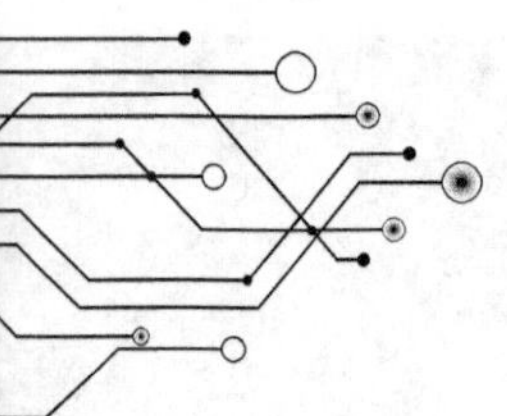

Chapter 16

THE BRUTAL FALL

Gwynn lay on her back and stared through the clear glass-like dome above her. She loved this view. She knew the name of every star, planet, and asteroid that could be seen from this angle, and on nights when she couldn't sleep, she went through the list, naming them one by one.

It had been a long while since she had been able to do this, take time to just lay flat and look up. The past year had been one giant event after another—celebrating her coming of age day, planning for and then hosting her wedding, receiving her honorary degree from Savenel, revealing her new Flaxen Moons Re-Dev station. When she was younger, she never could have even dreamed of a year like that. Sometimes she felt like she was living someone else's life, that all these wonderful things actually belonged to someone else. Sometimes she worried that she would go to sleep and wake up back in her old quarters at Flaxen Moons, spending her days in an endless repetition of the same experiments over and over again. She never really realized the hell she was living in until she was able to break free.

She pushed away those memories—she was free now. She'd paid her dues and she'd gotten out, and now her life was—not perfect. But good. And at times, even wonderful.

She rested her hand against her belly, rubbing light little circles over it. It didn't feel different yet, not on the outside. But she knew that inside her body was changing. She could feel the surge of hormones coursing through her, sending new messages to her organs, telling them to move and shift to make room for the growth that was to come. Her brain was creating new neuropathways, and her body was changing its composition, adding fat layers for energy storage. Gwynn giggled at the way she was dismantling her own body in her head, reducing it to chemicals and cells.

She was growing life inside of her.

She giggled again. It just sounded so absurd. It was easier to think of cells dividing than all the other parts of the process. She knew when the baby would have a heartbeat, and fingernails, and lungs. But when did the personality start? How did it get its sense of humor? What about dexterity, or drive?

There were so many parts to a person that she couldn't explain through biological impulses. One of the oldest mysteries of the human race was why people cry when they're sad. The sociologists beat out the biologists in this—human behavior wasn't predictable on the cellular level.

"There you are," Gair said, his footsteps heavy against the smooth wood floor of the ballroom. "Making yourself a picnic?"

"Come join me," she said, patting the spot next to her. There was a thick blanket stretched out under her, and a basket of fruit, bread, and cheeses next to her.

"Well this is lovely," Gair said, stretching out beside her, propped up on his elbows. "It reminds me of being planetside when I was a kid and my father would take us camping so we could look at the stars. It always seemed strange then—we'd come from the stars, why would we have to go out into nature to look back up at them? But the truth is, it's different."

"I haven't spent much time on planets," Gwynn said. "Never went camping as a kid."

"We'll do it now," Gair said, flipping on to his side to look down on Gwynn. He ran a finger down the side of her face. "Any time you want, any planet you want." He leaned down to kiss her, and she wrapped her hand around the back of his head, pulling him closer, deepening the kiss. When she finally released him, his face was flush, and his eyes bright.

"Maybe we need a more private spot," he said.

"I want to stay here," she replied.

"Are you sure?" he asked, bending to nibble at her ear, ticking her with his beard.

"Yes," she said, giggling and squirming away from him enough to look into his eyes. "Because this is the place where I want to tell you."

"Tell me what?" he asked, tracing his thumb along her hairline. She took his hand in hers and rest it on her stomach.

"I'm pregnant," she said.

Gair's face split into a huge grin, his eyes wide with wonder.

"Really? You're sure?"

Gwynn nodded.

Gair whooped with joy, and pressed his head into her neck, and alternated between kissing her neck and tickling her with his beard, working her sides until she was laughing so hard she was having trouble breathing. Finally his kisses became gentler as he moved up to her chin and traced her jawline to her ear, his teeth biting lightly on the lobe.

"That really does need a private place," she said, pushing his mouth away from her ear with a mock scowl.

"I am just so happy," he said. He kissed her lips, her forehead, each cheek, and her lips again. "You make me so very happy."

His com bracelet chimed then, and he pulled his wrist between them with a groan of complaint.

"A message?"

"A reminder—I'm supposed to meet with Enzo to go over specs for your father's newest investment."

"I don't know why you indulge him. None of his ideas ever pan out." Gwynn stretched her hands up above her head, twisting slightly from side to the other, working kinks out of her back. Gair's eyes followed her movements, a look in them that suggested there was a very good chance he was going to be late for his meeting.

"I think," he said, lowering his body over hers so that she could feel him pressed into her. "This is a private enough place."

Gwynn grinned.

"And we have a blanket."

Gair laughed.

"And we have a blanket."

Sometime later, Gwynn pulled her sweater on over her head, smoothing it down and watching with satisfaction as Gair slowly pulled his own shirt back on.

"I wish we could stay here forever," he said plaintively. Gwynn agreed.

"We could put our bed here," she said. "And the baby's crib over there."

"Raise our little one under the stars?"

"Better than a planet," she said, grinning. Gair laughed.

They took their time putting on the rest of their clothes, packing up the basket, and folding up the blanket, each in the mood to linger.

"We never get to do this," Gwynn said.

"We'll make more time for it. I promise." He entwined his fingers in hers and pulled her in for a kiss.

Another chime interrupted them, and Gair looked down at his com bracelet, then back up at Gwynn, shaking his head.

"Must be you," he said.

Gwynn frowned. She could have sworn she had set her com to silent, not wanting to disturb the peacefulness of her afternoon.

She had a message. She pressed her finger to the screen, unlocking her com and opening the message.

IT IS TIME.

It was signed IMP.

"Are you well?" Gair asked, his voice concerned. "You've gone pale. Is it hormone sickness from the pregnancy?" He led her over to a low bench on the outside of the dancefloor and helped her sit.

"I'll call Myles," he said. Gair took two steps away to speak into his com bracelet, and Gwynn took the opportunity to go back to the message.

Why was IMP contacting her now? It had been a year, and nothing. She had forgotten all about the promise she made her unknown benefactor. At times she had even forgotten that she had not actually created the tuotarium crystal herself. She'd done the work. For two years, she had done the work, all on her own. She knew that given enough time and resources she would have found the answer, knew it to the very marrow of her bones.

IMP had just sped things up, that's all. It wasn't like she really owed him anything.

Gwynn erased the message from her com. She'd ignore it, and IMP would go away.

Gair came back to her then, pressing the back of his hand against her forehead.

"You're clammy," he said. "If you are all right to move, Myles said we should go back to our quarters and he'd meet us there."

Gwynn nodded.

"It's probably nothing," she said. "This stage of pregnancy, I'm bound to have episodes like this now and then."

Gair didn't look convinced and kept her pressed close to his side in case she grew faint. Finally, they got to their quarters, and Gair helped her to their bed, insisting that she lay down.

"I'll get you some water," he said. As he left, Gwynn's bracelet chimed softly again, and she opened the new message with shaking hands.

YOU OWE ME. YOUR DEBT IS DUE. IT IS TIME.

Again she erased the message, and almost as soon as she did, she heard another chime.

I KNOW ABOUT THE BABY. WE NEED TO TALK.

Gwynn felt heat rush through her body, and her stomach roil. She pushed herself to the side of the bed just as she threw up.

Gair was with her in a heartbeat, smoothing her hair, wiping her mouth. Then Myles was there, taking her pulse, scanning her vitals. And then Enzo was there, and her father, and all the while they asked her how she felt and what her symptoms were, and none of them, not one, asked her what was wrong.

She might have told them if they did.

As she was tended to by a group of very nervous men, she realized that she was going to have to tell someone about IMP.

And that she didn't want it to be any of them.

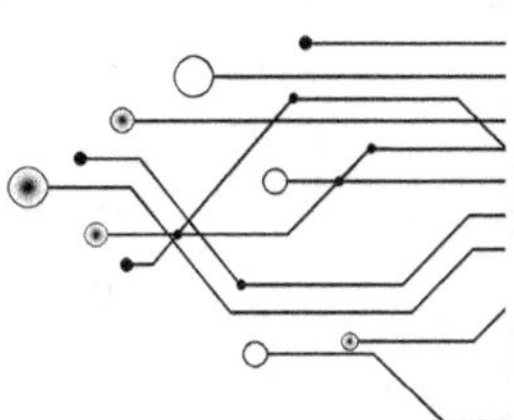

Chapter 17

THE OMINOUS MESSAGE

Tuari blinked hard, either in thought or in surprise. Gwynn couldn't tell which. Somewhere along the way, she had lost track of his expressions. At one point she could read his face as easily as words on a screen or cells through a scope. She had been attuned to his every mood, could interpret every sigh.

Now Gwynn felt frustrated that she couldn't tell what he was thinking, and it made it harder for her to know what to say next.

"I mean, it's not an impossible hack," Tuari said. "If you can get access to someone's com, sure you could probably change the settings."

"Remotely?" Gwynn asked. "Like, through the SatLink or something?"

"I don't know how remotely," Tuari said. "Like, what the range would be."

"Could you do it from a different solar system, or would you have to be local?"

"This really isn't my area of expertise," Tuari said. "I don't suppose you want to tell me why you're asking these questions?"

"I think someone's pulling a prank on me," Gwynn said. "I keep setting my com bracelet to silent, and someone keeps setting it to chime for every incoming message."

"Maybe something wrong with the bracelet," Tuari said. "Have you run diagnostics?"

"Twice," she said. "And then again through the lab workstation.

Everything seems to be in working order, except that the settings keep changing without me changing them. So that's why I just want to know—is it possible for someone to do this from far away, or do they have to be local?"

"I don't think distance matters so much as access. If they are getting to your com bracelet, they are probably accessing it through the station's network. Your bracelet will link with the closest, strongest signal, by default. When you're at the station, it links with the station. If you're in a ship, it links with the ship's communications sys. If you are in a space suit in deep space, it will find the closest satellite. But it won't reach for a satellite signal if there is a stronger signal closer by."

"So then, I should be looking at the station's security."

"Run a diagnostic of the station's internal coms, and then do a separate one to see if there are any issues in the connection between the station and the nearest satellites."

"What kinds of issues?"

"I really think if you're going that route, you should recruit help. Get Enzo on it."

Gwynn chewed her bottom lip, trying to figure out the best tack to take.

"Well, but it is possible, is what you're saying."

"Unless someone at Flaxen Moons has developed a very different sense of humor than they have previously shown, I'm almost certain it has to be happening from someone off-station. You have any enemies you want to tell me about?"

Tuari grinned at his own joke, and Gwynn struggled to smile appropriately back.

"Well, I'm married to one of the richest men in the galaxy, who runs one of the biggest corporations in the galaxy, during a time when people are growing ever more resentful of people who have both money and power."

"Point taken," Tuari said, frowning. "Maybe you should get one of Gair's people on this."

"It's just a nuisance," Gwynn said, shaking her head.

"Or a huge security breach. In fact, I'm going to upgrade that maybe. You need to get TenDek's security team on this. The more I think about it, the worse it sounds."

"And I thought you were going to make me feel better," Gwynn said.

"Sorry," Tuari replied.

"How's your father doing?" she asked. Tuari's face sunk.

"Hanging on," he said, "but barely. I don't think he has much more time."

"Oh Tuari, I'm so sorry." Gwynn wished she could reach through the vid-screen and hug him. She tried to think back to the last time she had even seen him in person. The wedding? "If there is anything I can do…."

"I don't suppose you have any good news? The work on Spres is taking longer than we anticipated, and the radiation levels inexplicably seem to have gotten worse in some parts. We think there's a local phenomenon that's combining with the pockets and triggered a chain reaction of some kind. Unfortunately, that level of vagueness doesn't really give us any clues as to how to find it, let alone fix it."

"You've been there over a year," she said.

"We're coming up on seven months over target."

"No end in sight?"

"It's still not safe for large-level habitation. Honestly, I'm not sure how safe it is for the people who stay on it."

"Do you need anything? Equipment, supplies. I can send a freighter."

Tuari laughed and shook his head.

"A whole freighter?"

"Honestly, yeah," she said, grinning.

"Must be nice," he said. "But we have all the equipment and supplies we need. I don't suppose you have any answers?"

"Fresh out," Gwynn said. "What about scientists? Maybe you just need a relief team. TenDek is full of bright young things with something to prove."

"Just send your good wishes," Tuari responded. "I think we could use those most of all."

"On their way," Gwynn said, smiling. "Thanks for helping me."

"Any time," Tuari said. Then he hesitated. "Is there anything else you want to tell me? Because you really can tell me anything, Gwynn."

Once upon a time maybe she could. Old Gwynn, with her neediness and her delusional search for grandeur, she would tell Tuari everything. But now she couldn't even read his eyes to know how he really felt about anything.

"Thank you," she said. "I really do appreciate it. Save your energy for yourself—sounds like you need it."

Tuari nodded.

Gwynn signed off shortly after, feelings of guilt washing over her. She wasn't sure what was worse—not telling him about IMP, or not telling him about her pregnancy.

She leaned back in her chair and tried to think about how to ask Enzo to run a diagnostic on the station network without raising his alarm. But he and Myles had taken to fussing over her whenever she raised even the slightest concern.

What she needed was someone knowledgeable, helpful, and discreet.

Elidor Ingram wasn't always on *Flaxen One*, but he'd come with Gair for this last visit to help him solve a problem with the farm that grew *umbraulva kuaweuweu*. Gwynn found him in her old lab, reading a data-pad.

"Gwynn," he said, standing up and bowing to her. "How are you feeling?"

"Well," she said. "But I had a concern that I hoped you might help me with."

"Of course," he said. "I am at your service."

He was one of the few people in the galaxy who could say that and always sound sincere, Gwynn thought.

"I was wondering when we last ran a station-wide systems diagnostic."

Elidor looked surprise.

"I'd have to check the logs, but that's not how it's usually done. Each system has regular maintenance checks, and any system that has been experiencing issues will get a diagnostic. Was there any specific system you had concerns about?"

"The communications network," Gwynn said, opting for honesty.

"Was there any specific issue you were having, or was this just a general concern?"

"Just a general concern," Gwynn said, finding herself spinning her wedding ring around finger with her thumb, a nervous habit she'd picked up in the last six months.

"It is my understanding that these sorts of concerns are normal during pregnancy. That being said, I will of course run a diagnostic on the communications system."

"And the station's network," Gwynn blurted out. "If you could."

"It would be my pleasure," Elidor said.

"And if possible, do you think you could keep this request to yourself?"

Elidor smiled.

"I don't foresee any circumstance in which someone here would question anything I do regarding the running and maintenance of this station, but in the rare occurrence that this might happen, I will be sure to remain discreet."

"Thank you!" Gwynn said, filled with such relief that she had to stop herself from hugging Elidor.

"I'll share the results with you once they come in."

Gwynn walked away feeling lighter, if still wary. As she walked down the corridor back to hers and Gair's quarters, her bracelet chimed.

STOP IGNORING ME, the message read. OR ELSE I WILL FIND SOME OTHER WAY TO GET YOUR ATTENTION.

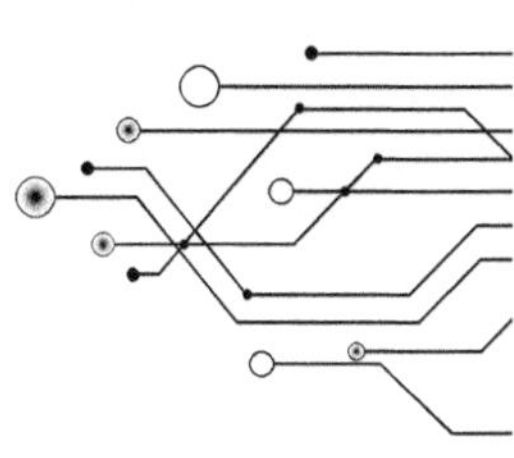

Chapter 18

THE UNEXPECTED RESULT

"Nothing wrong?" Gwynn asked again.

"Nothing detectable," Elidor responded. "There is always a chance that there could be something wrong with a system that isn't detected in the diagnostic. But for all intents and purposes, both systems are running as they should."

"Would these diagnostic tests be able to tell if someone was hacking into the systems?"

"Do you have reason to believe that someone is?" Elidor asked, his voice demonstrating his alarm.

"No, of course not," she said. "I just wanted to know what all these tests actually determine."

"If someone were to try to hack into our systems, any number of alarm bells will ring," Elidor assured her. "It was not always this way. Before the merger with TenDek, I'm afraid the *Flaxen One* network was very poorly defended."

"But it's better now?"

"Top of the line," Elidor said. "I oversaw the installation of the security protocols myself."

Gwynn nodded and wished she felt more relieved. In the past few days, she felt like she was going crazy. IMP was sending her messages throughout the day and night, and it was getting more and more difficult to hide what was happening from Gair.

"Is there something else I can help you with? Forgive me if I am being imprudent, but I have been wondering if maybe something was wrong, something you were afraid to tell me."

Gwynn shook her head.

"I appreciate your concern, but I am well. I think I'm just being more impacted by this pregnancy than I thought."

"If you ever do find yourself needing help, any kind of help, I hope you know you can come to me," Elidor said, his voice softer than even his usual soft tone. Gwynn was touched.

"I will," she lied. "I promise."

Back in her quarters, Gwynn sat down at her workstation and took a deep breath. She didn't want to be doing this, but she was afraid of what IMP might do next. Maybe the favor wouldn't be so bad, she thought. IMP had been a positive force in her life, helpful to her before now. What could her mysterious benefactor possibly ask for that Gwynn wouldn't be able to give? She had more resources at her fingertips than most entire solar systems.

Gwynn logged into the AltFeed, feeling the familiar rush of apprehensive rebelliousness flood through her. The first time she'd logged on, she only stayed on for thirty seconds before chickening out and logging off. She'd heard so many horror stories of entire networking systems being completely taken over the moment a new user logged on. Still, her curiosity had won out over her fear, and she logged on for a second time, staying long enough to start to get a sense of how people communicated through the feed.

This time felt scarier than any other time she'd logged on, including her first time. Gwynn opened up her messages and found the last one that IMP had sent her through the AltFeed: IT IS MY PLEASURE.

She had assumed at the time that IMP was just happy to serve. But Gwynn realized now that there was a second way to read that—ultimately whatever IMP did for others would serve IMP.

ARE YOU THERE?

Gwynn was surprised by how fast the reply came: WHY HAVE YOU BEEN IGNORING ME?

I'M SCARED. Gwynn wrote back honestly.

YOU MADE A DEAL.

Gwynn imagined that the voice behind that was harsh, cold, and cruel.

WHAT IS THE FAVOR? she replied.

I NEED YOU TO MAKE SOMETHING.

That didn't sound too bad. Gwynn nodded eagerly as she typed out: WHAT?

The next message included something that surprised Gwynn—an algae-based nutritional supplement. She looked over the instructions, which were very specific, and at first glance there didn't seem to be anything too difficult about it.

HOW MUCH?

FOR MASS DISTRIBUTION.

That would be more challenging, but not impossible. Gwynn wasn't as directly involved in product design as she once had been, but she was pretty sure no one would question her wanting to introduce something new.

She nodded her head and typed out the process: WE DO

A SAMPLE BATCH, MARKET TEST, THEN MAKE CHANGES, THEN DISTRIBUTE.

YOU CANNOT CHANGE IT IN ANY WAY. NO MARKET TESTING.

Gwynn frowned. That upped the difficulty level a few notches.

WHY? she wrote back.

YOU DO NOT GET TO ASK QUESTIONS. MAKE IT EXACTLY. START DISTRIBUTION IN A MONTH.

Gwynn blanched at that. Nothing got through development that fast. She looked back over the recipe and realized that Flaxen Moons had something that was similar to it already in distribution. New products couldn't roll out in a month, but "new and improved recipes" could.

I CAN DO IT, she typed.

YOU DO NOT HAVE A CHOICE.

WHAT HAPPENS IF I DON'T?

THAT IS A QUESTION.

CALL IT MOTIVATION, she wrote back.

I WILL DESTROY EVERYTHING YOU HAVE BUILT. I WILL EXPOSE YOU AND ALL OF YOUR LIES. I WILL DIG INTO YOUR LIFE AND FIND THE THING THAT YOU CARE ABOUT THE MOST AND TAKE IT FROM YOU.

Gwynn's heart pounded and her hands shook, and she knew tears were rolling down her cheeks.

BUT ONLY IF YOU DO NOT DO WHAT I SAY.

It took Gwynn a long moment to steady herself before she could write back.

AND THEN WE'RE EVEN?

YES. DO THIS, AND WE ARE DONE. DO WE HAVE A DEAL?

Gwynn choked back a sob. But it was just a food cube—how many of those had she helped make?

Yes. Deal.

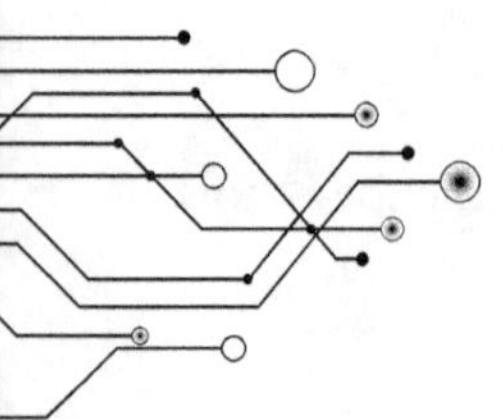

Chapter 19

THE FULL CIRCLE

"Gilda, start the launch sequences on the skip-hop!" Aderyn yelled into her com as she slid around the corner, slamming into the far wall shoulder first. She bounced off a sign with the evergreen tree logo of the Juniper Group and kept running.

"Starting launch sequence," Gilda said. "I am detecting a problem: you cannot launch the ship with the hangar doors closed."

"Can you get them open?"

"I will attempt to do so."

Aderyn glanced down at the map still displayed on her com bracelet, but it was hard to follow it while she was running. The mission to get data stored at the Juniper Group archives—the first lead she and Warren had about IMP in months—was not going well.

Something flew by Aderyn's ear and thumped into the wall next to her, leaving a large dent in the metal. Aderyn zagged to the other side of the corridor, ducking low, then zigged back, stretching herself as tall as she could go. If the security bots were programmed for headshots, she wanted to confuse their vertical aim as much as their horizontal. Mostly she wanted to put something solid between her flesh and their bolt-guns, and this hallway wasn't offering much in the way of choices.

"Gilda, am I close to the ship dock?"

"Are you feeling well, Aderyn?"

"Peachy," Aderyn said, ducking into a doorway and trying the handle. "Why do you ask?"

"You are normally much better at navigating than this."

"I didn't get a chance to study the map before the bots showed up." The door was locked, but she pressed herself against it, hoping there wasn't enough of her sticking out into the hall to make a good target. She brought her com bracelet up to eye height and studied the 3D map.

"Show me my location," she said, and a small purple dot appeared on the map. "That is not where I thought I was."

Another bolt thudded into the metal doorframe by her hip, answering two of Aderyn's questions: the bots weren't only taking head shots, and there definitely was enough of her sticking out to aim at. She wasn't too far from the next bend in the hallway, and she launched herself at it, rolling across the hall and coming back up on her feet.

"Ow," she said.

"Are you injured?"

"Metal floors are terrible to roll on," Aderyn said. "I think I bruised something." She risked a glance behind her and saw the first of the bots rounding the corner. She turned ahead again, getting her bearings and remembering the map.

Suddenly she dropped low, skidding across the floor on her hip, and grabbed the edge of a small square opening in the wall that was barely higher than the floor. Aderyn pulled herself through the opening feet first, crossing her arms across her chest, and slid down a chute.

"Aderyn, I think your tracking chip has failed. It says you have increased speed significantly and are moving through the walls at a diagonal."

Aderyn didn't have the breath to answer.

"Should I run a diagnostic on your tracking chip?"

"No!" Aderyn managed to shout. Her feet then hit open air, and she slammed her arms against the sides of the chute, the material of her jacket scraping and screeching as she tried to slow her momentum.

Then she was out of the chute.

Aderyn tried to brace herself for the landing, intending to use her momentum to roll at the bottom and keep going.

Instead she landed with a thud on her ass.

"Ow ow ow ow ow."

"Aderyn, are you well?"

"I am very much not well," Aderyn said. She rocked back and forth for a moment, trying to breathe through the pain. She was convinced she had broken something it hurt so badly.

Then her healing nanites kicked in, blocking her pain and, she assumed, getting to work on whatever damage she just did.

"Aderyn, you should be moving. This is your daring escape."

"Is any escape not daring?" Aderyn asked, rolling over to her knees and easing herself up one leg at a time. "Feels like the daring is built in. No one has a daring stay imprisoned."

"This is a joke," Gilda said. "A play on words. Very amusing."

"I miss Warren," Aderyn said.

"I do too," Gilda agreed. "I am still trying to track his whereabouts. I am worried about his com having gone offline."

"Me too," Aderyn said. "But he knows where to meet. How

we doing on those hangar doors?" Aderyn shook off her fall as she went over to the door of the recycling room and was momentarily grateful that she landed on the floor and not into a bin full of plastic and metal bits.

"I am fighting with a security program."

"Are you winning?"

"Yes."

"Win faster."

"I will endeavor to do so."

Aderyn pulled up the vid-feed for the hallway outside the recycling room, and not seeing any bots, slid through the door cautiously.

"I end up spending an awful lot of time in recycling rooms," she complained quietly, confident that Gilda would still hear her. The AI lowered her own voice in response, but she overshot it, and all Aderyn got was the sound of low murmuring.

"You are going to have speak just a bit louder than that," Aderyn said. "Repeat your last?"

"I said that I have beaten the security program into submission and the hangar doors are open."

"Atta girl!"

Now that Aderyn was on the right level, getting to the ship dock was much easier, and she managed to do it without running into any more bots.

"Are you scrambling their sensors?"

"Yes," Gilda said. "I thought it would be helpful if the bots could not track you."

"Very helpful," Aderyn agreed. "And that's exactly the kind of information you should feel free to share with me."

"Aderyn, I have scrambled the station sensors so that its bots cannot track you."

"Thanks for letting me know!"

"You are welcome."

Aderyn sighed. It was no use getting mad at an AI, especially one like Gilda. However brilliant they could be, they still tended to take things seriously and directly.

Aderyn was moving slowly enough that she could watch the purple dot of herself move through the 3D map on her wrist. There was another dot just past the door to the station dock, and Aderyn was in no rush to run into whoever it represented. Funny that it was a blue dot, Aderyn thought. Her com usually marked all other humans in red, and security bots in yellow.

Aderyn got to the door and pulled her taze-stick out, activating it. She took a deep breath and opened the door, swinging hard at the figure her map said was just behind it.

Fortunately, the map was slightly off, and Aderyn only barely hit the figure in the shoulder. Even more fortunately, the contact turned her taze-stick off.

"What the hells, Aderyn!" Warren exclaimed. She grinned and threw herself at him, squeezing him tightly.

"I missed you!" she said.

"I did too," Gilda added.

"I was offline for fifteen minutes," Warren said, hugging Aderyn back.

"It was a hard fifteen minutes," Aderyn said.

"*Apparen-tal-ly.*"

"You will stop saying it like that at some point, right?" Aderyn asked as she pulled away from him.

"Probably not," he admitted. "Not unless it gets you level ten mad. Anything under level three is fair game."

Aderyn shrugged.

"I go up to level four with you," she said.

"I've noticed."

"You two are very cute," Gilda said. "But I thought you should know that more security bots are headed your way, the hangar doors are open, and the skip-hop pre-launch has completed. I can help you launch when you are ready."

"That was exactly the kind of thing you should let us know," Warren said approvingly.

"Moving now, praising later," Aderyn said, pulling him toward the skip-hop. She opened the hatch and climbed in front, leaving Warren to take the spot behind her. He nestled in close, his arms unnecessarily around her waist.

"I missed you too," he said. "Tell me you got it. I would hate to have missed you for nothing."

She pulled a small disc from her pocket and handed it back to him.

"I got it."

"Launching," Gilda warned. Suddenly they were both thrown back, Warren against the seatback behind him, and Aderyn into Warren, and he scrambled to keep hold of the disc.

"We gotta teach her to countdown," Warren said.

"Just not from ten. Ten is too long."

"Five?"

"Sure," she said.

It was an uneventful trip to get back to the *Herald*, and Aderyn docked the skip-hop on the left side of the ship. Her STP was on the other side. She liked the symmetry. Then she and Warren were inside, curled up on her sofa, and shoving the disc into a reader independent from Gilda's systems.

It made a small whirling noise—loading. Then the screen on the reader came to life, various lines of data scrolling on it.

"And?" Aderyn asked. Warren rubbed his eye and squinted at the screen.

"Not English," he said. "And not a Latin alphabet. But...yes, we have it." He froze the screen and handed the reader to Aderyn.

"IMP," she read. "Hells! How old is this?"

"Old," Warren said. "My source said it came direct from the heart of the Planetary Alliance."

"And we're pretty sure it's the same IMP?"

"We are," he said. "Because of the ID tag. Look at the numbers."

"Another step closer," Aderyn said, wrapping her arms around Warren's. He took one of her hands in his and bent down to kiss the back of it.

"We'll get this bastard yet."

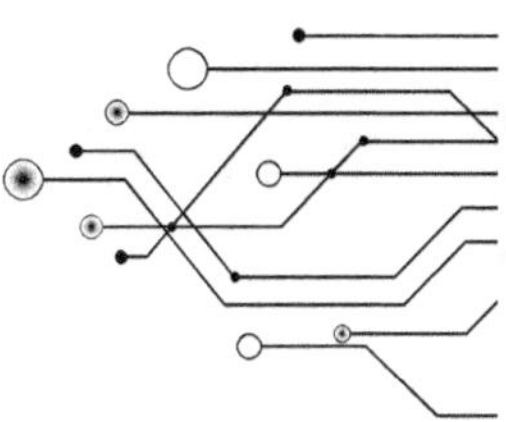

Chapter 20

THE ABSURD NIGHTMARE

"Hey, wait!" Gwynn jogged after the man in the tan suit, trying to get his attention. "You took the wrong thing!"

"What?" He turned around, and Gwynn could see something light blue sticking out of one of his ears. She mimed taking the object out, and the man complied.

"I said you took the wrong thing." She walked forward and switched out his data-pad for hers.

"Thanks! That would have made my day seriously bad."

"It would have made both our days seriously bad," she said. "Be well."

"Be well!"

He shoved his speaker back into his ear. Gwynn shook her head.

They were behind schedule. She'd been behind schedule before, but not with the same stakes, and she was feeling anxious all the time. She was sure that wasn't good for her pregnancy, but anxiety being bad for her pregnancy was just one more thing to be anxious about. She went back to the crate that had just been delivered and slipped its electronic leash around her com-free wrist. Then she turned the crate on and walked back toward her lab. The crate, thanks to the leash, followed.

Gwynn smiled as they passed the logo of the Flaxen Moons ReDev Center—three white moons orbiting a large green planet. She needed it to look different from the regular Flaxenhart logo, and she had never liked the yellow. But she made sure that the green was not the TenDek green.

Gwynn's lab was at the end of a long corridor that bisected two large open storage and testing areas. She walked through the door, taking the leash off her wrist and tossing it on an open hook against the wall. The crate obediently followed the leash, settling itself just below the hook. Gwynn turned off the follow function and typed in her unique customer code—complete with a DNA swab—in order to open the crate. A mechanism inside sprang into action, and a set of neatly stocked shelves rose up out of the crate. Each shelf had dozens of bottles of a particular additive that IMP had included in his recipe. Gwynn picked up a bottle and twirled it around in her hands, trying to see what was so special about this and why it had been so hard to find. It was something that Gwynn hadn't ever heard of before, but it was the last ingredient for the food cubes. This one crate had enough of the stuff to make over a million cubes, and she had an order for three more crates due by the end of the week.

Gwynn took the bottle with her over to her workstation and picked up the data-pad she had been using to look at IMP's instructions for the food cubes. Now that she had everything she needed, it was a fairly simple formula, and she was confident she could get a prototype completed by the end of her workday.

There was something about the recipe though that was bothering her. The more she worked on it, the more she felt that there was something off. Part of her really wanted to contact IMP again and ask about the cubes, but IMP had made it very clear that wasn't an action that would end well for her. Her biggest fear was that this wouldn't be the end of their arrangement, that IMP would hold whatever they had over Gwynn again and again, asking her for more and more. She tried to tell herself that she wouldn't let that happen, that she'd come clean long before she'd compromise her morals.

But she was already making a product—at no small cost to Flaxen Farms—that she didn't design, didn't believe in, and wasn't sure was exactly safe, all to protect her reputation.

And her marriage. And her child's future.

It was easy to justify almost any action with the right stakes.

Making the cubes themselves was easy, as IMP's instructions followed standard operating procedure. Gwynn almost enjoyed going through the steps—they reminded her of her childhood and how she used to beg to help the workers in the test kitchens.

Then there was nothing left to do but wait.

Gwynn curled up on the couch in her lab and tried to stay awake. She apparently had hit a tired spell in her pregnancy, and she drifted off anyway.

Gwynn woke with a start several hours later, her heart pounding and her back sweating. She'd had the same nightmare that used to plague her in college, that she had somehow created a sentient form of algae, which then went on a rampage to kill her and everyone else at Flaxen Moons.

She rubbed her hands over her face as if she could rub the images of death and destruction out. It was an absurd dream but that didn't stop it from being terrifying.

"Hello my sleepy-head," Gair said, walking over to her and sitting down next to her on the couch. Instinctively she curled up against him, and he pulled her close, stroking her hair. "Are you well?"

"I had a nightmare," she said. "One I haven't had in a long time."

"The dreams we have in our youth tend to stay with us—and be the scariest."

She nodded her head.

"You have been working hard all day. Your tired brain reached for something familiar."

"I wish it hadn't," she said.

"And what have you been working on?"

"A new food cube," she said. "Our selection is getting a little stale. We have to throw something new in the market every now and then to keep people interested."

"It is the same with every business," he said. "People crave novelty. And is your new food cube ready?"

Gwynn frowned.

"Should be." She checked the time. "Definitely. I need to get them out." She untangled herself from Gair and walked over to a large white device that looked like one stove stacked on top of the other. She opened the door to the top and pulled her tray of cubes out.

"They look the same," Gair said, standing next to her.

"It's a variation on a prior recipe," she said.

He reached for one and picked it up, and Gwynn watched him warily.

"Feels the same too."

"You know, these are just the prototype. It's probably not a good idea to try them until they go through testing and all that."

"I can be a good tester," he said, grinning at her. He took a large bite out of a cube and winked at Gwynn. He made a show of rolling the cube bits around his mouth.

"Same texture," he said. "Kind of meh flavor—sorry." He chewed and swallowed. "I think you may need to work on the recipe a bit more if you want them to be a hit. But then again, I have a refined—"

He started coughing, and Gwynn watched in horror as specks of blood flew out of his mouth.

"Gair!" she shouted.

He had his hands at his throat and kept coughing up more blood, his eyes wide with panic. He stumbled back, fell hard on the floor, and Gwynn rushed to his side as he began to thrash around wildly.

"Help!" she screamed. "Someone, help! Gair!"

When help came, Gwynn was still screaming, and people had to drag her off him. She followed them as they rushed Gair to Myles.

"What happened?" he shouted at Gwynn. "I need to know what I'm dealing with."

"The food cubes!" Gwynn said, sobbing. "He ate a food cube."

Myles injected various things into Gair, got his body to stop convulsing, got his heart to stop beating erratically, and got his breath steady.

The only thing his medications couldn't seem to do was wake Gair up.

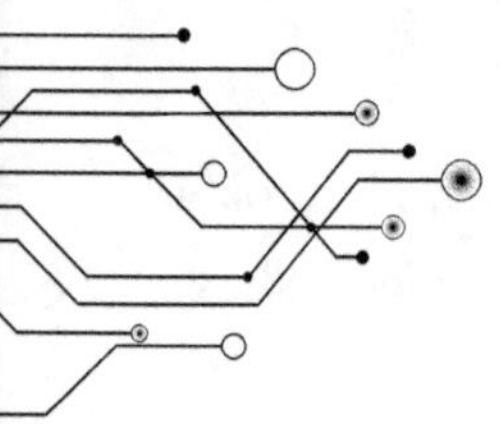

Chapter 21

THE SURPRISE RETURN

The message didn't change the more times Aderyn read it, but she read it again anyway: GAIR IS IN A COMA. PLEASE COME.

It was signed Bertram Flaxenhart.

"We could try calling," Warren said, holding her close, his chin resting on her shoulder, his chest pressed against her back.

"This feels like an in-person thing."

"Then we go."

"But she kicked me out."

"So we don't go, and we call."

Aderyn sighed.

"Those do appear to be all the options." She snuggled in deeper, scrunching down so that she could fit her head on his shoulder. She was a bit too tall for it, but it never stopped her from trying.

"You have an incoming message from Aunt Leona," Gilda told them. "Text only."

"Can you read it to us?" Aderyn pushed herself up, sitting up straight as though her aunt were actually with them.

"Sure," Gilda said. "She writes: Gwynn needs you. End of message."

"So it's settled then."

Aderyn nodded.

"We are going to Flaxen Moons?" Gilda asked.

"Set course," Warren said. "We're going to see Addy's cousin."

It took Gilda almost a full day of travel at top speed to get to *Flaxen One*. It had gotten bigger since the last time Aderyn had seen it, another large section added to it for Gwynn's ReDev Center, but the dome in the middle still stood out, transparent and magnificent. Aderyn couldn't help but think about what happened the last time she was at Flaxen Moons.

Part of her was still hurt and angry, but she pushed those feelings aside.

Docking was both easier and harder than last time the *Herald* came to the station, easier because she didn't have to wait in line, and harder because Gwynn had found out about her approach.

"Hold tight," Enzo said through the ships com. "We'll get this sorted."

"She can't seriously be denying me access?" Aderyn paced around the bridge of the *Herald*. "It's been over a year—how can she still be this angry?"

"Maybe it's something else," Warren said softly. "Maybe she's worried that whatever happened to Gair will happen to you."

"Or maybe she's just being a stubborn, power hungry—"

Warren put up a hand to stop her from completing her sentence.

"We're working on that clearance," Enzo said.

"Tell her Aunt Leona sent us," Warren replied.

"Really? I will."

"That won't work," Aderyn told Warren. "Aunt Leona doesn't have that same power over Gwynn that she does over the rest of us."

"Let's see," Warren replied.

"*Herald*, this is *Flaxen One*. You are clear to dock." Enzo's voice sounded amused, and Warren grinned.

"Aunt Leona for the win."

"She usually does," Aderyn said wryly.

She headed to the airlock doors, wiping her hands over her pants nervously. She had a half-thought that she ought to put her hair up, hide the purple, as if her hair was the reason why Gwynn was mad at her.

Warren squeezed her shoulder comfortingly as they waited, and Aderyn held her breath as the door to *Flaxen One* opened.

Bertram and Enzo waited for her on the other side, and Aderyn couldn't help but look around before she walked forward.

"She's by his side," Bertram said. "Always."

Aderyn nodded and hugged her uncle. He held her tight, fear and sadness in his grip.

Then it was hugs with Enzo, who was much more composed, and then their little group made their way through the near-maze of the *Flaxen One* corridors to med-bay. Aderyn slowed her pace, letting herself fall just behind the others so that she could prepare herself. She never did well with death and disease.

Gwynn's hair was longer. It was the first thing Aderyn noticed as she spotted her cousin standing just outside a sealed-off room, staring at the prone figure inside. Aderyn struggled to look at Gair with tubes and wires going into him, so she focused on Gwynn—longer hair, fuller figure, straighter spine.

Then Gwynn turned as the others approached and Aderyn saw—her purple stripe was out, free, loose, and uncovered. It was almost more shocking than the sight of Gair.

Gwynn looked past her father, Enzo, and Warren, and stared at Aderyn. Aderyn shrugged, not sure what else to do or say?

"That's it," Gwynn said, walking toward her. "You just shrug?"

"I didn't know what to say," Aderyn said taking a step back from her cousin's oncoming anger. "Except that I'm sorry. I just don't know if that's enough."

Gwynn stopped short, rage and sadness dancing across her face, the one chasing the other.

And then sadness won, and Gwynn crumpled, her knees giving out. Aderyn rushed to her side just as Gwynn began to sob, and pulled her cousin close, wrapping her arms around her and making cooing noises of comfort.

"I don't know what to do," Gwynn said, rocking back and forth. "I'm going to lose everything."

Aderyn smoothed her hand over Gwynn's hair.

"We'll figure it out," she said, "it's going to be all right. I'm here. We'll figure it out."

Gwynn buried her face in Aderyn's shoulder and cried for a good long while as Aderyn repeated herself like a chant: "I'm here. It's going to be all right. We'll figure it out."

Finally, when Gwynn's sobs subsided into small sniffles, Aderyn helped her get up and took her into another room with a low couch, away from the sight of Gair, and away from the anxious looks and pacing of the men.

"Do you want to talk about what happened?" Aderyn asked.

Gwynn wiped at her eyes and shook her head.

"I feel so lost."

"Start at the beginning. You were in your lab, right?"

Gwynn shook her head again.

"That's not the beginning," she said. "The beginning was over a year ago, when I got a message."

Aderyn felt herself grow still and tense.

"A message."

"On the AltFeed. About the crystals."

"From someone or something named IMP," she finished for her cousin.

"How....?"

Aderyn sighed deeply.

"Because Warren and I have spent the past year trying to track IMP down."

"Tell me you succeeded," Gwynn said, desperate hope dawning across her face. "Please."

"We're close," Aderyn said. "Why?"

"Because I think IMP wants to take out huge swaths of the galaxy and wants me to help."

Aderyn stared at her cousin.

"You better tell me everything."

PART 5: A Secret Revealed

On the third day the messenger came back again, and said, "I have not been able to find a single new name, but as I came to a high mountain at the end of the forest, where the fox and the hare bid each other good night, there I saw a little house, and before the house a fire was burning, and round about the fire quite a ridiculous little man was jumping, he hopped upon one leg, and shouted -

'To-day I bake, to-morrow brew,

the next I'll have the young queen's child.

Ha, glad am I that no one knew

that Rumpelstiltskin I am styled.'

You may imagine how glad the queen was when she heard the name. And when soon afterwards the little man came in, and asked, "Now, mistress queen, what is my name?"

"Rumpelstiltskin!"

Jacob and Wilhelm Grimm, Rumpelstiltskin

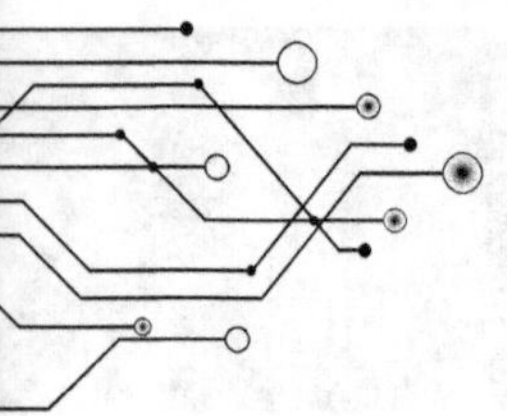

Chapter 22

THE UNUSUAL SUSPECTS

The pieces were starting to come together. Aderyn didn't know yet how they came together, or what the complete picture they formed was, but some things were starting to click.

"You were right about the crystal," Gwynn said. "I lied. To you, to everyone. It's just that I was so desperate."

Aderyn waved off her cousin's guilty confession as she traced the same path between the door of the room and the opposite wall, going back and forth like a guard drone. It wasn't that Aderyn didn't care about Gwynn's feelings, they just weren't useful right then.

"I need to see every com IMP ever sent you. And the downloads for the crystals and food cube recipes—all of it. You said that IMP hacked your com bracelet?"

"Kept setting it to chime when I got new messages, and then kept messaging me until I responded."

"And nothing showed up on the diagnostic scans of the station?"

"Elidor has those scans. I can get them for you. But he said everything was clear. He said he'd upgraded the security after the merger—that before that it wasn't very good."

Aderyn nodded and kept pacing.

"Yeah, I was able to hack into the station's sensors pretty easily the night of your engagement. It's what I had been trying to tell you—that night I saw someone going into what I thought at the time was your lab. But now I think it was your quarters."

"You saw them?"

"On the map," Aderyn said. She stopped and kneeled in front of Gwynn, bringing up the last 3D map on her com bracelet. "On a map like this," she said. "With little dots representing where people are. See? This one has a lot of people in it right now."

Dozens of little dots moved through the space.

"The people are the red dots?" Gwynn asked. Aderyn nodded. "And what about the yellow dots?"

"Security bots."

"Where is that?" Gwyn leaned forward, trying to get a better look at the 3D map. Aderyn used her fingers to zoom into a section of it and then pressed something on her com to turn the grid-line map into a live vid-feed.

"What's Juniper Group?"

"A medical company," Aderyn said. "They specialize in mods."

"And what do they have to do with IMP?"

"Not entirely sure," Aderyn said. "But they have been around for a long time, and Warren and I found a mention of IMP in their com logs."

"IMP was talking to someone at Juniper?"

"We think so," Aderyn said. "The weird part is that it was an old log—really old. Pre-war, at the height of the Planetary Alliance."

"IMP has been around that long?" Gwynn looked shocked.

"Possibly. It could be a code name, or an organization. It could be something that gets passed down from user to user."

"But you were saying—the night of my engagement—?"

"Right," Aderyn said. "So on one level, the internal sensors of every station, ship, and building track all the people and bots inside. And then on another level," Aderyn switched the view of the Juniper Group map again, "they track the functions of the station: water running, lights turning on and off, doors opening and closing."

"I'm following," Gwynn said, nodding.

"And the night of your engagement, there were no little dots near your quarters. But the doors from that part of the station were opening and closing. I tracked whoever was triggering the doors heading back to the ball." Aderyn snorted in frustration. "And then I lost them."

"And you think that was IMP?"

"Or someone working with IMP," Aderyn said. "From what you told me, someone had to physically leave that crystal in your room, along with the data disc. It's the only time there has been a physical connection to IMP."

"Hells," Gwynn said. "IMP was here. On this station—had to be."

"Or someone working with IMP. Here's the other weird thing about that night, and you're not going to like it."

"Hit me," Gwynn said, determined. "I feel like I can take anything now."

"I lost Tuari that night at the ball. That's why I hacked into the sensors—I was trying to track him down. The thing is, I couldn't find him."

"I'm confused. You couldn't find him, and then you couldn't find him?"

"I was tracking his ID chip. And it wasn't anywhere on the station. So either he went for a spacewalk—"

"Or he turned it off," Gwynn finished, her voice demonstrating her shock. "Making him a prime suspect for being, or working with, IMP."

"And he's not the only one," Aderyn said, taking a deep breath. This had been preying on her mind for the last year—the question she never asked and was afraid to answer. "Warren also didn't appear on any of the sensor logs."

"Oh Addy!" Gwynn said, reaching out take Aderyn's free hand. "You don't think that's really possible, do you? He's been working with you to track IMP down."

"Which could be a really good cover, while also making sure I never actually find IMP. I hate to think it, I really do. But is Warren any more shocking than Tuari?"

"It can't just be those two. It doesn't make any sense for either of them to be IMP."

"Or to work with," Aderyn reminded her. "It doesn't make any sense for you to be working with IMP, and yet look at what IMP got you to do."

"The cubes," Gwynn said, her face contorting with guilt and shame. "It's all my fault. If I hadn't agreed to work with IMP, then Gair…"

Aderyn sat next to Gwynn on the couch and put her hand on her younger cousin's cheek, looking into her eyes.

"You had no way of knowing that was going to happen," she said. "From what you've described, there was nothing unusual about the cubes. They were just food cubes. We still don't know why Gair reacted that way."

Gwynn wiped at her eyes and nodded.

"Myles said it was like Gair was poisoned, but he can't figure out from what. Whatever it is, its breaking down tissue faster than the nanites can restore. Myles said...." She took a deep breath and tried again. "Myles said that if we can't figure out what's doing this to him soon, he won't make it."

"Right," Aderyn said. "So we figure it out."

Aderyn noticed then that Gwynn's hand was on her stomach, almost as though trying to protect it.

"Gwynn, are you pregnant?"

Her cousin nodded, tears in the corner of her eyes.

"I need Gair," she said. "I can't do this alone."

"You can," Aderyn said. "But you won't be alone, no matter what." She pulled her cousin into a tight hug. "I promise, I won't leave you alone again."

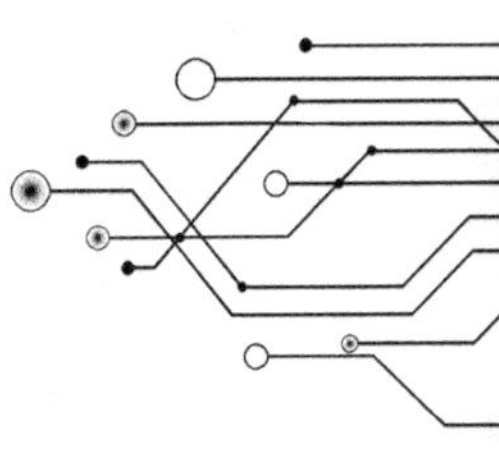

Chapter 23

THE RETRACED STEPS

Gwynn stared at the spot where Gair had fallen, shaking and bleeding, onto the floor of her lab. Some industrious cleaning bot had gotten to it, and there was no trace of blood left. But she could still picture where it had been, pooling under him, a trail from the side of his mouth and out of his nose. She closed her eyes against the image and took a breath. Then she opened them and turned to Aderyn.

"Here," she said.

"And these are the cubes?"

"Yes. We tested the space, looked for unknown pathogens. Nothing. We even tested the cubes and nothing seemed unusual about them either."

"All the ingredients were typical? It wasn't an unusual strain of algae or anything?"

"All the ingredients were typical," Gwynn said. "I had almost everything here already."

"Almost," Aderyn repeated.

"Hells," Gwynn said, picking up a bottle from the top of her workstation. "This," she said, handing it over to Aderyn. "It's an additive. Helps stabilize the solution, keep it solid at a standard range of temperatures. All the recipes have additives. But this one? It was hard to find."

"How hard?"

"Only one manufacturer makes them, and I had to buy from

a third party," she said. "Here." She walked over to a crate at the side of the room and typed in a code and brushed her thumb over a DNA scanner. The crate opened, a pop-up display of bottles rising up from inside. Gwynn showed it to Aderyn.

"Do ingredients normally come like this?"

"Most," she said. "Smart crates are pretty standard in manufacturing. But you know what's not standard about this?"

Aderyn shook her head. Gwynn grinned, happy to have an answer her older cousin didn't have for once.

"Glass," she said. "These are genuine, authentic glass bottles."

"And that's not standard?"

"For cross-space shipping? Even with smart crates, there is still a higher chance of the glass breaking than metal canisters, which are the norm."

"So one, and only one manufacturer makes this specific additive, and they also happen to be old fashioned enough to use glass containers."

"Maybe we can use this to figure out where this stuff was made," Gwynn said hopefully.

Aderyn looked at the bottle in her hand, turning it around slowly and studying every part of the label. Then she turned the bottle over and looked at the bottom.

"Here," she said, moving next to Gwynn to show it to her. "I know this logo."

"Seriously?"

"Yeah, my parents sent me some wine in glass bottles that had this logo at the bottom."

"The people who made the additive make wine?" Gwynn asked, confused.

"No, but the people who made these bottles also make wine bottles," Aderyn said, grinning. "And if we can get their customer list, we can find the makers of the additive, find out more about it."

"Great!" Gwynn said. "How do we do that?"

"We call my dad," Aderyn said.

"Uncle Coburn?"

"He just happens to be in the same place these bottles came from, a place where metal of any kind is considered precious: L'Mondeau."

Gwynn stared at her cousin, the expression on her face apparently worrisome because Aderyn frowned in response.

"What?" she asked.

"Do you know what else is on L'Mondeau?" she responded.

Aderyn shook her head.

"The Thirteenth."

"That's old news—they were wiped out in the first waves of the war."

"A hate group like that isn't easily wiped out," Gwynn said. "And there's something else—The Thirteenth specialized in biochemical warfare. They probably have some of the best chemists in the galaxy."

"Ironic considering how they loathe technology."

"They loathe modification," Gwynn corrected. "Not all tech, just tech that changes people or places."

"Which is every tech," Aderyn said, shaking her head. "The

ability to communicate across vast distances changes people. The ability to cook food—hells, even the ability to make clothes. All of that is tech. Old tech, but still tech. I don't know why people suddenly got to a point where they thought, no, this advancement, this one is too far."

Gwynn shrugged.

"I guess if you think there needs to be a line, you have to draw it somewhere."

"My point exactly—why does there need to be a line?"

"There needs to be balance," Gwynn said. "Unchecked tech gets us Earth, a planet losing its ability to support human life. Humans did that."

"Balance, sure," Aderyn said. "But I don't see how murdering mods restores it."

Gwynn shook her head.

"Me neither."

Aderyn reached out then and ran her fingers down a lock of Gwynn's purple hair.

"You wear it out now," she said. "It looks nice. Longer, too."

Gwynn nodded, a familiar mixture of emotions churning inside her. The shame, the anger, the resentment, but also, the pride.

"I'm trying to learn to accept all parts of who I am."

"You know there is nothing wrong with you, right? Wrong with this?" Aderyn tugged lightly on Gwynn's hair. "That's just Naturalist propaganda."

"Yeah, except that growing up with this was torture," Gwynn said. "It made me a target. Still makes me a target."

"I know," Aderyn said. "But that means there's something wrong with the people targeting you, not you."

Gwynn took a deep breath to try to settle her mixed emotions.

"It's amazing how easy it is to learn to hate who you are," she said. "But I'm trying to unlearn that hate." She put her hand over her belly again. "I don't want this one to feel the way I felt."

"We won't let that happen," Aderyn said, putting her hand over Gwynn's. "And I'm sorry—we should have been there for you more when you were little. The Ryder clan, all of us. I know Mom has regrets about that, and Aunt Leona. Bertram was very protective, but we should have tried harder."

Gwynn nodded.

"That probably would have been good," she agreed. "But that's all in the past. We have to worry about the future now."

"We should get this to Myles," Aderyn said, looking back down at the bottle. "Maybe this will help him figure out what's happening with Gair."

"Do you think?" Gwynn asked, hope burning in her chest.

"I really do," Aderyn said. "And then we need to do something we've both been putting off."

"What's that?" Gwynn asked.

"Talking to Warren and Tuari about the night of your engagement."

Gwynn swallowed hard, and then nodded. "But first, Gair."

"Agreed."

Back in the med-bay, Myles took the bottle from Gwynn with a perplexed look.

"You think something in this may be hurting Gair?"

"It's the only ingredient I can say with any confidence he's never had before—it's the only one we've never used before," Gwynn said. There was no need to bring Myles into all the rest just yet.

He nodded.

"I'll test it," he said. "Thank you. This helps."

"If it is what's hurting him?"

"Then there is a very good chance I can synthesize something that will counter it."

Gwynn let out a breath she didn't know she had been holding, and Aderyn patted her on the back.

"We'll leave you to it," she said.

As they walked back to Gwynn's quarters, Gwynn felt lighter. Doing something felt so much better than doing nothing. She pulled Aderyn into a side-hug on impulse.

"I am so glad you're here," she said.

"Me too," Aderyn replied.

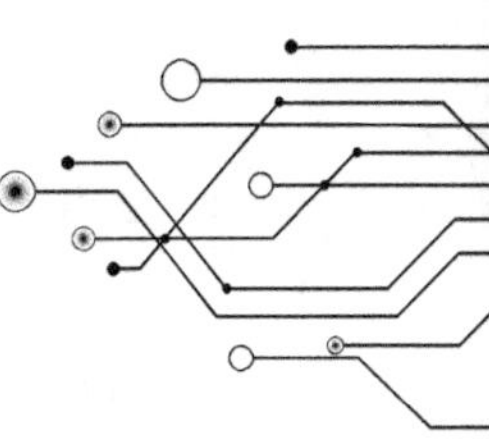

Chapter 24

THE REGRETFUL IMPASSE

Aderyn slipped her arms around Warren's waist and nuzzled her head into his back. He took her hands in his own and pressed them into his body, his way of returning her embrace.

"Is Gwynn well?" he asked. He pulled her out from behind him and spun her around to face him. "And are you doing well?"

"Both as well as can be expected," she said. "But you and I need to talk."

She had been putting this off for as long as she could, reaching out to her father first, checking in with her aunts and cousins and updating them on Gwynn, even checking in on Gilda and Ruby on her ship before coming to find Warren. If she was being honest with herself, she had been putting it off even longer than that, never once in the year plus they'd been together asking Warren about that night.

"Is this going to be a hard conversation?"

"Most definitely."

"Do we need alcohol? Soft things to throw at each other? A bed to fall into after?"

"Probably all of those things," she said. "But instead we're going to go for a walk."

He didn't question her, and just nodded, slipping his hand around hers as she led him away from the *Flaxen One* med-bay.

Then again, he never questioned her. He was probably the

easiest-going person she had ever known and seemed to be perpetually calm and endlessly amused.

But he also had his secrets, things that he did before they met that he wouldn't talk about, filling any attempt to do so with so many cracks and jokes that she would end up dropping the conversation. She had never managed to get him to stay on a topic he didn't want to talk about, and there was only one topic he didn't want to talk about—his past.

"Are we going to the ballroom?" he asked.

She nodded.

"Feeling nostalgic?"

"A bit," she admitted. "So many things happened that night. It feels like it was the end of one major chapter in my life and the start of a new one."

"With me," he said smiling. "I'm part of the new one."

"You *are* the new one," she said. He pulled her to him to kiss her on the forehead before letting her walk forward again. Soon they were at the ballroom, and Aderyn let his hand go, needing space for this conversation. In fact, she needed so much space, she picked the biggest room she had ever been in to have it.

"We need to talk about the night of Gwynn and Gair's engagement," she said at last, when she felt like he was far enough away to not read every emotion that crossed her face.

"I don't think I've ever heard your voice sound like that before," he said. He paced a few steps toward one of the low benches on the outskirts of the room and pulled on the leaves of the potted palm next to it.

"What's it sound like?" she asked, mirroring his movements and moving to the bench parallel to his.

"Vulnerable."

Aderyn swallowed hard.

"So, that night, after we ran into each other the first time—"

"And you chased me, attacked me, and got all suspicious at me."

"Yes," Aderyn said, smiling despite her anxiety. "And then you stole my taze-stick from me."

"And then gave it back!" he said.

"And then gave it back," she amended. "You disappeared from the sensor logs. Or rather, your ID chip did."

She watched as he leaned back against the trunk of the tree and crossed his arms across his chest.

"Am I allowed to ask how you know that?"

She shrugged. "I was trying to track down Tuari."

"So why were you looking for me?"

"A test search."

"Why did you need a test search?"

"We're getting off topic," she said.

"I'm pretty sure we're not," he replied. "You were running a search for Tuari—and then you searched for me. Which means you didn't find him. Which means we both disappeared from the sensors."

"It wasn't a glitch in the system," she said, suddenly feeling defensive.

"Oh, I know," Warren said. He uncrossed his arms and shoved his hands in his pockets. "I'd turned my tracking chip off.

And from the sound of it, so did Tuari. And based on everything else that is happening, I can't help think that maybe you are worried that all of this has to do with Gair being in a coma."

"Which, if we want to connect all the dots, I'm worried has something to do with IMP."

"Hells," he said, turning and taking a deep breath and letting it out slowly. "It always comes back to IMP."

"Apparen-tal-ly," she said, stealing the word he liked to mock her with.

He turned and smiled at her, but his eyes looked sad. He took another deep breath before speaking to her again:

"Addy, do you think I'm IMP?"

"Or maybe working for IMP," she admitted.

"Do you think Tuari is?"

"One of you. Both of you. I don't know. But I have to ask."

"I could just lie."

"True."

"You'd need some sort of proof." He meandered over to the other palm on the other side of the bench, and Aderyn did the same on her side of things.

"I was kind of hoping you'd have a good alibi, something verifiable, something that made it impossible for you to be IMP."

"Why do you think IMP was part of things that night?"

"Because Gwynn didn't make the tuotarium crystal. It was left in her quarters, along with a disc with the formula to make it. And there was someone in that area that triggered all the doors but didn't show up on the security logs."

"Someone who presumably turned off their ID chip but forgot about the general sensor logs."

"Tell me you're not that dumb."

He laughed.

"I think you're just that smart," he said. "I have to admit, I wouldn't have thought of doing that."

He moved back toward the other palm and then sat on the bench, directly in the middle. Aderyn sat opposite him.

"Here's the thing—I can't tell you where I was. And I can't give you an alibi."

"Why?"

"Because those aren't my secrets to share," he said.

"You were on a job."

"I was working, yes."

"For Elidor?"

He smiled.

"Remember how you aren't supposed to ask certain questions?"

"You won't kill me," she said, scoffing.

"No, I just won't answer them. Because you promised not to ask."

They were at an impasse, and Aderyn ran her hands over her thighs, trying to manage the tension in her body.

"Are you IMP?" she asked.

"No," he said, meeting her eyes.

"Are you working for IMP?"

"Not that I know of."

"Have you ever worked for IMP?"

"Again, not that I know of."

She rolled her shoulders and took a deep breath.

"And you won't give me an alibi."

"I can't."

She took another deep breath.

"Even if it costs you us?"

He shook his head sadly, and Aderyn couldn't tell, but she thought he might be fighting back tears.

"I made promises to other people long before I made promises to you. I want to tell you everything, I really do. But I can't."

Aderyn nodded. Her nails were digging into her knees in her effort to stay calm, to not explode or sob or scream.

"Will this cost me us?" he asked, his voice cracking.

"I don't know," Aderyn said, struggling to keep it together. She couldn't help thinking about the first time they met, about his casual smile, his easy way of seeing through her disguise. "Want so rarely comes into it."

It was his turn to nod solemnly.

Aderyn waited for a long moment, hoping something would happen, that something would change this moment, change this feeling of despair crawling into her gut and making itself at home.

"I can't trust you right now," she said.

"Right now," he echoed, clinging to the one thing that might give him hope—both of them hope.

"If I find IMP, find out you had nothing to do with any of this…."

She probably shouldn't have said that. If he was really IMP, she definitely shouldn't have said that.

But part of her couldn't help but think that if he was IMP, she wouldn't care anymore. Not about anything, possibly not ever again.

"Do you want me to stay here? Stay on the *Herald*? What can I do to help?"

"Here, I think," she said. "A locked room likely wouldn't hold you. But if you stayed where other people always saw you, that could maybe work. I need witnesses."

"I can do that," he said, nodding.

"And that means you won't be able to help me," she said. "And I won't be able to talk about this anymore, and I don't know how long any of this will take." It was her turn for her voice to break. She took several breaths and composed herself.

"Can I ask you to hurry?"

She snorted.

"Trust me, I will be working as fast as I can."

She stood up then. She wanted to run to him, jump on him, hold him. Instead she started to walk toward the ballroom entrance, back to where all the other people were. He followed suit, staying parallel with her as long as he could, until they both had to veer toward each other to get through the door. Even then, he kept his distance. He walked slightly in front of her, kept his hands out his pockets. Just as they got to the med-bay, he stopped, and she stopped too, her hands open and ready.

"Here," he said, reaching his hand slowly under his jacket and pulling out a taze-stick, the one she had made just for him. Then he bent awkwardly, still keeping his hands up as much as possible to show her he had nothing to hide. He unstrapped his knife from his ankle and handed both weapons to her. "In case you need them," he said.

"Thanks," she said. She took both from him carefully, avoiding touching his hands. She watched then as he walked into medbay and settled himself on a couch just outside of Gair's room and in plain view of everyone and anyone walking through.

Aderyn knew it was probably stupid to trust him even this much, but she just couldn't bear not to trust him at all.

She strapped his knife, which was a good thumb-length longer than hers, around her own ankle. It felt awkward and heavy, but also comforting. She shoved his taze-stick in her belt and went to find Gwynn.

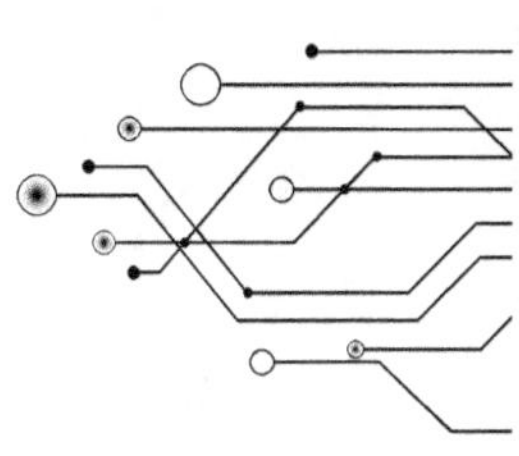

Chapter 25

THE HATEFUL POISON

Gwynn watched Gair breathe in and out and wished he could do so without a tube helping him do it. The additive had been the key after all, and Myles was able to create an antidote to what was poisoning Gair. But he still needed help to breathe, and he still wouldn't wake up.

The rest? She was still trying to wrap her head around all that.

"It targets genes?"

"Certain genes, yes. You'd have to have that particular genetic tag, for lack of a better term, in order for the poison in the additive to activate. And then it's quite fast moving, as you saw."

"And if you don't have that genetic tag?" Aderyn asked.

"The additive, and anything made with it, is harmless."

"Any idea how prevalent that tag is?" Aderyn walked around the edge of the bed, looking down at Gair with a thoughtful expression. "Was this specifically targeted at the Ingram family?"

"Possibly," Myles said, shaking his head. "Though it's kind of a scatter-shot approach. There is no way of knowing if Gair or anyone with the tag would consume the additive. On the other hand, a genetic tag like this could be found in any number of people: hundreds, millions, even billions."

"Yeah, and if you put something like that out in the mass market, eventually a lot of people are going to eat it," Aderyn said.

"Particularly if you put it in more than one product," Gwynn said.

"So we're assuming that this was on purpose," Myles said, shaking his head in a way that made the curls around it bounce. "That someone created something specifically to try to hurt—kill—as many people with this genetic tag as possible."

"That's what we're assuming, yes," Aderyn said. She looked at Myles as if she was assessing him and shot Gwynn a questioning glance.

"Myles fought in the war," Gwynn said. "It's how he and Enzo met."

"Whatever it is you're worried I can't handle, I can handle it," Myles said. "Don't let my soft appearance fool you."

"I never did," Aderyn said, smiling. "There's steel in you—anyone can see that."

Myles seemed taken aback by her comment, and Gwynn could swear he was blushing.

"To summarize: we think there is a powerful force out there who has been working for a long time to put a plan in action that will wipe out an entire group of people for reasons known only to said powerful force—so far. And we think that force is targeting vulnerable and desperate people, trading them something they need for something that will serve its own purposes."

"And we think that because I was one of the vulnerable people it targeted," Gwynn said, swallowing hard. "I made the food cubes because this force asked me to."

"Gwynnie, why?" Myles shook his head. "What could this thing possibly have over you?"

"Because I didn't figure out how to make tuotarium crystals," she said, relieved to get it out. "Whoever this force is—it did. But I traded the formula for a favor."

She looked down at Gair's unconscious body.

"And this is where that led."

She was shocked when she felt Myles pull her into a hug, and she turned into it, burying her face in his shoulder, just like she had when she was little.

"Oh sweet-one, I'm so sorry," he said. "I am so sorry that all of this is happening to you. You never should have been under that kind of pressure, never made to feel that desperate. We failed you. Enzo and I—we were supposed to protect you, and we failed you. And I am so very sorry."

Tears were running freely down his face, and Gwynn realized that hers matched.

"You didn't," she said. "I did."

He shook his head again and pulled her into another hug. It was a long moment before either of them were composed enough to separate, and Gwynn wiped at her eyes.

"I don't mean to interrupt, but I really feel like time is against us on this," Aderyn said.

"Of course," Myles said, wiping at his own eyes and standing up straight. "There will be more time for all of that after. What do you need my help with now?"

"We need to mass produce the antidote," Aderyn said. "Just in case. I can't help but feel that Gwynn wasn't the only one tasked with something like this."

"It wouldn't be a very efficient system if she was," Myles

agreed. "As popular as our food cubes are, you'd only get so much of the population. If you really wanted to make sure that the additive got out into the galaxy, you'd need to hit multiple products at once."

"And you'd want them all out at the same time, to make sure that as much of the market was saturated before anyone caught on to what you were doing, what was actually killing people." Gwynn shook her head at the audacity of IMP's plan.

"We need to find out who else bought this additive, stop them from sending their products out. And then we need to find out where this stuff is made and turn it into a fireball," Aderyn said.

"And I know one place we need to start," Gwynn said.

"Spres Prime."

Myles seemed feel the tension between both women.

"What's on Spres Prime?" he asked.

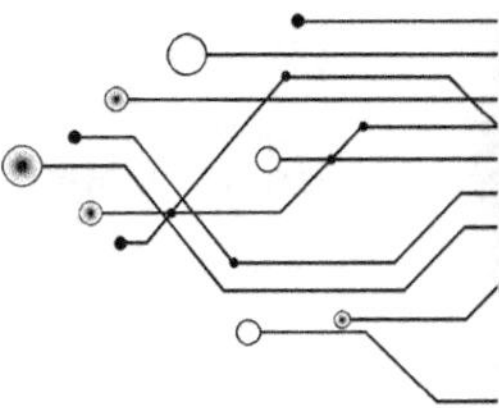

Chapter 26

THE IMPOSSIBLE CHOICE

Several hours later, Gwynn still struggled with her choice to leave *Flaxen One*. She wanted to be there in case Gair woke up, but Myles reassured her it would be days yet, that even with the antidote, it was going to take some time for Gair to heal, and he needed to be in a medically induced coma during that time.

Myles had been so kind to her, so sweet. Gwynn ran her hands over Ruby, Aderyn's pet genet, and thought about how amazing it was that Myles would be so willing to forgive her so quickly. She'd wanted to take the time to tell Enzo and Elidor, but Aderyn didn't think they should. She thought it would be best to keep as few people involved as possible. Gwynn knew it was because Aderyn didn't trust any of them, was still not sure who might be working for IMP. She had eliminated Myles as a suspect on account of how quickly he made the antidote. Anyone who had really wanted Gair—or people like him—dead would have found a way to muck that up.

Gwynn shook her head. She was amazed and a little scared that Aderyn could think like that. She also noted that Warren was no longer with them and that Aderyn didn't say goodbye to him before they left. When Gwynn asked, Aderyn just said that he was still on the suspect list.

Gwynn realized that she never really understood Aderyn before now. She had seen her older cousin as this bright, vivacious force in the world, and then as the bright, vivacious force that snuck around sleeping with Gwynn's best friend and secret crush and lied to her family about it. It hadn't really occurred to her to think about Aderyn as someone who struggled in any way, or who lived life thinking about all the worst-case scenarios all the time and made plans for dealing with each and every one.

Including, Gwynn knew, what she would do if she found out that the man she loved was a potential mass murderer.

Gwynn shivered, and Ruby stirred under her hand, opening one eye to look at her before rolling on her back and resuming her slumber. Gwynn scratched lightly at Ruby's belly, and then quietly got up to leave the small, furry cat-like creature's sanctuary.

"Sleep well, little one," she said to the genet. Aderyn had suggested some time with Ruby could be good for Gwynn, and she had been right.

As Gwynn made her way from Ruby's closed-in and plant-filled corner of the ship to Aderyn up on the bridge, she tried to picture what she was going to say to Tuari. How did you go about accusing your best friend of being evil?

"How far out are we?" she asked Aderyn, taking one of the seats in the command area and noting a pair of men's slippers tucked up against the workstation next to it. Aderyn caught her looking.

"He doesn't like to wear shoes and his feet get cold," she said. "And he's kind of a messy person. We're only a few minutes out. You feeling all right?"

Gwynn nodded.

"Not sure what we should say to Tuari though," she said.

"We'll be direct, ask what we need to ask, and hope he has a good explanation," Aderyn said. "But you should do the talking. Things didn't end well the last time he and I spoke."

"How long ago was that?" Gwynn asked.

"Your engagement."

Gwynn stared at Aderyn. Her head filled with questions, but she didn't think this was the time to ask them.

"Final approach," Aderyn said. "You're sure he's on the station and not planetside?"

"That's what he said," Gwynn replied.

It didn't take long for them to dock at *Spres Retreat*, the largest station orbiting the planet below. They were greeted by station security at the airlock, and then issued visitor badges along with having to register their ID chips with the station's AI.

And then they were taken to Tuari, and Gwynn was surprised that their guide led them to the station med-bay.

Akechata, she remembered. He was probably being treated here.

Tuari sat next to his father's bed, holding his father's hand. Gwynn had assumed his face would be wrecked with worry, but instead he seemed at peace, happy even. He jumped up as soon as he spotted Gwynn and pulled her into a tight hug, lifting her off her feet.

"Gwynn, it's so wonderful that you're here. We just found out—my father's illness is in remission! The doctors say he will be fine."

"Oh Tuari, that's wonderful!" Gwynn hugged him back. "I am so glad."

Then the smile on Tuari's face changed to something

unreadable, and Gwynn followed his gaze to the source of the change: Aderyn.

"Hi," she said and waved. He waved dumbly back. "Really good news about your dad. Is there someplace we can talk?"

It was an awkward few moments after that as Tuari led the women back to quarters he had taken up on the station in order to be near his father.

The conversation after was even more awkward.

"You want to know what?"

"Why you turned off your ID chip the night that Gwynn got engaged," Aderyn repeated.

Tuari looked for a moment like he was going to argue with her, and then he seemed to deflate.

"When you told me you could track Gwynn that night, I had been worried you knew what I'd done," he said.

"And what did you do?"

"Put the tuotarium crystal in Gwynn's quarters."

Gwynn felt her knees grow weak, and she sat hard on Tuari's couch.

"What?"

"The data disc too?" Aderyn continued, as if everything they knew hadn't just been split apart.

"Yes."

"And where did you get them?"

"The bottom of a smart crate that had carried party supplies," he said.

"And who told you where the crystal and disc would be?"

"You won't believe me," Tuari said.

"I bet we will," Gwynn said in a tone of voice that got a sharp look from him.

"I was told by someone named IMP," he said. "I've never met them. And it didn't feel like a bad thing to do—a little dishonest maybe, but not bad. I knew how much it would help Gwynn."

Aderyn nodded and Gwynn buried her head in her hands. If she had told Tuari about IMP, none of this would have ever happened. They both would have known what the other knew, known that IMP was playing them.

"And what did IMP give you in return?"

"My father's cure," Tuari said. "And mine."

Gwynn looked up in time to see Aderyn also sit suddenly on the couch, close her eyes and take several deep breaths.

"I knew it, I knew there was something wrong," she said. "I'd even guessed illness, probably *the* illness. Your family is susceptible."

"Because we don't believe in modification, which would help make sure we didn't get it." Tuari nodded.

"But there is no cure," Aderyn said, shaking her head. "No medicine you can administer."

"You have to be modified," Tuari said, nodding again. "I know."

"Wait, what?" It was Gwynn's turn to be shocked again.

All of what Tuari just said finally came together.

"You modified your father? You modified yourself?"

"We had to," Tuari said. "Our people, doing the work we do, in the conditions we do it in. Without those modifications, we'd all just keep getting sick, dying. It was getting worse, more and more people were getting sick, and my father refused to do anything about it."

"And then IMP told you they could help," Aderyn said. "And then I delivered the information on how to do whatever it is you did to Chianna. And you did it to yourself, whatever it was, but you hesitated to do it to your father. You hoped he would recover on his own. Until he got worse."

"I was desperate," Tuari said, his face a mask of anguish. "I couldn't just watch my father die and do nothing."

Aderyn stood up and paced across the room. Gwynn noticed that her cousin tended to move when she needed to think.

"We need records of all your coms with IMP," she said. "And I need a copy of that disc I gave Chianna—all the information on it. And I need it now."

Tuari stood up slowly.

"Addy, I need to explain."

"There's no time for that," Aderyn snapped. "Just get what I asked so that we can get out of this damned system!"

Tuari looked at Gwynn as if looking for help or support. Gwynn shook her head. She wasn't ready for that yet.

Tuari did what he was told, handing over a disc with everything he had on IMP. True to her word, Aderyn headed for the *Herald* as soon as she had it in hand, refusing to look at Tuari as she took walked away. Gwynn met Tuari's eyes and tried to think of what to say.

"I wanted to help you," he said. "To help my people. All I wanted to do was help."

"Adapt, and survive," she said. "I get it. And I'm sorry, because I know what that must have cost you."

"Gwynn," he said, reaching out a hand to her, clearly in agony.

"You betrayed your family and your friends, and I know what that's like, too," she continued. "But I think we're all going to need some time before we can move past it. Be well, Tuari."

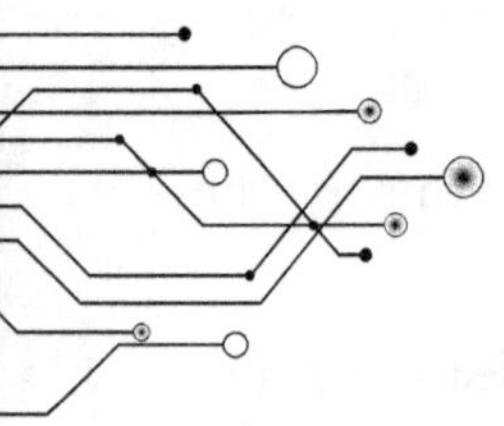

Chapter 27

THE THIRD NAME

Aderyn knew she should probably say something to Gwynn, talk about what happened with Tuari on *Spres Retreat*, but she didn't want to. She wasn't in a processing-her-emotions mood, she was in a kick-all-the-ass mood. Unfortunately, she was short on assess to kick.

Tuari had lied to her. More than that, he had made her feel small and petty and horrible, all because he couldn't handle his own choices. He wasn't the man she thought he was, and it was going to take a long time for her to deal with that.

"Incoming message from L'Mondeau. Text only, with an attachment." Gilda said. "Shall I read the message to you?"

"Sure," Aderyn said.

"My sweet Aderyn, I have the information that you asked for. It wasn't easy to get, but it was fun. I hope it helps you and whatever adventure you're on. May the gods hold you. Love, Dad."

Aderyn grinned.

"May the gods hold you," Gwynn repeated. "That's nice."

"Local greeting," Aderyn said. "Sounds like Dad has gone a little native. Gilda, have you downloaded what he sent yet?"

"And analyzed it. It appears to be detailed records on every product ever sent out from a company called S'Glass, which specializes in mass producing glass containers, as well as information on the manufacturer of a specific item that the company bottles."

"Does that item happen to be an uncommon additive?" Aderyn asked.

"Yes."

"And?"

"The additive is made by TenDek Corporation."

"Hells," Aderyn said.

"I don't understand," Gwynn said. "Gair made the poison that nearly killed him?"

"Not Gair, TenDek," Aderyn corrected. "Gilda, did Dad send information on how it's distributed, and to whom?"

"It is sold to multiple companies, who each in turn sell it to even more companies, who in turn sell it to consumers."

"That's how I got it—I had to track down a distributor, and there seemed to be no direct link between that distributor and the manufacturer. I had to go through a second distributor to get the rest that IMP asked for."

"We'll assume that everyone else IMP has working on this had to do something similar."

"How do we even find it all?" Gwynn asked. "We'll never be able to track every purchase to every product, not before the distribution deadline."

"We'll announce a recall," Aderyn said. "Or rather, Gair will, once he's awake, and Myles is already working on mass producing the antidote through Flaxen Farms, and we'll hope we get enough—save enough."

"It would seem prudent to also stop IMP," Gilda said.

"Yes, it would," Aderyn said. "Gilda, change course to the Dekken system."

"I already have," Gilda said. "You have another incoming message, this time from Flaxen Moons. Should I put it on screen?"

Aderyn looked at Gwynn, who nodded, her face tense.

"On screen," Aderyn said. Enzo's nearly-bald head filled the view-screen, his brows knit tightly together.

"Enzo, is Gair…?"

Gwynn couldn't finish the sentence, but Enzo's face softened.

"No dear-heart. There has been no change with Gair. I actually need to speak with Aderyn. Privately, if I could."

Gwynn nodded, giving Aderyn a curious look as she left the bridge. Aderyn waited until the door chimed close behind her before turning back to Enzo.

"There is something you should know about Warren," he said. "He told me what happened, that you…are suspicious of him."

That felt like an understatement to Aderyn, but she nodded anyway.

"Because he turned off his ID chip the night of the ball," Enzo said.

"Yes," Aderyn agreed.

"He did so because I asked him to," Enzo said, looking embarrassed. "I can go into details why, but…."

"You're Blue Band," Aderyn said, finally putting the puzzle piece into place. The short hair, the time in the war, the same military precision that carried over into all parts of his life. She'd never seen the tattoo on Enzo's arm, but she had become intimately familiar with the one on Warren's. It was one of the things that he *never* talked about.

"I am," Enzo said. "Or was. Though, we don't really do *was*." He shifted his weight nervously, his head bobbing on the view screen. "I can answer any questions you want to ask."

"He wouldn't," Aderyn said, still feeling the hurt of it.

"We don't betray our comrades," Enzo said sternly. "He wouldn't even tell me why he wasn't with you. I had to guess. This is my choice. I don't want what he did for me to get in the way of what he has with you. I can't let him sacrifice like that."

Aderyn closed her eyes for a moment, warring with her own emotions. Finally she opened them, nodding with her decision.

"Can you account for all his time at Flaxen Moons where his chip was off?" she asked.

"I can," Enzo said.

"And do you think that he is, or has been working with any malevolent force?"

"IMP?" Enzo asked. "Myles told me. And no, I can say with every confidence that Warren Frey is not IMP. I am not sure that any of us can say with any confidence that we have not worked for IMP."

Aderyn nodded again.

"I believe you," she said, feeling the relief of it make her knees weak. "We're on our way to Dekken. We have a lead."

"Warren and I can meet you," Enzo said, straightening up, looking every bit the soldier.

"You'd be hours behind us," Aderyn said, shaking her head.

"He'd want to be there," Enzo said softly.

"I know. But right now, he's better off where he is, keeping you, Myles, Gair, and Bertram safe. We still don't know if this was a targeted attack against the Ingram family."

"We still haven't been able to get in touch with Elidor," Enzo said, frowning.

"Exactly," Aderyn said. "Gwynn and I will find out what we can. I promise, we will try not to do anything too dangerous without you."

"And you don't have any questions?"

Aderyn shook her head adamantly.

"None of my business," she said. "I just needed a witness, and alibi. Thank you for exposing yourself to tell me."

Enzo smiled.

"I think you may be the best thing that ever happened to him," he said. "I have never seen him like this before."

"We'll do a dinner," she said, trying not to blush. "Trade war stories."

"I promise," Enzo said. "Be safe, Aderyn."

"You too, Enzo." She clicked off the view screen feeling much lighter than she had before. Enzo could still be lying, and Warren with him, but, for once, Aderyn wanted to believe in the best of people, and not the worst.

Two jump gates later, and the *Herald* entered the Dekken Solar System. Fortunately it wasn't a large system, and they didn't have far to go to get to the TenDek ReDev station. Aderyn had Gilda put the ship in a high orbit around the station and headed for her skip-hop.

"Obviously I'm coming with you," Gwynn said.

"I would like to come as well," Gilda said. "I thought our last time working together went very well."

"It's going to be dangerous," Aderyn told them both.

"I will not be in any physical danger," Gilda said.

"IMP, whatever else they are, is a genius hacker. You don't have to have a physical body to be in danger, Gilda."

"Glenda has been helping me build up my defense subsystems," Gilda said.

"Well, you're pregnant," Aderyn said, pointing at Gwynn's stomach.

"Yeah, but not defenseless. I'm going."

Aderyn put up her hands, clearly exasperated.

"Fine," she said. She took Warren's taze-stick out of her belt and opened a part of it up. "Put your finger here," she told Gwynn.

"What is that?" she asked.

"Bio-lock—makes sure that it can't be used on you." She pulled hers out, and also presented it to Gwynn to touch. "Better to be safe than sorry," she said. Then she closed up the seal on both sticks and handed Warren's back to Gwynn. "And now you're armed with a weapon that can't be used against you. Well, the taze part anyway. It's still a stick."

Gwynn took it and seemed pleased as she looked it over before clipping it onto her belt.

"Unfortunately I didn't have time to build us detailed covers, so we're going in as Savenel students doing informational meetings with some exec to see if they'll hire us," Aderyn said. She pulled out two blue and silver jackets from her ships storage and handed one to Gwynn. Gwynn handed it back.

"I'm the wife of the owner of TenDek, I have blonde hair with a large purple streak in it, and I go to all the staff parties. I am our cover."

"Oh," Aderyn said. "Right. But how will we explain the skip-hop?"

"I never use fancy transport," Gwynn said.

"Great," Aderyn answered, completely thrown off. She pulled a satchel over her head, wearing it with the strap across her body. "Gilda, is your interface downloaded into the skip-hop yet?"

"Yes," she said. "And linked to both your coms. This is exciting."

Her flat voice seemed to belie her stated emotion, but Aderyn didn't doubt that Gilda was excited. At some point she was going to have to remember to upgrade Gilda's voice module.

"All right ladies, we ready?"

"Let us go kick some IMP ass," Gilda said.

Aderyn shook her head and led the way to the skip-hop. They were underway shortly, and with Gilda's help, Aderyn was already in the docking database, marking her ship as approved to land and updating the schedule to make it seem like Gwynn's visit was put on it several days before. Soon she was getting clearance to dock, and she managed to land without incident.

"So far, so good," she told Gwynn behind her. She opened the hatch and pulled herself up, stepping over the side and onto the ledge below while the built-in ladder descended.

"Hi, and welcome to TenDek Corporation!" a familiar voice said.

"Hells!" Aderyn said, turning around, her back to the person walking toward the skip-hop. "You need to go down first," she whispered urgently to Gwynn.

Gwynn looked confused for a moment, and then nodded, and it was an awkward dance for them to switch places. Then Gwynn was down the ladder and Aderyn looked over her shoulder as Batilda, the galaxy's friendliest dock attendant, greeted her cousin.

"I would be very pleased to help you with anything you need," she continued. "Oh! Ms. Flaxenhart, it's you."

"Hi!" Gwynn said. "I'm going to show my cousin, Aderyn, around the facilities."

"Of course," Batilda said, looking over at Aderyn curiously. "Will you be needing a guide?"

"Not today, thanks," Gwynn said.

"All right. If you need anything else, I can be reached through any com box. I hope you enjoy your visit!"

"Thanks," Gwynn said, smiling at her. "You've been so helpful!"

Batilda beamed as she walked away.

"If you get the chance, you should probably see about getting her promoted," Aderyn said.

"Definitely," Gwynn agreed. "Now what?"

"Gilda, you in their systems yet?"

"I am. But not all of them. There is an area at the planetside part of the station that is separate from the rest that I cannot get access to. Should I try harder?"

"No, leave it alone," Aderyn said. "Just find us a path there and patch it to my com."

"Sure," Gilda said.

"You think that's where IMP is?" Gwynn asked.

"I think it's a promising place to start," Aderyn said. Soon her com bracelet chimed and Aderyn was able to pull up a 3D map of the station. Gilda had laid out their path in a purple line.

The path took them down several floors from the shuttle dock and past at least three other sections of the station. They were stopped a few times by folks in green and gold security uniforms, but Gwynn's open friendliness and confidence in her right to be doing exactly what she was doing won the guards over every time, and they never had any problems.

Aderyn envied Gwynn her ability to get people to trust her instantly.

Finally, they were at a section that was closed off, thick security doors blocking their way.

"Gilda?" Aderyn asked.

"This is where I lose access," she informed them. "The door has a DNA lock and requires a passcode, both of which I do not have."

"I do," Aderyn said.

"How?" Gwynn asked. "You didn't even know this existed before today."

Aderyn patted her bag.

"I have a tendency to collect DNA samples," she said. She

rifled through her bag, hesitated, and then pulled out a specific DNA sample.

"Whose is it?" Gwynn asked.

"Mine," a voice behind them said. Both Gwynn and Aderyn whirled, Gwynn with her taze-stick out and ready in front of her. Three security bots were coming up behind them, the one in the front displaying a face on a view-screen built into its chest. "Unless I have overestimated you, Aderyn."

Aderyn turned the sample kit around to display the name on the front: Elidor Ingram.

"Ah," he said from the center of the bot's chest. "I see that I have not."

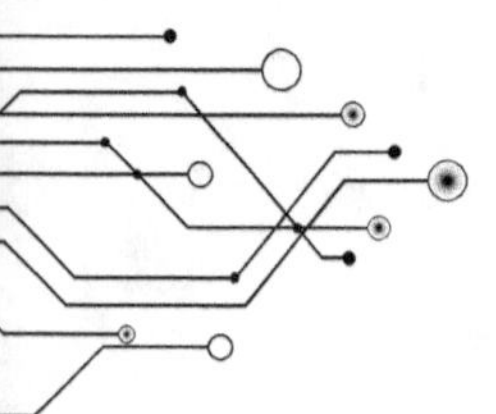

Chapter 28

THE TRAGIC HERO

Elidor's bots opened the door for them and led them inside, while Gilda apologized to Aderyn for not detecting the bots sooner. These were not the green and gold security bots they'd passed earlier but seemed cobbled together from spare parts and several different metals, giving them a patchwork look.

"I do not seem to be able to track things where you are," Gilda informed Aderyn. "I cannot give you any information about these bots."

"Keep trying," Aderyn said. "But be careful."

The bots in question seemed to be a variation of worker bots, with hover technology keeping them afloat and multiple arms on each side of their bodies, no two having the same amount. Each arm seemed to hold a weapon or tool of some kind, and Aderyn kept her hands out and ready, unsure of what to expect.

"I need you both to know that I never intended for my brother to get hurt," Elidor said, his voice floating out of the bot in front of them. It led them past an open storage area that had crates and other containers randomly scattered about, and down a wide hallway that passed several other rooms, each with some sort of mechanical and electrical thing inside that looked only partially finished.

"This is my personal lab," Elidor's voice explained. "My sanctuary."

"You like to build things," Aderyn noted.

"Always did. I like to see how things are put together. My grandmother in particular liked to indulge my interests, gifting me with puzzles to solve, each one more complex than the last. Almost like she was training me. Or maybe Ix was, through her."

Aderyn looked at Gwynn to see if she knew what Elidor was talking about. Gwynn shrugged back. Neither of them knew who Ix was.

The bots brought them into a large open space that had several tables and workstations in it. Aderyn could see the pale green shards of shattered crystals—failed attempts. There were beakers full of liquids and an impressive looking chemistry lab set up, as well as a table full of soldering irons and wires. One table looked like it was used for metal working.

Elidor was perched in a chair vaguely in the middle of the room, another bot standing over him. He had something in his hand that he pointed at the bot, as though he was trying to keep it away from him. He didn't look good. He was wearing strange coveralls over his clothes, and he was sweating profusely. His chair was in front of a large rectangular box that took up a third of the wall it was up against and rose at least a foot taller than Aderyn. There was a monitor embedded into it, and a type-pad resting on a stand roughly three feet in front of the monitor.

"This," Elidor said, gesturing to the box. "Is IMP."

"Hells," Aderyn said.

"What?" Gwynn asked. "What am I missing?"

"IMP is an AI," Aderyn said.

"A very old AI," Elidor amended. "IMP was built even before the height of the Planetary Alliance and was an expensive investment even by those standards. And then the war started, and IMP was abandoned by the wealthy family that created it."

"What was IMP designed to do?" Aderyn asked walking cautiously closer.

"Be helpful," Elidor replied. "And IMP is very helpful. You give IMP any problem—say, how to create a tuotarium crystal from algae—and enough access to relevant information, and IMP solves the problem. I have to help too, of course—do the physical things."

Aderyn walked the length of IMP and tried to imagine the level of processing power something this size had. Gilda was a pretty advanced AI, for all that she was young and growing, but even her processor was a fraction of this size.

"Why does IMP want Gair dead?" Gwynn asked. Aderyn noted that her cousin was still holding her taze-stick, though she hadn't activated it yet.

"That was a mistake," Elidor said, sounding genuinely remorseful.

"Aderyn, I believe I am being probed," Gilda said. "IMP is testing my defenses."

"Tell IMP to stop," Aderyn told Elidor.

"I am afraid that IMP no longer listens to me."

Aderyn looked up in surprise and exchanged an uneasy glance with Gwynn. She suddenly very much wanted to get her cousin out of there.

"Why not?" Gwynn asked.

"Because I tried to kill it, in a manner of speaking. After I found out about Gair, I came down here to speak with IMP, and then I tried to kill it. And then you two showed up. IMP let me use the bots to talk to you, but I don't control them, either."

"I really don't understand. You didn't make IMP, but you used it to solve problems, like mine, like Tuari's. But then you also used it to hurt Gair, only you didn't mean to hurt Gair."

"What did you mean to do?" Aderyn asked.

"Make him sterile," Elidor said, matter-of-factly, as if that wasn't a weird thing to want to do to your brother. "To save the universe."

He slumped in his chair, tears in his eyes.

"My grandmother—well, the woman who called herself my grandmother, gave me a task. I had to stop Ix from reassembling the control box, so that he couldn't escape. But I didn't know how. It was much too big a problem for a young man to handle all on his own. And I didn't know how to talk to people, how to ask for help. And then I found IMP, and then I had all the help I needed to solve my problem. And IMP created a plan. We worked together, for years, putting all the pieces in place."

"To stop something called Ix from assembling a box?" Gwynn asked.

"The control box for the tesseract he is trapped in. If that gets assembled, he can escape."

"So we just won't assemble it then," Aderyn said, talking softly.

"You don't understand!" Elidor said, suddenly shouting. "We'll do it! We won't even mean to, but we'll do it! He'll control us! Ix is in us! The only way to stop Ix is to stop the bloodline, make sure there are no more of us left to do his bidding."

"You want to kill all of your family?" Gwynn shook her head.

"Not kill," Elidor said sadly. "That wasn't my plan. But I didn't design it."

"The additive," Aderyn filled in. "IMP wanted to distribute it, en masse. To stop the bloodline." She shook her head at the insanity of it.

"In drinks, in food cubes, in anything that could be processed, packaged and consumed, all across the galaxy, everywhere that TenDek has business partners, all going out at the same time to get as many of them as we could at once."

"Everyone with the genetic tag," Gwynn said. "Gods!"

"My grandmother's family," Elidor said. "You have no idea how long she lived, how many children and great great grandchildren she had. And they are all spread out, all over the galaxy, and each and every one of them is tainted."

"Tainted?" Gwynn said, her hand covering her belly. "By what?"

"By Ix and the deal she made with him," Elidor said.

"That doesn't make any sense," Aderyn said.

"Aderyn," Gilda warned. "IMP has broken through my defenses. I am sorry."

"How do I make it stop?" Aderyn asked, picking up the typepad and staring at the monitor.

"Type," Gwynn said.

PLEASE DON'T KILL MY AI, Aderyn wrote and watched as words showed up on the screen.

A new line below them was IMP's response.

I WAS NOT GOING TO.

WHAT DO YOU WANT WITH HER?

TO KEEP YOU FROM ESCAPING, WHICH I HAVE. WOULD YOU LIKE TO MAKE A DEAL?

"Don't!" Gwynn shouted. "You can't trust it."

"Aderyn, the ship is locked down. I cannot move it, and I cannot call for help." Gilda's voice was flat as always, but she still managed to sound defeated.

WHAT DEAL? Aderyn typed.

ELIMINATE ELIDOR, AND I WILL LET YOU LIVE.

Aderyn stared at the screen.

"Why does it want you dead?" Gwynn asked.

"Aderyn, I now have access to information about the station I didn't have before," Gilda said. "IMP has allowed me this access."

"What are you reading?" Aderyn asked.

"IMP has shut off all life support in the station. IMP is overriding the security protocols and is starting a process to open all the airlocks. I am trying to fight him but I estimate that in ten minutes time all airlocks will be open."

"IMP's going to vent everything into space?" Gwynn asked.

"That'll kill everyone!" Aderyn said, looking around the room to see what their immediate danger was. There didn't appear to be any airlocks in this area, but without life support, it wouldn't much matter. She picked up the keyboard.

I CAN'T KILL ELIDOR IF I AM DEAD. TURN LIFE SUPPORT BACK ON, she typed.

"Oh, oh no," Elidor said. "That's not going to work." He clutched whatever was in his hand tighter.

"We have to stop IMP," Gwynn said. "Tell us how!"

"The additive was just supposed to make people sterile," Elidor said. "The line would die out naturally then, with enough time. Then a few decades later, we'd do it again, and once more a few decades after that. They could still live out their lives, still be happy. Just without children. And that way the curse wouldn't spread, and the box wouldn't be rebuilt, and the universe would be saved."

Aderyn saw then that something inside of Elidor had broken. Whatever his grandmother told him, whatever he had been living with to make him work with an AI like IMP and take all these steps, it had eroded him down, made him less than what he probably once was. All those half-finished projects they passed on the way in.

"I gave IMP the problem, and we agreed on a solution. And then IMP came up with a different one."

"Kill them all." Gwynn stared at her brother-in-law in shock.

"So you tried to kill it," Aderyn said. "How did you try?"

"I wanted to remove the power source," Elidor said. "But I couldn't do it."

And that was when it hit Aderyn, what she had been missing.

Her scalp was tingling.

"The power source is nuclear," Aderyn said.

"I didn't build IMP," Elidor said apologetically. "I tried to disconnect the power source, but I couldn't. I wasn't strong enough."

Aderyn stepped to him then and touched him, feeling directly just how much radiation he had absorbed. She saw slashes in his suit, and realized he'd been fighting.

"How strong is the radiation?" Gwynn asked. "How much were you exposed?"

"Gwynn, look."

Aderyn pointed to the purple streak in Gwynn's hair, which was changing hues.

"Enough that he's giving off some of his own."

Do not attempt to disconnect my power source, and I will not kill the people of this station.

Aderyn stared at the screen.

"IMP appears to have also accessed our coms and can now hear what we are saying. I can only talk to you because IMP lets me. I am sorry. I wish I had been stronger," Gilda said.

"Gwynn, we have to get out of here," Aderyn said, grabbing her cousin's arm.

"We have to stop IMP!" Gwynn pulled her arm away.

"I don't think you're going to be able to do that," Elidor replied. "And in the meantime, Aderyn, if you don't kill me, you, Gwynn, and the thousands of souls that work here will die."

"We need to take out IMP's power source." Gwynn said. "Shut IMP down."

If you attempt to remove my power source, I will kill you.

The bots closest to them started waving their arms menacingly, the tools at the ends whirring or shocking. None of the bots had blasters, but that didn't mean they weren't dangerous. Elidor was proof of that.

"Why haven't the bots killed you already?" Aderyn asked.

Elidor showed her what was in his hand.

"Short range EMP," he said. He pressed the button and all the bots in their immediate area shut down tanks to the electromagnetic pulse. "IMP will send more," he said. "I couldn't use it before because I couldn't risk my only chance."

"How do we remove the power source?" Aderyn asked him. He gestured to the side of IMP's case where an access panel had already been removed.

"It's in there," he said. "But you'll never make it. The radiation is too high."

"I'll do it." Gwynn started to walk to the access panel.

"No," Aderyn said, shaking her head and grabbing Gwynn's arm. "The radiation level is going to be too high for the baby. You can't."

"But we filter, don't we? Isn't that whole point of this?" Gwynn flipped her hair.

"You're not doing it!" Aderyn said adamantly.

"I will," Elidor said.

"The radiation will kill you," Gwynn said, shaking her head.

"It already has," he responded gently. "Let me do this. For you, for Gair. To show him how sorry I am."

He reached out and touched Gwynn's face with genuine affection. Aderyn could see that Gwynn was fighting back tears.

"You and Gilda try to block access to any incoming bots and get life-support back on," Aderyn told Gwynn. "We're going to try to take out IMP's power source."

There was a creaking noise near them, and they turned as one to stare as part of the wall in the side of the room creaked open, a large section of it falling to the floor with a thump. Half a dozen bots began to pour out, each one hovering, arms whirring with tools they'd used to cut through the wall.

"Hells!" Gwynn exclaimed.

"I guess they were closer than I thought," Elidor said. "I should have waited. It will take time for the EMP to recharge."

"Give me that," Gwynn said, taking the EMP and shoving it into her pocket.

Aderyn ran for the nearest bot coming at them and whipped out her taze-stick, slamming it down against the joint where the bot's head met the rest of the body. The electric shock was designed for humans, but she was hoping it might short something out in the machine. She watched at is fell and flailed, evidence that the taze-stick did something.

On the other side of Elidor, Gwynn swung her own stick at a bot in front of her, taking out one of its arms, before kicking it bodily away.

"I'll handle these!" she said. "Get the power source!"

Aderyn turned back to heave Elidor up to his feet and drag him to the service hatch. She couldn't help but glance at IMP's screen:

YOU WILL ALL DIE FOR THIS, it read.

"The first airlocks are opening," Gilda said. "People have noticed that life support has shut down and are trying to board ships and escape pods. There are not enough for all the occupants, and IMP is locking down doors to prevent people from escaping. Security bots are firing on TenDek employees."

"Try to access the bots, get them to stop," Gwynn said.

"I am trying," Gilda said. "IMP is very powerful."

"Use my security override!"

"Excellent suggestion," Gilda said.

Another bot whirred toward Aderyn, and she swung her stick again, knocking it over. But it bounced back up almost right away, its hover tech righting it, and it came for her again. Aderyn had to let go of Elidor and shove him away from a particularly sharp tool, dodging under the bot's arm and swinging up with her taze-stick, aiming for the head-joint. Again, the electrical current seemed to do the trick, and the bot shorted out.

Aderyn looked over to Gwynn, who had another bot disabled at her feet and was aiming the tip of her taze-stick expertly at a sensor in the bot in front of her. It went down with a satisfying crackle of energy.

Another half a dozen bots poured through the opening in the wall and Gwynn took out Elidor's EMP.

"Almost," she said to Aderyn. "I can take them out. You two need to go!"

Aderyn grabbed Elidor by the arm and dragged him up toward IMP's casing.

As she got closer to the hatch, she could feel her scalp tingling even more. She looked back at Gwynn just in time to watch her hit the button on the EMP and take out all the bots in the room. Then Gwynn bent over the one nearest to her, obviously looking for weaknesses and preparing for another battle with the bots.

Aderyn focused on her own task. Inside the access panel, protective gear hung on hooks, and Aderyn pulled on a jacket and gloves, feeling strange to pull a mask over her face. A protective force field spread out from her jacket to cover her legs and feet. She helped Elidor with his mask and he handed her a tool belt which she slung over her shoulder. Once inside, he seemed to regain strength, and he led her down a short corridor. Aderyn realized then just how far gone Elidor already was—he'd left all the doors and seals open, exposing the entire room to radiation.

"The plan will work," he said. "The plan will work."

He seemed to be chanting it to himself. Aderyn could feel her skin getting hot, even under the suit. Finally, they reached the core of the computer. Here too was evidence of Elidor's prior attempt, as some connectors had been removed while others were still attached. There seemed to be twelve in total and only three had been removed. Aderyn watched as Elidor tried to disconnect one and fumbled the wrench he was using, dropping it. The radiation was too high for him and was messing with his coordination. She pushed him out of the way and picked up the wrench, undoing the connector he was working on. Then she went after a second one, and a third. As she worked, the radiation levels increased.

"I can still monitor your health," Gilda said. "You should know that your radiation levels are getting dangerously high."

"Just a few more," Aderyn said.

"You should also know that more bots found Gwynn. She is fighting them now. If you can hurry, that would be good."

Aderyn tried to hurry, but sweat was pouring into her eyes, and she could feel her muscles start to weaken. Elidor was slumped on the floor, not moving, but she didn't have time to think about that. She stepped over him to try to get to the last three connectors.

Her hand slipped and she dropped her wrench. She struggled to feel it with her fingers and pick it up.

"Your radiation levels have surpassed your ability to mitigate them. If you don't leave right now, you may be subject to serious and permanent damage."

Aderyn ignored Gilda, her fingers finally finding the wrench. She dragged it to her, picked it up and put it back on the connector. One more twist, and it was free.

Two more connectors to go.

"Aderyn you need to leave. I am very concerned about your health."

One twist, two twists, three. One more, and the second-to-last connector was off.

"Aderyn. Aderyn please. You are going to die if you do not leave."

Aderyn took a second to try to slow her breathing and then counted down the twists, focusing hard so that she wouldn't drop the wrench again. Her arms felt weak and her eyelids heavy.

"Help me count!" she shouted at Gilda. She twisted the wrench. "One."

"One," Gilda dutifully repeated.

It took a second for Aderyn to reattach the wrench, and then she yanked it.

"Two!"

"Two. What number are we counting to?"

"Two more," Aderyn said. "Just two more."

She fumbled with the wrench, finally locking it in place, and this time it felt like it took all her effort to make the bolt move.

"Three," she whispered hoarsely."

"Three," Gilda said. "One more Aderyn."

"One more," Aderyn mumbled. "One more," she said again.

"Aderyn, one more. Aderyn, you need to move. Aderyn, you have one more in your count. Aderyn."

Gilda's voice was a persistent buzz in her ear, keeping Aderyn from just drifting off to sleep.

"One more!" Gilda said again, full volume.

Aderyn snapped her eyes open. Her skin hurt. Her bones hurt. Hells, even her teeth hurt. She couldn't find the wrench, and then she could, but it had slid under some cables and she couldn't get to it.

She tried to stretch her arm out, but the wrench was too far away. She fumbled on her body, looking for something to extend her reach, and pulled her knife out of its sheath, through the protective force field that probably wasn't able to protect her anymore. She shoved her hand under the cables, the knife point sticking out.

Still, she was not close enough.

She pulled her arm back and fumbled some more, tears pouring out of her eyes making it hard for her to see, searching for something, anything that could help. Then her hand found Warren's knife strapped to her other ankle. She pulled it out, and laid flat against the floor, stretching her arm and the knife at the end of it under the cables.

There! It was just long enough! She carefully snagged the

edge of the wrench with the tip of the knife and dragged the wrench closer to her. It felt very heavy as she lifted it and put it in place against the connector. She took a deep breath and pulled.

"Four," she said.

"Good Aderyn, you made your count. Now you have to leave, Aderyn. Leave."

Again, Aderyn found herself drifting, and again, Gilda used the top of her volume: "Leave!"

Aderyn dragged herself away from the nuclear core and through the first outer door. She knew she should seal it behind her, but she didn't have the strength. She focused on moving, her body banging into walls and door frames, her knees feeling like they were filled with glass. Two doorways.

She got halfway to the third doorway when she collapsed and blacked out.

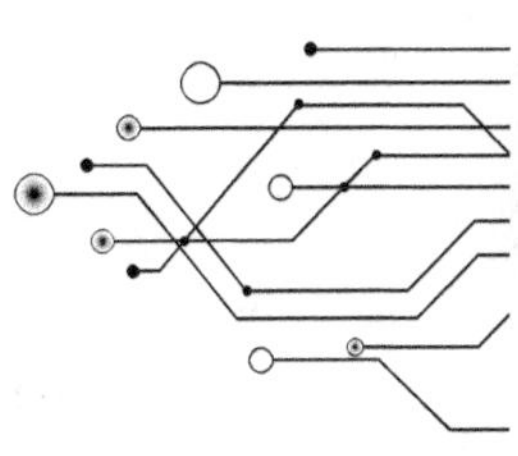

Chapter 29

THE HARD GOODBYE

Gwynn stood in the center of the Flaxen Moons ballroom and tried to think about how long it had been since she told Gair she was pregnant.

Her once flat belly was round now, and she could feel movement inside. It was a strange, wonderful, scary thing.

The galaxy was full of strange, wonderful, and scary things. And sad things too.

"Gwynn Flaxenhart," Warren said, walking toward her from the other side of the ballroom. "Fancy meeting you here."

"Well, I do own the place," she said.

"How's that going for you?"

"Well, TenDek had a massive recall on a bunch of products, lost a ton of revenue as well as its reputation, and has been providing free inoculations against any potential harm our tainted products could possibly cause." She shook her head. "And despite that, people are still dying. Too many other products with the additive went out."

"Which isn't your fault," Warren said.

"I played my part."

"We all did."

She watched as he looked up through the top of the dome, maybe looking at the stars on the other side, maybe looking at nothing at all.

"I'm the one that hired Addy, did you know that?" Warren

said. "For that first job, when we stole the program for the advanced search engine so that Elidor could add it to IMP. From what I can figure, that search engine is what helped IMP find all the information it needed to do what it did. It played an integral role. And I helped steal it."

"You didn't know," Gwynn said.

"Neither did you," he countered, looking at her. "And you know what the worst part is about that, me helping steal that program?"

"What?" she asked.

"I would do it again. Because that's how I met Addy. And I don't know what kind of person that makes me. I did something that probably helped lead to all these deaths, and I would still do it because that's how I got to be with the love of my life."

"I don't know what kind of person that makes me either," Gwynn said. "Because I kinda think I would do the same thing." She rubbed her hand over her belly protectively.

"I think that makes us the human kind of people," Warren said. "Like Tuari, and Addy, and Gair, and even Elidor. We all made huge mistakes. But I don't know that any of us are evil."

"Not even Elidor?"

"He was a kid when he first started working with IMP, did you know that? His grandmother had just died, and from what you told me, it sounds like she did a number on his head."

"He thought she was ancient, that she had all these descendants. He thought that is why all these people had that genetic tag."

"And not only that—cursed! And the only way to free them was to kill them."

"No, he didn't want them dead," Gwynn said. "He just wanted to end the family line. He was adamant about that, until the end."

"Yeah, the end."

They both grew quiet then, contemplating what the end meant, and how Elidor died.

"Your Aunt Leona is looking for you," Warren said after a moment. "It's why I came to find you."

"Oh?" Gwynn looked down at her com bracelet, frowning.

"She specifically sent me in person," he said. "Maybe she had one of her feelings, thought we needed to talk."

"I think she was right," Gwynn said. She smiled at him, and he smiled back, but the sadness between them didn't dissipate.

"Shall I escort you?" he asked, walking over to her and holding out his arm. She nodded and put her hand in the nook of his elbow. "Which way do you want to go?" he asked.

"The long way."

The long way took them past her old lab, past her old quarters, and past the entrance to the Flaxenhart Museum. They kept walking around the station, taking their time and enjoying the silence, until at long last they got to the docking bay. Then it was a relatively quick wait for the station airlock to close behind them and her aunt's ship's airlock to open in front of them, and then they were on the *Cardinal de Richelieu.*

"Welcome, Gwynn, welcome back, Warren," Glenda, the ship's AI, said as greeting. She had a high, friendly voice that belied how powerful she was. She had been with the family for generations. "Mistress Leona is in Medical. Would you like me to show you there?"

"I know the way," Warren said. It was a long walk, as it was a large ship, and they continued to pass the time in companionable silence. Finally, they reached the entrance to Medical, which was large enough to hold a dozen beds, three surgery suits, and two intensive recovery units. Gwynn unlinked her arm from Warren's before she went inside, sad to lose the comfort of his closeness. He stayed with her as she entered Medical.

"Gwynn," her aunt said, coming to her and pulling her into a hug. "It's going to be all right, I promise." She was a tall woman, soft around the middle and broad in the shoulder, her hair 100 percent purple.

"It's not," Gwynn said. "Because you're going to tell me it's time, that we've done everything we can, and I'm not sure I'm ready to hear that."

"You will never be ready to hear that," Leona said. "And yet, it is time."

She held Gwynn's hand as they walked toward one of the intensive recovery rooms. Gwynn faltered at the doorway before being able to step inside.

Gair lay on the bed, motionless. Even with the antidote, even with time and nanites, even with all the advanced medicine that money could buy, he was never going to wake up.

Aunt Leona confirmed it, using her gift—his body was with them, but that other part of him, the part that laughed and sang and tickled Gwynn with his beard, was gone.

"Would you like to say anything?" Aunt Leona asked. Gwynn shook her head. She'd said it all in the months that she sat by his side, hoping and praying, and finally, accepting.

"Actually, yes," she said, leaning down over Gair's body to whisper in his ear. "May the gods hold you." She kissed him on the cheek, and then stood up and nodded to her aunt.

Aunt Leona pushed some commands into a console, and all the machines that were keeping Gair alive shut down, one by one. Gwynn and Leona stayed until his heart stopped. And then they stayed a little longer after that.

When Gwynn was ready, Aunt Leona took her hand and led her away, out of Medical and to another part of the ship. The genet sanctuary on the Ryder family base-ship took up an entire wing, and was filled with trees, grass, and ropes and pillars for the furry creatures to climb on.

Today it was also filled with Enzo, Myles, Bertram, Treasa, Tuari, Warren, and Aderyn. Gwynn watched as Aderyn rest her head on Warren's shoulder, smiling and looking content while watching the genet. But when she looked up and saw Gwynn watching her, her face changed, and she immediately walked over. Gwynn finally let go of the tears she had been holding on to and began to cry.

Aderyn pulled her into a hug that was strong, proof that Aderyn truly was on the mend, and let Gwynn cry it out while the others found benches or patches of grass to sit on and give them space.

"Hard day," Aderyn said, wiping tears off her cousin's face.

"Hard several months," Gwynn said, "for both of us."

"But I'm still here," Aderyn said, squeezing Gwynn's hand. "Thanks to you coming in after me. And this little one is still here, thanks to her Ryder heritage." She lightly touched Gwynn's belly. "And you're still here," she continued, touching her cousin's cheek. "And that means good things are still possible."

"I still can't make sense of what happened," Gwynn said. "What Elidor and IMP were trying to do."

"You mean that whole thing where some ancient evil was controlling all of Elidor's relatives, and he needed to wipe them out—by making them sterile—to save the universe? He'd gone completely insane by the end."

Gwynn frowned.

"He wasn't insane when he put those plans in place. I worry." She rested her hand on her stomach. "What if there really is some ancient evil that will take control of his family? My family?"

Aderyn squeezed her hand again.

"Then we'll figure that out, too," she said.

"One day at a time, right?" Gwynn asked.

"That's not our motto," Aderyn chided. Gwynn repeated the words with her:

"Adapt, and survive."

Dear Reader

Word-of-mouth is crucial for any author to succeed. If you enjoyed the book, please leave a review on your favorite book sales or review site. Even if it's just a sentence or two. It would make all the difference and would be very much appreciated.

Search for: *J.M. Phillippe* on any book review site such as Goodreads, BookBub, Amazon and more.

Thank you!

Learn more

about the Flaxenhart descendants in

The Seventh Swan from Bethany Maines

Take a sneak peak at Chapter One on the next page...

PART 1: The Swans & the Queen

The boys, seeing that someone was approaching from afar, thought that their dear father was coming to them. Full of joy, they ran to meet him. Then the Queen threw one of the shirts over each of them, and when the shirts touched their bodies they were transformed into swans, and they flew away over the woods.

The Queen went home very pleased, believing that she had gotten rid of the children. However, the girl had not run out with her brothers, and the queen knew nothing about her.

Jacob and Wilhelm Grimm, The Six Swans

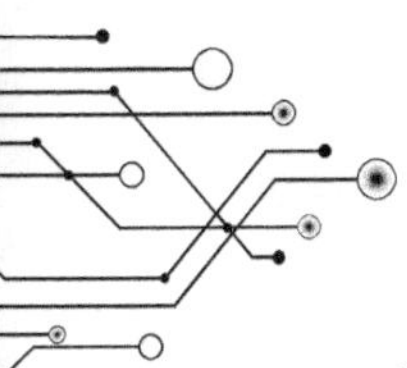

Chapter 1

KEELIA BLACK AND THE END OF THE BLACK LIGHT

Keelia Black of the Swan Clan watched through the domed glass of the hanger deck as her ship, the *Black Light*, exploded in a fiery blossom, beautiful and silent against the inky blackness of space. In front of her, Easton, her second oldest brother, dropped to his knees and began the Prayers for the Damned.

"You have just violated intergalactic law," said Niall, the eldest, his voice hoarse with rage.

Fang Nazari laughed. It wasn't a mad laugh. Or even particularly evil. Fang was delighted, as if Niall had promised her double desserts after dinner. "I know!" She drew a deep breath, as if inhaling the smell of victory. "And wasn't it fun!"

Keelia turned and examined their captor more closely. Fang was nearly eight feet tall—either space-born or modified—and she didn't walk so much as glide. Or perhaps it was her dress that moved? The fabric, if it could be called that, moved around Fang as if made of millions of tiny green iridescent insects. Occasionally, bits of her dress broke away from the mass and crawled up into her turquoise hair and sometimes into her mouth, where she ate them with an audible crunch.

Keelia and her six brothers, Niall, the twins Easton and Graves, Jedidiah, Anwell, and Mataxlen had arrived in the quadrant earlier in the week. Alliance surveys had indicated that it was uninhabited, but likely to hold profitable asteroids. The Black children had harvested two ice rocks and were looking for dwarf star alloy when their scans picked up an asteroid the size of a small moon with multiple alloy pings. They had landed, prepared to do a survey and a little exploratory digging with their father's newest invention—a sonic drill.

What they had found was a moon base, a mad woman, an army of robots and what appeared to be a seven-foot man-alligator. Fang Nazari, as she had introduced herself, had wasted no time in launching one of her robots armed with a detonator and a cubic meter of the highly explosive dwarf star alloy at their ship.

And now their ship, and their way home, was dust and debris.

The circular hanger was a donut shape. At the center was a shaft dug into the side of the asteroid—meant for venting engine exhaust into space. A force field kept the atmosphere in the hanger deck and out of the shaft, allowing them all to breathe. Deep below them, Keelia could see that the turbines and grav-shields were inert, meaning the shaft wasn't in use at the moment. She couldn't imagine what kind of engine would require a vent shaft that big. Above them, inside the shaft and exposed to space, a complex arrangement of scaffolding, handles and cables proliferated, allowing only glimpses of the dark expanse of space beyond.

Around them stood a cadre of robots, led by the commands and tail flicks of the alligator-looking creature that was almost as tall as Fang. He snarled at every move the Blacks made, but once their mistress had called a halt, neither he or the robots had moved.

Behind Fang stood three humans, none of whom had taken part in the fighting. The first was a man with dark-fringed eyes, a thick beard, and long black hair tied up in a knot on his head. He held his hands in front of him as if they were in chains, although no cuffs were in evidence. The second was a woman with broad shoulders and green hair. The third, an older man, had short white hair, red-rimmed eyes, and gnarled hands. All three of them were filthy with dark dust and watched the Black children with flat, impassive expressions, as if they had seen this show before.

"Your actions indicate that you would like war with the Alliance," said Niall. It was a stall. Everyone knew that this far out, the law of the Alliance wasn't worth the data stream it was imprinted on. It was really just to give Easton time to make contact. Every morning the telepaths on each ship of the Swan Clan received an image of who the Swan Emergency Beacon would be that day. Today it had been their mother, her hair, red like Keelia's own, vibrant in the rendering. Easton was attempting to calm his mind and send a distress call. They all knew what the odds were. Their mother was a very long way away and no one could possibly reach them for months. But, at the very least, the Swan Clan would descend in fiery retribution. That seemed like cold comfort at the moment.

"The Alliance doesn't exist here," snapped Fang. "There is only me or space. So now you have a choice. If you'll notice, there are escape pods around the room."

"Mat," said Niall, pointing at their youngest brother. Mataxlen jogged to the nearest pod, jostling past the cylindrical robots who creaked in protest.

"The pods are standard issue: enough fuel for a short directional thruster burst, twenty-four hours of air, and only short-range communications," said Fang pleasantly. "Or so I'm told."

"Air and fuel tanks look full," said Mat, running back. "She's not lying. Also, Dura-flex coating and a docking arm." There was an exchange of looks. Dura-flex coating was resilient, flexible and could withstand the outer corona of a sun, such as the one located a short distance from their position. A docking arm meant that the pods could be linked. Their possibilities for escape had just expanded.

Easton chanted softly, leaning against his twin's leg for stability.

"You got here in a very lovely, very large ship with a lot of air and fuel. I'm sure you know exactly how far those pods will take you," said Fang, smiling gleefully, unaware of the subtle shift of mood in the Blacks. "I'm sure you will acknowledge that the pods are simply a prolonged method of suicide. But I do have another option for you."

"What's that?" asked Niall.

"Work for me," said Fang, crunching a piece of her dress between her teeth. "I'm in need of experienced diggers."

"Pods," said Niall, without hesitation.

Fang looked mildly surprised. "Interesting choice. You did hear me state twenty-four hours of air, right?"

"Pods," said Niall again.

"Before you commit, I feel I should point out a few little… problems with the pods."

"Such as?" Niall's face had hardened into angular planes, his jaw clenched so hard that Keelia was worried for his teeth. Of all of them, he looked like a true Swan—thick, white-blonde hair, light brown skin, aquiline nose and a square jaw. Her brothers were all variations on the theme—some more brunette than others, but all with the same blue eyes. She was the one who stood out, with her mother's fiery red hair and her father's green eyes.

"Well, for instance, there is no internal release. In order to eject, someone has to manually release each escape pod. And of course, there is the fact that the release buttons are all inside the exhaust shaft." She pointed upward.

"You mean, someone has to stay behind," said Niall.

"Is that what it means?" asked Fang with a wicked grin. "I should also point out that whoever stays behind would have to use this air canister and it only has three minutes of air." She patted a breather mask and canister next to her.

"Our suit tanks all had more air," said Niall pointing to the collection of canisters that had been ripped from their suits along with their helmets when they had surrendered.

"What tanks?" asked Fang, and the droids promptly began to crush the tanks in pinching claws, the tubes popping and leaking the air out in angry gusts.

"Right," said Niall.

"The other problem," continued Fang, "is that the computer estimates that it would take someone five minutes," she traced an arc from right to left in the air, "to make it around the entire circle. Five-minute trip. Three minutes of air. You might want to factor that into your decision making."

Keelia looked up at the path that Fang had traced. It made sense that the computer would estimate that route—it was the safest. But safest also meant slowest. She could do it faster. But how much faster? Within three minutes?

Niall turned his back to Fang and surveyed his siblings. Keelia did the same. They were all fighters. Even Jed, who was their medic, was a better fighter than Keelia was. They all had more skills in piloting, flying and ship maintenance than she did. She did have one thing that they didn't—a childish talent based on stubbornness.

"Easton?" Niall asked.

Easton abruptly stopped chanting and stood up. "Mother says: *Quicquid capit.*"

They all nodded—they knew the family motto.

"Who stays?" asked Niall.

"That's me," said Keelia.

"Can't be you," said Anwell. "Everyone knows Dad wants to leave you the business." It was a family joke. Everyone knew Dad didn't have a business. He had a lab, mad dreams and crazy inventions that Mom turned into a business. Langston Black invented things. Rayna Black kept them all flying. Keelia had been the first in the family to go to an official school. She was only working with her brothers until the Engineering Guild reviewed her test scores and approved her license.

"I'll be faster," said Anwell. "I'll do it."

Keelia shook her head. "Yes, you and Niall are faster than me in low grav, but I can hold my breath the longest," said Keelia. "The best shot for everyone is if I do it."

They all looked to Niall. She didn't have to add that she would be counting on them to come back for her. That was a given.

Niall reluctantly nodded once and then all nodded together and began to move, running for their pods.

Niall hugged her tightly, for only a second.

"You stay alive," he whispered in her ear. "Whatever it takes."

Quicquid capit.

Then he was gone.

Keelia turned back to Fang who was watching open mouthed as the brothers dispersed. Behind her she heard the sound of running feet and the first pod slam shut.

"You must be just the biggest wet blanket at crew parties," said Fang, staring down at Keelia as if she were a new and disgusting form of mold.

Keelia steadied herself, trying not to feel the loss of her wall of brothers as she stared up at the pale face of Fang Nazari, with her red slash of a mouth and deep black eyes. Keelia didn't answer Fang. Her voice would probably shake anyway and she didn't want to embarrass the family. Fang would never know that she was scared, that her mouth was dry and her palms were wet inside her space suit. She marched past the towering woman and picked up the breather apparatus, weighing it in her hands.

Fang slid around in front of her, watching her with eager eyes. As if genuinely interested to see what Keelia would do next.

"Three minutes of air?" Keelia asked, looking up at the levers and buttons.

"Three minutes," said Fang reassuringly. Behind her, the man with the long black hair shook his head in a small negative gesture and held up two fingers.

"Good to know," said Keelia, and strapped on the face mask.

Niall was stepping into his pod. Keelia tightened down the straps on the mask, started her watch and hit the oxygen apparatus to start the flow. Then she sprinted across the access ramp to the exhaust shaft and launched herself upward into space.

READ MORE IN THE SEVENTH SWAN FROM BETHANY MAINES

Galactic Dreams

Volume 1

Volume 2

About the Author

J.M. Phillippe has lived in the deserts of California, the suburbs of Seattle, and the mad rush of New York City. She worked as a freelance journalist before earning a masters' degree in social work and becoming a therapist in Brooklyn, New York. She spends her free-time playing fetch with her two cats, drinking cider with amazing friends, and catching up on the golden age of TV.

Find out more at:
JMPhillippe.com

Other Works by J. M. Phillippe

Perfect Likeness

The Christmas Spirit

GALACTIC DREAMS VOL. 1
Aurora One

SHORT STORIES
Plane Signals
The Sight

www.ingramcontent.com/pod-product-compliance
Lightning Source LLC
Chambersburg PA
CBHW071505110726
47908CB00003B/729